An outrageous free spirit meets her match in an introvert with a secret leather business

"Would you—" She ran a finger over her lower lip. "—play the next round with me?"

"No." His answer was almost a grunt.

Her frown deepened.

"Er, no, thank you, Miss Jenkins." He gave an abbreviated bow.

"I beg your pardon for disturbing you." *Another man less interested in me than I am with him, for godsakes.* She turned to go, dropping her hand to her side. She'd play again anyway, and damn his sensibilities.

"No."

The urgency in his repeated response made her look over her shoulder at him.

"Don't go. Please. I simply do not"—he waved a hand, and his lip curled in a small sneer—"perform these games. I prefer my play to be private."

"Oh." She turned fully back around, gratified when his gaze flicked to her décolletage before returning to her face. "Would you prefer private play with me?"

flavors of sex and punishment are sure to excite even the most discerning of kinky-historical readers."
> ~ *Annabel Joseph, NYT and USA Today bestselling author of* The Properly Spanked *series*

~*~

"*Penelope's Passion* is…a wonderful story of forbidden romance from two people in very different life circumstances just trying to do the right thing for both themselves and their families…readers who like an extra spicy historical romance will not want to miss out!"
> ~ *Golden Angel, USA Today Bestselling Authorof the* Bridal Discipline *series*

Other Books by Maggie Sims

The School of Enlightenment Series
Roslynn's Rebellion (prequel novella)
Sophia's Schooling (Book 1)
Penelope's Passion (Book 2)
Althea's Awakening (Book 3)

Spin-offs
Helen's House
Ann's Angel (a Christmas short story)

The Control Series
Charlotte's Control
Lyon's Lover
Folly's Folly

Spin-offs
Duke's Diversion

Books written as Debbie Charles

The Texas Tornadoes Series
Second Chance Puck (exclusive newsletter novella)
Dances with Pucks
Net Pucks and Chill
Spicy as Puck
Intentional Offside

For Love or Money (a spin-off novella)

Beth's Behavior

by

Maggie Sims

School of Enlightenment
Book Four

Beth's Behavior

Cover by *Lisa Dawn MacDonald*

Publishing History
First Edition, 2023
Trade Paperback ISBN 979-8-89044-401-1
Digital ISBN 979-8-89044-402-8

Published by *Maggie Sims, LLC*

Dedication

To my readers
Those who have been with me since the beginning and
those just finding me
Thank you

Prologue

Beth Jenkins extended her legs and arms in a languid, satisfied stretch. She rolled over, hopeful but found the space next to her empty. The angle of the sunlight streaming through the crack in the curtains gave her the reason.

I suppose Lisa had to report for work downstairs. Ah, well. I would have enjoyed round two of teaching her the joys of intimacy with a woman.

She sat up and extended her arms overhead. The sheet dropped to her waist, her exposed nipples pebbling in the cool room. Heedless of her nudity, she leaned over to sip the tea left by Emma, her personal maid, before slipping out of bed. As she meandered to the washbasin for her morning ablutions, she heard the rap of knuckles on her door before Emma slipped inside.

"Lady Althea wishes to see you."

"Right-o. Fetch me a day gown, please?" Beth knew not to keep her cousin and guardian, Lady Althea Egerton, waiting. She yanked a comb through her chin-length cinnamon curls.

Moments later, she bounced into the library to where Althea's desk occupied one end of the room.

"You wished to see me, cuz?" Thankfully, Althea found her affectionate nickname amusing rather than annoying.

The dark-haired woman stood to lean her knuckles

on her desk, using her several inches and six years over Beth's to her advantage. Althea's spine was rigid, her pen tapped on the desk where she'd been working. "A second maid has given notice. She would not tell me why until I pressed her. Can you guess what the reason was?"

"Godsakes," Beth swore under her breath. Louder, she guessed, "Lisa?"

Althea nodded, lips pressed together.

"I am very sorry, Althea. I promise to do better." Beth ducked her head, scuffing her toe in front of her.

"You said that last time." Althea sighed, her shoulders dropping in defeat. "I understand. I do. I've told you before, I don't disagree with your parents' approach to life, but we must balance it with society's rules for the sake of your reputation. In part so we do not run off all the help."

Beth peeked up at her. "She was lovely. I resisted for ages, tiptoeing around, making sure she understood my attentions and returned them. I swear she did... I suspect she shocked herself with her interest and is running away."

"Which is her prerogative. She'll have an easier time of it if she doesn't pursue any interest in girls, sadly. She hasn't your freedom to ignore social mores when you like, as she needs a job."

"I hope you gave her a good reference. I certainly would. She was a magnificent kisser. And those breasts!" She hid her grin by twirling to pace past the seating area done in burgundy with gold accents.

"Beth. Focus. Please."

"Right. I beg your pardon again. I thought you were looking into servants from the school?" She referred to the School of Enlightenment, where Althea had sent her to attend multiple courses exploring independence, relationships, and her sexual identity.

When Althea had first brought her home, Beth had been eighteen with newly awakened yearnings in her body that she didn't fully understand. She'd seen enough at her parents' house, even as a younger child, to view physical intimacy as fun and self-control as overrated.

When her open-minded, spiritual parents had died suddenly a year ago, Althea's father became her guardian. Beth had enjoyed all the liberties and outlooks of a boy, free of society's views regarding proper etiquette for women. The abrupt change to the strict and religious household Althea had been raised in was too much for both Beth and the earl. She'd fought his very strict rules before succumbing to depression, at which point Althea had stepped in.

Althea had rescued her from that hell, and Beth had celebrated her newfound freedom. So when she'd found herself attracted to servants, visitors, or even, in one awful case, one of Althea's shop employees, she'd acted on it.

Within weeks, her cousin had realized she could not handle Beth and the store and had cast around for help. Althea had been invited to join a group who called themselves the Enlightened Salon but had been unable to attend a meeting due to overseeing the shop. Nevertheless, she'd reached out, and upon their recommendation, enrolled Beth in the School of Enlightenment.

Beth had joined the introductory course, then the advanced course, and thrived. Most of the advanced classes were about various forms of relationship building and physical intimacy. These were her people. While she knew she'd maintain friendships with the less judgmental of the introductory course group, these girls would be lifelong sisters.

Indeed, her closest friend Penelope had been in the advanced classes with her.

"I am waiting on a response from the headmistress. Could you not behave for a few more weeks?"

"I have said before, it depends on your definition of behave. I always pose it as an invitation, making it their choice." Beth arched her brow as she turned back toward the desk from the fireplace, trailing a hand over the soft wine velvet of the settee cushion top.

Althea sighed again. "I gave her a good reference and some funds. I also told her I thought you could help place her if she was interested, given your extensive network. She declined." She lowered her chin to give Beth a stern look.

"I can still make inquiries. I shall try to limit my affections to men for the time being, as they hardly ever feel the need to depart the premises afterward." Beth was proud of her wide range of contacts.

Althea barked a laugh despite herself.

"How is the expansion plan going?" Having wound her way through the seating area, Beth wandered over to the desk to look at her cousin's paperwork. Math was not her strong suit, but she wanted to show her support. She'd also found a way to help Althea, but her cousin would not like some aspects of it, so if Althea had solved the issue, Beth would not mention her idea.

A product of her father's strict upbringing and newly widowed from a similarly strict marriage, Althea still often had no idea what to do with her wild cousin, and Beth hadn't known what was expected of her.

Despite that, mutual respect and willingness to hear each other's points of view had led them to a loving friendship.

The paperwork was for a second apothecary. Althea had inherited a London shop from her merchant husband and had grown its success significantly, but she'd still need outside investment to open another location. Finding resources was Beth's strength, and she was determined to help this woman who had done so much for her.

They'd tried a few paths, including contacting alumna of the school. Unfortunately, despite their enlightenment, most of the women did not control enough funds in their household to help. The London Season was also ending, which meant a number of their missives had gone unanswered.

Just yesterday, Beth had found another path for her cousin. One man who could fund the whole venture with a flick of his wrist and knew a number of other investors if he was not interested. Conveniently, he hosted a house party each August with a reputation for debauchery and exclusivity, a perfect combination in Beth's mind. Penelope, who was now married to one of the earl's closest friends, had provided her with two much-coveted invitations. However, Althea would not like being absent from the store that long, nor would the nature of the party appeal.

When Althea shook her head in answer to Beth's question, Beth dared to get her hopes up.

"I've found a solution. You'll need to take a fortnight away from the store. We have a house party to attend." Beth grinned, snickering when her cousin's expression turned to alarm. She barely refrained from

rubbing her hands together in anticipation.
Mayhap there is a party in my future after all.

Chapter One

Robert Orford, second son of an earl and known as Ford to his acquaintances, sat with his best friend watching guests arrive.

He had met Evan Gardner, Earl of Cheltenham, in secondary school when Evan had come to his defense against classmate bullies. They'd continued on to Oxford together.

On this rare warm and dry day, they lounged on the balcony of Robert's guest room as carriages pulled up on the circular drive below for Evan's house party. It would last a sennight, with games becoming more carnal each evening. Evan had made it an annual post-Season tradition these past few years since he gained his title, and invitations were in great demand. The guest list was one of the best-kept secrets in the Ton.

"I had the servants clean your workroom this week." Evan referenced the space where Robert created custom leather apparel. Greenborough Park was enormous, with dozens of guest rooms. In addition, Evan's business acumen had made him one of the wealthiest men in England. Thus, Robert maintained a permanent guest room with the sitting room done over as a workroom in the family wing.

Robert grinned. "Excellent, thank you. I have a new cuff configuration I think will sell well, so I started a few and will place the buckles accordingly on the lengths to order."

Another carriage pulled up. Two ladies emerged, along with a maid. When each had leaned forward to find the step from the carriage's small opening, the balcony's height gave the men a perfect view of cleavage. The dark-haired woman didn't have much to share, and when she straightened on the ground, Robert realized she was a giant, almost as tall as Evan.

The second, though. His gaze narrowed as recognition sparked. He'd seen these women before. The taller woman was Lady Althea Egerton, and this beauty was Beth Jenkins. He'd attended a demi-monde party in London with Evan a year ago. The girl had entered in a whirlwind, unable to stand still for long. Her beauty and energy had created a magnetic pull, and he'd tracked her with a hungry gaze. Her bosom had drawn his admiration as it did now.

And just as it had before, saliva pooled in his mouth as he imagined testing the weight of those magnificent breasts in his palms or seeing if the color of her nipples was the same burnt rose shade of her lips.

Mayhap she'll catch her hem on something in the carriage and be stuck there. Those bosoms are spectacular. He licked his lips.

When she stood, he smiled at her petite but rounded deliciousness. He'd found skinny women, like the brunette, preferred Evan's lean build. Hellfire, who was he kidding? Most women did.

Miss Jenkins' energy was palpable, even from a floor above. She bounced on her toes once, her eyes bright as she peered around her, then leaned in to speak to the other woman, her lips moving quickly. She had an hourglass figure and the coloring of a porcelain doll, all creamy pallor with lips and cheeks that matched her peach-colored gown.

He'd been mesmerized by her energy and beauty a year ago as well. She'd remained oblivious, rushing to speak to Penelope Wood, accompanied by his friend Michael. Then Miss Jenkins had sidled up to Evan and rubbed the side of her breast against his arm as her hand made a slow pass along the outside of his thigh.

Robert's heart had plummeted. As always, he had been invisible, the quiet, rather square friend in the shadows, while Evan's long and lean plumage drew peahens of all shapes and sizes. His friend could not help his good looks. He should be used to it, should stick to tupping working-class girls and those at Sarah Potter's Spanking Club. They were always willing to test his leatherwork for him—and with him.

So he had put the succulent peach of Beth Jenkins out of his thoughts…until now.

Sitting on the balcony, Robert considered the games Evan often chose and the licentious behavior at these fêtes. Mayhap he'd see those breasts after all, possibly even touch them. About to ask Evan about her, the arrival of another carriage distracted him.

A man even taller and thinner than Evan alighted, sweeping his top hat up onto his head with a flourish. The gent was attractive, but Robert knew from past interactions that his eyes were small, sharp, and mean.

Robert groaned. "Really, Bags? Did you have to?"

Evan glanced at the drive, then over at him. "Sorry, old chap. I need him for an investment. Didn't you tell me he'd mellowed with age?"

"No." Robert answered in clipped tones. "I wouldn't know, I don't talk to him. He only ever greets me when

I'm with you."

"Mayhap he's embarrassed by his behavior as a youth?"

"He should be." The man, a boy back then, had stolen Robert's pin money every day for weeks, claiming Robert looked like he did not need lunch. Little did the privileged earl's heir know that Robert's money had to stretch to books as well as lunches and he often skipped meals to pay for tutoring when he needed it.

Robert could not help his frame, but it seemed others expected it of him. If he dropped a fork and rose to replace it, snickering and oinking had broken out as students assumed he was returning for seconds. If he was running late to a class, boys jolted as though he was causing tremors in the ground.

"Any others I should know about?" he asked Evan, referencing the other elitist Ton members who had shunned him as a child and whom he now avoided.

His friend shook his head.

Half of them now weighed more than he and had likely forgotten the childhood pranks, but seeing the bully turned earl in attendance put Robert off from further thoughts of the delicious curves of Miss Jenkins, and he moved on to other topics with Evan. He'd play with her if he had an opportunity, but odds were that she'd try for Evan like the rest of them.

****

Beth meandered through the halls of the main floor in the sprawling country home. She was restless, her needlework abandoned in the room where many of the ladies had gathered to gossip and stitch.

She'd been so excited to attend the most infamous house party in England, but this first day dragged interminably.

Lingering in the main hallway to watch servants' activities as they readied rooms for the evening's entertainment, Beth contemplated the gossip she'd heard about earlier parties at Cheltie's. The whispers had covered everything from naughty versions of parlor games to orgies. But even her exceptional network and ability to ferret out information on all sorts of subjects had not unearthed more details.

Although...Cheltie hires from the school. She had recognized more than one housemaid. *Oh. I hope the footmen are like-minded. That one is magnificent.*

She scanned the particularly muscular footman's form. The Cheltenham livery strained across his shoulders and was tight around his biceps. His rear made her mouth water, bulging in his knee breeches as he lifted and carried furniture to accommodate the night's games. And his calves in those white hose.

I would love to test their firmness, then see if he is hard elsewhere. And why not, at this party of all places?

First, she must do her best to gain a meeting for Althea with Cheltie. Then she could play. But there was nothing stopping her from asking questions.

"Pardon me." She tapped his arm as he returned from moving another chair into the ballroom.

"Yes, miss?" Even the tenor of his voice warmed her.

"Can you tell me what games will be offered tonight?"

He grinned. "'Fraid not. His lordship insists on secrecy until after dinner."

"Is there nothing I could offer to convince you to share?" Beth licked her lips and trailed her hand over the neckline of her day gown, drawing his gaze.

He wiggled his eyebrows. "You are welcome to try."

Well, I guess that answers my question about the footmen's availability—and their loyalty.

She tried one more question. "I'd heard that Cheltie's friend designs and makes leather goods that might be demonstrated for custom orders. Is that true?" She was partially seeking confirmation, as she'd heard about his skills from a contact rather than Penelope.

He seemed to debate whether he could answer her safely before nodding. "Yes."

"Have you seen them? What are they like?" She was dying of curiosity, given the nature of the fête.

Penelope had mentioned Robert Orford, who she called Ford, as the other friend in Michael and Cheltie's closest circle. Beth could not remember him. She'd likely met him at one or more of the London events they'd all attended, but the earl's star burned bright, and it was difficult to see past him. Cheltie's reputation matched hers, albeit with more acceptance than the Ton gave hers.

"I'm afraid I cannot share that information either, miss." The footman shook his head. "I must return to work now, but I'll be free later and I'll look for you, shall I?"

"That sounds lovely." Right, then. Learning about Robert and his leather work would have to wait. Between that delicious calfman—er, footman—and the prospect of new toys, she was excited. She'd do her best to garner Althea a meeting with Cheltie, and of course, she was always gathering information on people's needs and skills to match them. But mostly, this trip was all about fun.

If only the fun would start. This must be how Cheltie builds suspense. Who needs that when we've all been looking forward to this since we were invited? Or invited ourselves, as the case may be.

She looked outside. Raining again. Beth had never sat still well, and with the more circumspect daytime activities being indoors and sedentary, she could not feign interest. She wondered what the male guests were doing.

"Beth." Althea's voice startled her. "I wondered if you were lost. Your needlework is here. Are you coming back?" Althea hovered in the doorway to the sitting room where the ladies had congregated.

"Cuz, I can't sit still another minute." Beth decided then and there. "I'm going to take a walk, rain or no rain. I'll try not to dampen our room with wet clothing afterward."

"Take a servant with you."

Oh, good idea. Where did Calfman go?

She should learn his name. Mayhap there was a mature willow to protect them from the rain.

After grabbing her cloak and requesting a footman and an umbrella, she took her meandering outdoors. Sadly, this footman was older and skinnier than her choice, but he was willing to hold the umbrella for her and venture outside, so she was satisfied. Following one of many paths around the estate, she held her cloak tightly around her against the chill and enjoyed the scenery.

At least tonight, she was likely to get relief. Meanwhile, she needed to burn some energy. Spying a smaller house with a pretty glassed-in conservatory in the distance and smoke coming from the chimney, she headed in that direction.

As Beth neared the smaller house, she saw two figures in comfortable wing chairs in the conservatory. When one of the women waved to her, she quickened her steps. "I think this calls for a visit."

The footman mumbled something about Cheltie, but Beth ignored him. She never passed up a chance to meet new people. Behind orgasms, it was her favorite activity.

A stout woman who may or may not have seen thirty years answered Beth's knock, nodding to the footman over Beth's shoulder.

"Hullo. I am Beth Jenkins, one of Cheltie's guests."

"How can I help, miss?"

"That house is so crowded, I needed to stretch my legs. Then I saw smoke from the chimney." Beth fumbled for words when the woman did not step back and welcome them inside.

"Lucy?" An older woman's voice called from within. "Do we have guests?"

Lucy flashed Beth a warning look. "Watch how you step, miss. She doesn't have many visitors." Finally, she held the door wider and gestured them inside.

The footman lingered in the entryway, tucking the umbrella just outside the front door.

Beth followed Lucy through the kitchen and parlor to the conservatory.

"Lady Rose, may I present Beth Jenkins, a friend"— she shot Beth a look as she said the word—"of Evan's."

"Come, dear. Won't you sit with me for a spell? I saw the carriages arrive yesterday. That son of mine and his parties." The woman's burnished gold and gray-streaked hair was pulled into a bun at the back of her head, and she wore a simple day dress. Despite that and the knitting in her lap, her resemblance to Evan and her posture told Beth that this was the Dowager Countess.

I can learn more about Cheltie and mayhap even find a way to ensure Althea gets her audience.

"'Tis lovely to meet you, my lady."

"Oh, I am Rose, dear. We do not stand on formality here." Evan's mother smiled.

"Thank you, and I am Beth."

Lucy called from the kitchen, "Tea?"

In unison, they responded, "Yes, please."

"How do you know Evan?"

"A friend of mine married his friend, Lord Mansfield," Beth stated, assuming Rose knew Michael as he and Evan had been friends for so long.

"Michael? He's married?"

Lucy bustled in, despite the tea kettle not having boiled yet, and shot another warning look at Beth. "Yes, Rose. He married last winter."

"Hmm."

"And you? Where is your family?"

Beth regaled Rose with a few stories of her childhood with her free-thinking parents over tea until the older lady's head nodded.

Standing quietly, she took her tea cup to the kitchen, where Lucy was pretending to wipe the counters within hearing distance of the conservatory. "How long have you been with Lady Rose, Lucy?"

"Almost two years."

"Does she often have memory loss?"

"More and more these days. Please, this must remain confidential. I would lose my job if Lord C knew I was discussing it."

Beth patted her hand where it had stilled on the counter. "I understand. I am sorry I intruded, I was responding to her wave. Truly, this has been far more entertaining than the afternoon of needlework at the manor."

Lucy laughed. "We haven't begun teaching you to knit yet."

"No chance." Beth giggled. "Two years is a long time to be out here in the country with only Lady Rose, though. Where is your family?"

"Up north. And my mother fell recently and needs my help. She worked as a baron's housekeeper-cook, but she cannot be on her feet that long now."

Beth's ears perked up. *Even better. I can offer to use my network to help Cheltie find Lucy's replacement in exchange for him granting Althea an audience.* More, this was what she loved to do. She'd help Lucy and Cheltie and Rose even if Althea was not here. Her hobby—if only she could be paid for it and not be a burden to Althea—and passion was connecting people with reciprocal needs. "Is Lord Cheltenham working to relieve you here, then?"

"Yes. He's been lovely about it. I am simply anxious to get to my mother." Lucy shrugged one shoulder.

"I cannot promise anything, but I help at a charity school in London, and I may know some girls who have gone on to nursing training. When we return next week, I shall see what I can do."

"Oh!" Lucy looked surprised that a stranger visiting for a party would offer to help so readily. Then she frowned.

Beth patted her hand again. "Never fear, my skills at matching people with needs are far superior to my stitching or knitting."

The women laughed together as Beth donned her cloak and gathered the footman from the hall to return to the manor house.

Chapter Two

Robert was on edge. The first evening's entertainment of strip whist and dancing had gone smoothly. As he usually did at soirées, he followed in Evan's shadow, unnoticed. As host, Bags—as Michael and Robert had nicknamed Evan at Oxford—slipped in and out of both ballrooms, ensuring his guests were having a good time, then danced with a variety of ladies and lords.

He'd asked Evan for more information on Beth Jenkins, and his friend's reaction had seemed strange. Brows raised in surprise, he'd pursed his lips like he wanted to share information about her but said only, "Good choice. You'll have fun with her."

The prior night's close-hold dancing, partners' bodies brushing each other as they'd never be allowed at a Ton ball, pushed him to consider dancing with Miss Jenkins. However, after a brief but intense internal debate with his timidity, he could not find her. He left obsessed with the idea of her curves against him.

Mayhap I'll get a dance with Miss Jenkins tonight. His cock twitched anew at the image of those magnificent breasts pressed against him, that luscious arse just below where his hand would rest. Robert spied the object of his desire. She was dancing with a muscular footman, a favorite with guests, as he enjoyed men and women alike.

Of course, she likes his physique. Who wouldn't? No one is going to choose the blocky bloke hiding in the shadows.

Frowning, he continued to scan the room. Evan had led Lady Egerton to the other ballroom for his crazy interpretation of blindman's bluff.

Robert lingered to watch the dancing, torn between desire for the curvaceous chestnut-haired girl and defeat at the knowledge that yet another woman he found attractive had eyes for everyone except him. When it seemed the group in this room was happily engaged and the orchestra segued into the next dance, Robert turned to follow his host.

He snuck into a corner of the room to observe Bags weave his magic with the guests. The earl observed tradition by stepping in as the first blindman, and it appeared he was required to identify players by their arses.

Robert shuddered. He could not fathom what someone might think of his rear end, after the jeers and unflattering comments during his school years. Worse, in Evan's naughty version of the game, Robert could be forced to guess people's identities by touching a body part and be judged for his accuracy, even if it was all supposedly in play.

What if it was bosoms? And that curvaceous beauty was a participant? His pulse leaped. He clenched his fists, torn between desire and fear as he considered the tradeoffs.

Then the round was over.

The door opened and Robert's focus shot to the bouncing bosom of the guest he'd been contemplating, who he already thought of as Beth.

Without warning, Bags tossed the blindfold at him. "What? No." He scowled.

"Come, please, for me. They're warmed up. They will play along nicely. And look at the curves on that one."

Damn Bags for knowing his type and remembering he'd asked about her. "You owe me, Bags."

His friend's demand solved the question he'd been pondering. Even for Beth, he would not risk the disparaging remarks as the blindman, but he would certainly oversee the play. He wasn't certain he could bear to watch her be petted by someone else, even if the person were blindfolded, but nor was he willing to give up his hope to get to know her better. For the moment, he'd live vicariously, watching from the shadows as always, as he gathered his courage to approach the lovely Beth.

As Evan rushed out the door, Robert searched for the servant assigned to this room. Evan required someone on hand to help facilitate games and ensure nothing got out of hand. Finding the maid, he handed off the cravat-blindfold and called, "Right, then. I believe I heard chests and breasts. Who wants in?"

****

After she'd met with Cheltie and arranged Althea's interview by offering to find a new nurse for his mother, Beth felt freer to explore on the second night. She was overjoyed when Calfman—whose name she'd learned was Franklin—bowed over her hand.

"May I have this dance, milady?"

Her eyebrows shot upward in surprise.

"We may join the festivities at our discretion once our duties were done. His lordship even gives us time to practice the dances before the house party each year."

As the orchestra struck the final notes of the waltz, Calfman—er, Franklin—bowed, thanked her for the dance, and turned to the next lady.

She'd go home at the end of the week and not miss him, but her pride stung at him moving on first. She was tired of not being anyone's choice. She always felt as if she had to pursue partners, rather than the other way around. It did not help that her body was clamoring for more attention after rubbing against his for a dance.

'Twas time to try door number two.

Raucous laughter spilled out as she opened the other ballroom door. Guests stood in a circle, exclaiming over Cheltie's prowess at whatever game had just finished.

Damn me, I am sorry I missed that.

Her nipples were hard and chafing against her chemise, and her belly quivered from rubbing against her dance partner, echoing her thoughts. Then again, she doubted she'd be Cheltie's choice either.

The sandy-haired man she suspected was Robert Orford stood with mouth agape as Cheltie brushed by Beth. She had searched for this creator of ingenious leather apparel last night to no avail. Close to Althea's height, he was twice her width. A neatly trimmed beard covered the lower part of his pale face, and hazel eyes watched the crowd through strands of dark blond hair hanging in his face.

Those shoulders and arms could hold my weight for up-against-the-wall fun.

A strip of cloth dangling from his fingers, the man's eyes moved to her, trailing up and down her curves as he announced the next round of the game.

Her eyes widened. A female servant rushed to

explain their take on blindman's bluff, where the person in the circle guessed names by fondling body parts. Beth bounced. *How fun!*

The gentleman eyed her chest as it jostled, so Beth pranced in place once more, giving him a saucy glance and a hand on her hip as she waited for him to either don the blindfold or join the circle.

He did neither.

She'd observed Cheltie talking in hushed tones to him earlier in the day, and now he'd been made delegate host, which made it likely that this was Cheltie's best friend, Robert Orford. Despite her interest in his leather goods, the game beckoned, irresistible to her free spirit.

She gave a mental shrug. *Let the wallflower watch.*

Stepping into the circle, she became immersed in the game. The blindman, another guest whose name was Owen something-or-other if she remembered correctly, made his way around the loop, players snickering and whispering in anticipation of being touched. Proud of her breasts and as eager as the others, Beth arched her back to thrust out her chest. She peeked at likely-Robert. His focus was riveted on her prodigious assets.

Her gaze returned to the blindman when someone in the circle moaned. He was touching the third player in the circle, the servant directing his hands to the right height so he could not determine the guest's name by fingering clothing.

The guest moaned low a second time, and the blindman laughed, his hands cupping her breasts. "With these lovelies, I don't care how low you pitch your voice."

She giggled, and he moved on.

As the blindfolded player touched the next guest's

waistcoat and starched linen covered chest, the man looked around, winked, and said in a high breathy voice, "Oh my dear Owen, oh yes. More, please."

Owen scowled, his forehead above the mask wrinkling. But then he smiled slyly and tweaked the man's nipple through his clothes.

The player gave a mock high-pitched shriek. "Yes, yes!"

Beth's eyes fluttered shut as she conjured an image of the spectator as the guesser, burning a hole through the blindfold with a lustful look at her breasts as he tweaked one. A leather strap in his other hand tapped against his leg, matching his dark jacket and trousers. Her nipples beaded against her chemise, just as Owen reached her.

His hands cupped her sensitive flesh, thumbs cheekily brushing her nipples. He grinned with pleasure.

She gasped as a lick of heat coursed through her. She tilted her head to stare at likely-Robert, still imagining the hands stroking her were his.

He'd stepped away from the wall, frowning, his hands clenching and unclenching at his sides. He regarded her face now, rather than her breasts.

She licked her lips, holding his gaze, and he inhaled sharply, his eyes closing for a long blink. When they reopened, his brow smoothed and his fists loosened.

She winked at him.

"Possibly the best yet," Owen murmured with a last thumb swipe. "But not familiar. I'd wager this deliciousness belongs to a new guest."

After Owen had completed his rounds, named who he could and received a score, Beth stepped out of the ring. She'd always enjoyed breast play and was disconcerted that she had not taken it at face value from a fun and attractive man. Instead, she'd needed to fantasize about a wallflower.

Deciding this mild obsession required further investigation, as did his leather goods, she sauntered toward him, taking in his stocky figure. Looking at his shoulders, his middle, his thighs, even his arms, the perception of strength resonated in her mind. He looked solid, prompting a wish to test her theory of whether those biceps really could indeed hold her against a wall.

His eyes and mouth were pinched as though he was nervous. As she approached, he blinked twice, looked behind him, then straightened as she stopped in front of him.

Bobbing a curtsy, she said, "Sir, I don't believe we've been introduced. But as nothing about this party is conventional, may I dare to offer my name for yours?"

Taking her hand, he raised it to his lips as she rose. "You are Beth Jenkins, cousin of Lady Althea Egerton, and friend of Penelope Wood."

"Oh. Yes. Yes, I am." She was taken aback until hope bloomed that he might know who she was because of an interest level that matched her own. "And you— Are you Robert Orford, friend of Lord Michael Slade and Cheltie?"

His lips quirked, and he slid fingers through his hair to comb it off his face. "Indeed I am."

"'Tis lovely to meet you. I've heard delicious things about…" She hesitated as his dark eyes widened but could not restrain herself. "Er, your leather goods."

His lips twisted, but he remained silent.

Wait, did he want me to have heard delicious things about him? Or is that simply my hope?

Frustrated at his unwillingness to actively participate in the conversation, she frowned. Was the man going to deflect every answer? She might yet have to go find Calf—Franklin. At the moment, though, she wished to learn about Robert more than she wanted the sexual adventures offered by the other guests, so she gave it one more try.

"Would you—" She ran a finger over her lower lip. "—play the next round with me?"

"No." His answer was almost a grunt.

Her frown deepened.

"Er, no, thank you, Miss Jenkins." He gave an abbreviated bow.

"I beg your pardon for disturbing you." *Another man less interested in me than I am with him, for godsakes.* She turned to go, dropping her hand to her side. She'd play again anyway and damn his sensibilities.

"No."

The urgency in his repeated response made her look over her shoulder at him.

"Don't go. Please. I simply do not," he waved a hand and his lip curled in a small sneer, "perform these games. I prefer my play to be private."

"Oh." She turned fully back around, gratified when his gaze flicked to her décolletage before returning to her face. "Would you prefer private play with me?"

There. No one could confuse her intentions now. Even this semi-mute handsome brute.

His eyes widened again, and he sucked in a breath.

Have I shocked him speechless? A friend of Cheltie's? That seems unlikely.

She pursed her lips.

"One moment." He signaled to the servant running

the game that he was leaving, then offered Beth his arm.

She inhaled a faint scent of leather that she didn't think was from his boots.

Slowing outside the ballroom, he asked, "Are you sure?" even as he clutched her hand on his arm.

His hand, rough and scarred from tooling such a tough material, was large and strong on hers. A shiver of anticipation shook her.

Apparently, one could confuse my intentions. She rolled her eyes.

His brow creased.

She pressed her bosom against his arm, and he sucked in another breath.

Ha. Men are so easy. "Do you really care? And why would you even ask?"

His chin drew back. "Of course, I care. I ask because it seems unlikely given your beauty and my…not."

She blushed. Few things made her as uncomfortable as compliments. "Thank you, but you'll allow me my own opinion of your appearance, I hope. However, I find I am unwilling to pass judgment until I've seen more of it."

"Right, then. Shall we…" He appeared at a loss.

"Come now, Mr. Orford. You must know this place inside and out after being friends with Cheltie for so many years. Surely, there is somewhere we won't be disturbed." She raised her free hand to trace patterns on the back of his with one fingernail.

"Ahh." He flushed.

"Mayhap you could show me your…leather?"

How can a friend of Cheltie's not be able to read a woman's nonverbal signals? Biting her lip, Beth waited for his answer. She'd pushed as hard as she was willing.

At his silence, her confidence waned. *Is he no longer interested?*

"My workroom is this way. 'Twas the sitting room to my bedroom, and Evan kindly had it outfitted for me."

"How—" She squeezed his arm. "—convenient. For you. You have a permanent suite here, eh? I suppose 'tis like my rooms at Althea's house. Do you live here year-round, then?"

"No. I have a home in London also. I spend much of my time there because the raw materials for my pieces are more accessible there and are cumbersome to lug around."

They gained the landing of the staircase and turned away from the wing that held her room. She suspected this was the family wing, which was surprising even for a close friend.

"Mr. Orford—"

"Please, I am Robert, or Ford, at your preference."

"And I am Beth."

"If your raw materials are in London, why do you have a workroom here?"

"Most of my pieces are custom orders. The customer's location plays a factor if fittings are needed. For new designs I am testing or accessories that are—" He cleared his throat. "—adjustable, once I have the leather cut and know what fasteners I need, they are easier to transport. And I get a significant number of orders from this party each year."

"How long does a design take, on average?"

"A few weeks." He stopped at a door and opened it, gesturing her inside.

She smelled it before she saw it all. The rich, unique scent of leather permeated the air. Then the various shaped leather goods draped over almost every surface in the room registered. She stopped short in awe, her mouth agape.

Chapter Three

Robert bumped into Beth when she stopped abruptly. Stepping to the side, he closed the door and set a shaking hand against her lower spine to guide her forward.

Do I offer her a drink? I should offer her a drink. "Would you like a drink? Er, I only have whisky and ale, or I could call for something different."

"Yes, please," she murmured, running her hand over a piece laid across the chair closest to her.

He wondered what to do given the vagueness of her reply. He desperately needed a whisky, so he poured two at the sideboard. Then what? Mayhap they could sit— Oops, he needed to move a few things to make room for that.

She wandered the room and fingered strips of leather.

He placed the drinks on a table near the settee and stepped to hover next to her.

She picked up one piece that was six strips of leather emanating from a metal ring. The harness was an experimental design, and he hadn't visited Sarah Potter's to have any of the girls model it for him for comfort or fit.

Those black straps across her soft, peaches-and-cream skin, her pliant belly, breasts, and arse in contrast to the stiff hide…

His cock stood up, saluting the vision, and he tugged on his waistcoat as she turned to face him.

"How does this work?" Her tone was breathy, her eyes slumberous, and her nipples stiff.

Her reaction is for my designs, like everyone else's. His cock did not care. Nor, on second thought, did he. Moving forward, he centered the ring at her waist.

She leaned forward an inch to watch him manipulate the arrangement.

"One pair goes around your waist. Another circles your neck." He placed them as he spoke, although he did not fasten them, allowing each to drop as he moved to the next. "And one…" He tugged it downward. "I cannot show you this part whilst you're wearing clothes."

"Ohh." The word held wonder and interest.

"Would you like to try it?" Feeling brave enough to push, he nonetheless stepped back to ensure his bulk did not feel threatening. He'd asked her downstairs to be sure, but he still wanted to hear her agreement.

"Yes, please."

Picking up the whiskies, he held one out to her, forcing his hand to steadiness. "Cheers. Would you like help with your dress? I am no ladies maid, but I'm sure we can muddle through."

Beth claimed one of the whiskies and gave him her back. He fumbled with the buttons until they were undone. Turning around, she held the dress in place below her breasts and set down her glass. She shrugged her shoulders, and the dress fell, separating from her chemise at the sides of her breasts but catching on those lush mounds.

It was all he could do not to pant like a dog. He licked his lips, and that must have been the reaction she wanted.

Her hand lifted, and the dress dropped to the floor. Her sheer muslin chemise, in a barely-peach color that matched her skin, did nothing to hide the rose-tipped points poking through it. Just below, her waist cinched in with quilted satin stays cascading to a petticoat.

Unable to tear his gaze from her bosom, he watched her magnificence quiver as she stepped out of the pool of dress around her feet. They were lost to his sight when she presented her back for him to untie her stays.

He needed two tries to grasp the ends of the bow and untie it. Then, reward in mind, he made quick work of loosening the criss-crossed laces.

The garment hit the floor, and she sighed. Finally, his knowledge of corsets and women flooded back, and he pulled her chemise up, slipping his fingers beneath it to smooth across her flesh, soothing the creases left from her stays.

"Yesss. Goodness, that feels marvelous."

Undoing the tapes of her petticoat, he shoved it off her hips and spun her.

"Would you like to try the garment now with your chemise on? Or do you prefer to remove that as well?" The hope in his voice was undeniable.

****

Beth had never cared about nudity or even being discovered in *flagrante delicto*. Preferring to feel that supple leather against her skin, Beth whipped the chemise over her head.

Robert did not move. She wasn't sure he even blinked.

Am I too round? Or was he offended by my lack of modesty? Beth was proud of her curves and knew her breasts were a draw for most men, but the perversity of the Ton, criticizing her behavior even while more than half of them were enthralled by it, made her question his reaction. She cared little for most people's acceptance, but her vulnerable position made her crave his.

The nature of the party and her reputation guaranteed his interest would not last past this night or mayhap this week. She could bemoan that later as she always did after her conquests ended, even knowing her actions reinforced her partners' beliefs that she was unsuitable for more than tupping. However, she needed validation that her naked form was acceptable for the evening, at least.

Then she spied movement. The rigid outline of his cock pulsed against his breeches, reaching toward her. With a sigh of relief, her shoulders relaxed an inch.

His shoulders twitched, and she realized her sigh had jostled her bosom, where his gaze now focused.

"Do you plan to remain fully clothed? I had plans to opine on your appearance if you recall."

"Uh." His brow furrowed, and he glanced at the fireplace.

"Mayhap at least your jacket? Cravat? Waistcoat if you're feeling daring?" She teased, hoping to loosen his demeanor.

His expression cleared, and he stripped off his jacket, uncaring that the sleeves turned inside out in his haste. The cravat flew.

After all, what need do we have of that when we are surrounded by sturdier options in leather? She suppressed a giggle.

His waistcoat disappeared.

She picked up the spidery leather contraption and

held it against her waist as he had done. "Show me, please?"

As he circled around her, he caught one strip of leather and brought it with him, then leaned around her other side to gather the corresponding piece to buckle around her. He then took the longest pieces and ran them up between her breasts to secure behind her neck.

The two remaining lengths hung along her front. Both had buckles. She had no idea how they'd fasten.

Coming to stand before her, Robert took one in his left hand. "Please tell me if you become uncomfortable." After a beat, he added, "Physically or mentally."

Beth smiled. "I will, but you needn't worry." She placed a hand on his linen-covered chest to reassure him.

He sucked in a breath, holding still.

Despite loving the solid feel of his muscles under her hand, Beth was dying of curiosity. Sliding her palm down his front slowly, she allowed her hand to drop to her side. "Right then. I wish to experience this. Please?"

"Yes, of course." He moved to her right and squatted next to her. "Widen your stance a little for me?"

"Of course." 'Twas almost a question. *Will that length of leather rest along my core? That could cause some erotic rubbing. Oh my.*

She'd been damp since her gown had loosened, and Beth worried her juices would mark the leather, but she was too embarrassed to warn him. Realizing his head was level with her most secret folds further inflamed her.

He passed the strap between her legs to his other hand, then leaned around to cinch it to the belt around her waist so it angled outward toward her hip and cupped one cheek of her bottom. Rising, he quickly replicated the configuration on her other side with the remaining strap.

He'd set these last two in the crease of each leg, so the pressure mounded her intimate folds outward. She wanted to see the whole picture in the mirror, to run her hands along the straps, and to pull them and see what that did to her. But most of all, she wanted him to pull that bulging cock out and stick it inside her.

I hope I can get to the bed—or nearest available surface—in this.

But Robert retreated a step to make a slow circle around her to evaluate every angle.

Tugging on her "belt" gently, he muttered to himself. "Mayhap a few more holes in each strap for different shapes."

Coming back around, he put his hands against her ribs just under her breasts. "A length here that meets in the center back and connects to the neck? Mayhap sold separately. But is it fixed or made to measure? Hmm…"

Beth shifted, impatient. She'd viewed the leather as a means to an end, and she hadn't pictured that end as lengthy sensual torture. Was he going to fuck her?

Robert shook his head, refocusing on her face. "My apologies, Beth. 'Tis the first time I've seen it on someone. Does anything pinch?"

"A bit." She gestured downward.

"Where? Are the straps too wide? Did I catch a tender part?" He knelt and inhaled a deep breath.

Is he smelling me? Oh my. "No, not exactly."

"Where does it hurt?"

"I'll show you." Smirking, she held her hand out for his. She turned it palm up and brought it between her legs to slide it through her wetness to the raised bundle of nerves at her center. The glide of skin to skin sparked her nerve endings, and she jolted when his finger found her most sensitive spot.

Goodness, I am sopping. I hope he takes that as the compliment it is.

He bent his finger a hairsbreadth.

She moaned in pleasure, her hand falling away. He didn't seem to need guidance. She was so swollen and sensitive, she'd need only a few strokes. If he didn't move soon, she'd take herself over. Or better yet, mayhap she'd use one of those leather straps conveniently placed. But no, she craved his touch. Her pleasure bump pulsed against his hold.

"Sounds like more of an ache than a pinch," he said, even as his fingers turned and pinched her nub.

"Aaiyee!" She clutched his hair, ready to direct if need be or hold herself upright if he was as skilled as she was starting to think he was. *'Tis always the quiet ones. I should—*

He put both his hands on the front of her thighs and spread her lower lips with his thumbs.

Yes, please. She stared downward at him in hopeful surprise.

"Hold on to me if you need to," he said and pushed his face against her, his tongue finding the nub he had just pinched to soothe it with gentle licks.

Ahh. His tongue seemed connected to every nerve ending in that area, as well as her nipples. Bolts of lightning shot from her core to her stomach muscles and breasts. Even her ears buzzed. Beth wasn't sure a man had ever found her pleasure point quite so well, quite so quickly.

"Robert—" If only she could find her words to finish the sentence. One of her knees buckled, and her hand dropped to his shoulder for balance.

"Mmm?" Her flesh muffled his question.

"Do y'think I can sit or mayhap lay, in this?"

"In a moment."

In another minute, I won't need help. I'll be lying on the floor. She quivered, sucking in a breath. Every muscle in her body tightened, except her legs, which went noodley.

He took one last lick before releasing her and kneeling back.

"Let us adjourn to the other room, and you can lay on the bed." He gestured behind him. Standing, he took her hand. "Can you walk in it? Without it pinching anything?"

She tried. The smooth leather straps slid one way with one step, then the other with her next motion. She moaned.

"Yyowwch!" she yelped in pain and froze, mid-step. The two straps had caught her nether lips in the back-and-forth movement.

"I was afraid of that. Ah well. This will be for use in situ then. I shall soothe your tender flesh." Stopping, he pressed her down on the settee. "Do I need to loosen any straps?"

"Yes, please." The ones running between her legs were now pulling. She was amazed he'd realized that might happen. His knowledge of women's bodies and apparel was astounding.

"Right, then."

He knelt and undid them both, then took one and slid it up through the strap circling her waist. With his free hand, he pulled her wrist close and looped the leather around her wrist, fastening the buckle to holes she hadn't noticed. Her wrist was essentially pinned to her side. He repeated his actions with the other wrist, creating cuffs.

Oh my. Beth could not remember an intimate encounter when her partner had managed to surprise and impress her this thoroughly. And they hadn't even reached the good part yet. *I take that back. This has all been glorious. I could spend hours seeing what he imagines next.*

Not one to sit passively, she opened her mouth to ask about his soothing reference, but he beat her to it.

"Now, what needs massaging?" He did not wait for an answer. Instead, he hooked his hands behind her upper calves and tugged her forward, then pushed them wide.

Without her hands to support her, Beth slouched with her spine curved against the seat and back cushions of the sofa. She wasn't sure it was the most flattering position, but as he did not seem to notice, she didn't care.

Then his lips touched her flesh again, his breath warm on her sensitive bundle of nerves, his teeth pressing gently as his tongue sought her opening.

Her sprawl was forgotten. Throwing her head against the rise of the couch, she moaned again. Her imprisoned hands twitched with the desire to feel his hair, to press him against her, to tug him away. Her eyes flew open, wanting to watch, and her gaze went to the movement of his head between her legs.

Somehow, seeing his hair sway but not being able to read his expression elevated the sensations from each minute swirl of his lips and tongue…and oh, lord, fingers now too.

Her orgasm circled up from where he touched her into her belly and breasts, curling her toes. Her hips lifted, trying to thrust into mouth. *There, there—*

He pulled back. His lips were less than an inch from her, his breath wafting over flesh that needed one more touch, one more lick.

"Please," she whined.

"Patience. You wanted to see how this worked. I am not done showing you."

"Yes, but you can show me more after you touch me a bit more. Please?"

"Certainly. I shall touch you here." His fingers ghosted along her inner thighs—in the wrong direction, damn him. They feathered toward her feet, where he gripped her arches and bent her toes back in a gentle stretch before sliding upward. He tested the plumpness of her calves, then curled his hands around her knees and slid them up the top of her thighs and onto her belly, drawing her attention back to her posture.

She narrowed her eyes, watching his face for signs of distaste, but his gaze was hungry as it followed his hands.

He weighed her breasts in his palms, fingers prodding the crevice underneath them.

"Bountiful. Delicious." His words were breathy, his eyes hot. He flicked his tongue over his lips.

She relished that tongue but wasn't sure he remembered there was a person attached to the breasts he cupped, a common issue with men who saw them. Squirming, she attempted to remind him of where she wanted his touch.

"You see? I can touch what I want now, without being rushed." He caught her gaze and smiled, his voice firmer again. "I can"—he leaned closer, his breath washing over one tip—"lick where I desire." His lips closed over the hard point of her breast.

She tried to dig her elbows into the settee to push against him but had no leverage.

"Ah, Robert. Will I get to touch you?" *And if I get my hands free, will I get your cock in play to put this inferno out?*

"We shall see." His tone was noncommittal. "Now, shh, or I shall see if I can find a strip of leather for a gag."

Beth's eyes widened, and, surprisingly, her center pulsed hard. She'd never been gagged.

The quiet one has a spine. And mayhap even a plan.

Did her reaction mean she wanted a gag? She wasn't opposed to it. Then she realized debating her options was futile; she had no choice but to sit back and take what he offered. That was the purpose of this strange apparel he'd concocted.

He raised his head, trailing one hand up to curl his fingers around the back of her neck. "You are marvelous, gorgeous."

She did not have time to formulate a reply before his mouth met hers, his hand holding her immobile. Soft and lush, his lips nonetheless moved with intent, parting hers to thrust his tongue inside to tangle with hers. The man kissed as expertly as he did everything else.

Tasting her essence on him threw another log on the flames of desire burning inside her, and she moaned into his mouth, returning the kiss with enthusiasm.

He trailed his lips along the side of her neck to her other breast and, from there, back down her body.

She had never been the center of prolonged attention while naked. Being proud of her curves and having them subject to this level of scrutiny was quite different, but his continual worship of every part of her did not allow for self-doubt. Even when he reached around and squeezed what he could palm of her bottom, his awestruck expression excited her.

The contraption's goal was achieved. She was the happy passive recipient of whatever attention he wanted to give her.

And give, he did. Over and over, he put his mouth to her most sensitive spots and licked and sucked until she was shaking with need.

Each time, ecstasy gathered in her, coiling tighter and tighter. Her heartbeat pounded in her chest and wherever his mouth touched. Every time she neared the precipice and could taste the explosion on her tongue, he shifted his fingers, hands, and lips to a less erogenous area on her body. When her shaking subsided, he returned, slowly and softly at first. Then his lips would suck her nub or his tongue would spear into her, and she'd writhe and gasp. And again, he'd stop.

Finally, she screamed in frustration, and began to beg in earnest. "Please, please. I cannot take anymore. Please. I'll do anything."

"Ah, you're ready." He stood.

She managed a weak glare. She'd been ready for over an hour, damn him. But more important was—"Where are you going?"

"Just here." He reached for two throw pillows and put them on the ground in front of her, undid his breeches, and knelt.

Damn him, I did not even get to see his cock.

The pillows put him at the perfect level to fuck her. His hand was out of sight, but she thought it was on his cock. His other hand extracted a sheath from his discarded jacket and brought it between her legs.

Another first. *Stupid, Beth.* She, who always ensured she was protected, hadn't thought to ask.

Then the head of his cock was at her entrance, even as she felt wetness drip between her bottom cheeks.

He thrust forward.

All her nerve endings fired. She was so swollen that the fit was tighter than she remembered ever feeling. Flames erupted from every tiny spot he touched, rolling up through her, igniting everything in its path. Her breasts ached, her nipples stabbed the air, her hands clenched. Despite her awkward position, her hips rose against him, and she keened once before the explosion darkened her vision.

He thrust again and again. The ecstasy did not abate as it raced through her body, burning her, on and on.

"Ah, yes, my little peach. Come for me." His thumb touched the bundle of nerves already throbbing, and a new wash of fire exploded from her belly to behind her eyes.

That was the last thing she felt.

Chapter Four

Robert might not be able to read women's intentions or thoughts or even most of their actions. But he prided himself on reading their bodies and strumming them like a harp.

He'd never been athletic and still had no idea what had prompted Evan Gardner, the most popular boy at school, to befriend him. He'd never be the best-looking man in the room, even without Evan present. That did not mean he could not be the best lover in the room, even if no one knew.

This was his secret skill, giving a woman the most pleasure she'd ever experienced. The girls at Sarah Potter's fought over him. Rarely did he choose to focus his skills on a member of the Ton or even one on the periphery, like Beth Jenkins.

He'd been unable to resist her luscious curves, though. Evan's party gave him an opportunity for a short-term affair. He would not invest his feelings, he would not be hurt when she inevitably wanted to find someone more comfortable in social gatherings, more handsome, simply more. This dalliance had an end date built in when the party concluded in a few days.

His enjoyment of Beth's softness and responsiveness had been so fervent, the intensity of his focus helped stave off his need for release. Even when she was spread open and at his mercy, he'd wanted to slow down, to savor this feast before him.

Only when she begged and cried for release did his mind register his rampant need for her. He remembered to protect them both from pregnancy and then…

He was home. No woman had ever fit him so perfectly. Her flesh gripped him but gave way generously. Her body's lubrication, still sweet and salty on his tongue, helped him slide in to join pelvis to pelvis.

She arched as he surged, meeting him.

Lava flowed through him, gathering at the base of his spine and in his bollocks. Holding there, he felt her contract around him, milking his cock. He thrust through it, hoping to elongate her pleasure, gritting his teeth against his own. Then he succumbed to his body's demands, unable to stave off orgasm any longer. Both fire and relief shot up his spine as he pulsed against her contractions, groaning.

"Here, you can do more." He narrated for himself as much as for her. Bringing his thumb to her most sensitive spot, he pistoned his hips faster, chasing his pleasure as hers mesmerized him.

Holy hell. He could not form words or thoughts beyond that phrase. He'd never before been left speechless by passion. It was rather disconcerting.

He hung over her to catch his breath, braced on his hands. As he came back to himself, he realized she had passed out. From pleasure, he hoped.

Pulling out, he set the French letter aside on his handkerchief and, without fastening his breeches, began undoing the buckles on the leather harness she wore. He knew from prior testing that muscles stiffened after too long in his contraptions, and while passion would mask that, the discomfort kicked in afterward.

He massaged her thighs as he lowered them.

She murmured and her eyelids fluttered, but she remained lax.

Once the whole contraption was off, he turned her to recline along the length of the settee, covering her with a quilt from the bedroom. Then he fastened his breeches and stood to search for his whisky.

He lifted it to drink and rang the bell for a servant to bring tea to restore her. Such a bold young woman would not need smelling salts, just tea and a few moments to recover.

Returning, he perched on the edge of the settee and stroked her cheek with a knuckle.

Her eyes flickered open and focused on his.

"Whisky? I've rung for tea as well."

"Yes, please."

He offered her glass to her, waited while she sat up and sipped, trying to ignore the blanket falling away from her magnificent breasts. His cock twitched in renewed interest, but he ignored it, knowing she'd had enough for the night.

"Are you quite all right?"

"Ha." She barked a laugh. "No, I'm not 'all right.' I'm amazed, satiated, and ever so slightly disconcerted. That was the most—" She seemed to search for the word. "—intense experience of my life. 'All right' does not begin to cover it."

He was grinning by the time she was halfway through, pleased with himself and her response.

"Excellent. Do you need to return to your room or would you like to stay here?" He was shocked to hear those words coming from his mouth. He never invited women to stay the night.

She ran her gaze over his still-clothed form and licked her lips. "Stay. Definitely stay, please."

Ah, mayhap she hasn't had enough. We'll have all night as well as the morning.

****

Robert woke to sharp knocks at the door and Evan's voice calling his name. Beth was curled around his back, her luscious breasts pressed against his shirt-covered spine.

Damnation, Evan never bothered him first thing. What was with the fellow this week? He'd fallen asleep anticipating what position he could bind her into next. Mayhap whilst she was still sleeping—

Bangs sounded on the door again.

Beth mumbled and rolled over, pulling the covers over her delectable curves.

"Stay under there," Robert whispered before rising. Frustrated, he yanked on his breeches from last night and strode through the workshop to crack the door.

As usual, his friend tried to push in, assuming he was welcome. Meeting with resistance, he complained, "I need your help, man. Let me in."

"No. I have a guest."

"*Really*? Who is it then?"

Robert sidestepped to stop his friend from peering around him.

"I helped you last night. You've used up your requests." He went to shut the door.

"Come on, please? Meet me downstairs in… Uh, how long do you need? Is she sleeping, or will I need to wait for another round?"

Robert arched a brow. "Maybe both."

"Right. I will take breakfast in my office. Join me

when you can." Robert was thankful as always for their friendship that made these kinds of interactions easy.

Robert tiptoed into the bedroom and found clean clothes. Grateful men's clothes did not actually need a valet if he opted for more comfortable boots and a simple cravat tie, he dressed quietly in his workroom and slipped out. He hoped his friend's request was brief and he could ease back into bed with the ripe little peach to fulfill the fantasies he'd been building overnight.

When he ambled into Evan's office a quarter hour later, his host snorted. "That was fast. I hope you at least got a good suck."

He folded his arms. "Oh, I thought you needed something. I can come back later."

"Teasing. Teasing." Evan held up his hands in surrender. "Thank you."

Robert accepted the cup of tea handed to him and sat, crossing one ankle over the other knee. "What's this about help?"

"You remember Penelope's friend? And her cousin? From the ball in London where Michael proposed? And here, this week?"

"Yes." Robert remembered—from five minutes ago when he left one of them in his bed. But he'd never been one to brag about his conquests.

"Beth and Althea. Althea wants investment help. Which is why Beth requested their invitations." Evan shook his head. "So much impudence in so small a package."

"Why did Beth seek the invitations? And why does that make her impudent?"

"How isn't she? That girl knows almost everyone and their servants. She's already met my mother, if you can believe it, and has offered to find Lucy's replacement."

Robert wondered how that had happened. Evan did not allow anyone unvetted near his mother.

"Her parents were unconventional, to say the least," Evan continued. "They died in an accident when she was around seventeen. She ended up as Althea's ward until she reaches her majority. Anyway, Althea is not like Beth, or you or I, or Penelope, for that matter. She is reserved and unaccustomed to—" He coughed. "—our type of fête, shall we say."

"Ah. So, you need me to entertain the quiet mouse? I can do that. Especially after you threw me into the thick of it last night." If he could not spend time with Beth, he wanted to lick his wounds in solitude.

What wounds? I can't be hurt from one night of fun, a night similar to any at Sarah's. Can I? I should not have had her stay. It muddies the waters. I cannot become invested.

Evan glared, his jaw tightening.

Robert stared in surprise as his friend growled, "No, thank you. I need to find out more to see if the investment makes sense. I need you to keep her rather energetic cousin entertained."

Ah, an excuse to— No! Attention from the mean-spirited Ton is the last thing I want. Gor, I knew that girl was too bold for me. But those breasts were nigh on irresistible, and she did not wait for my invitation.

"No," he barked. "I can't. No."

Evan's eyes widened.

It was rare for Robert to feel strongly about anything, rarer still for him to raise his voice to almost a shout. He cringed, expecting his friend to question him on his vehemence.

Instead, Evan stared at him for a moment, then continued. "I am not asking for every moment of the day, only the evenings. Remember what I said to you when you arrived? This wom—ah, opportunity—is the first thing to catch my interest in months."

Robert sighed, deflating. A few days was not much to ask, especially when Evan rarely needed help and had done so much for him. "Yes, of course. I'll do my best."

"Now that you've agreed, I should probably warn you about her." Evan grinned at Robert's hard stare. "She grew up learning that the same rules that apply to boys and men should apply to girls and women. That she should have the same rights as you or I and not care what the Ton thinks. So her behavior is often bordering on the outrageous. When I say she knows a lot of people, I mean intimately. I imagine Althea keeps her somewhat reined in, and they seem close, so Beth likely tries to remain circumspect for her cousin's sake, but that little body bursts with vivacity, so she struggles. You'd think, as she knows half the Ton and their secrets, they'd be kinder to her."

Robert grunted. "Doesn't seem to work that way." He'd had enough horrible experiences with society's view of him, his shape, and his untitled standing, even after Bags's investments had assured his ability to buy and sell almost any of them. Another thought occurred to him. Evan knew he hated to risk gossip. "That wasn't fair, asking me to squire a wild chit around who is going to cause mischief."

"No need to squire. Simply keep a watchful eye so she doesn't interfere with me getting to know Althea. Please. If she finds games or men—or women—to occupy her, your duty is done."

Given his knowledge of Evan's sexual history as well as his own, promiscuity did not bother him as it might another man. However, he hated the idea that she would replace him.

Buck up, man. You're being childish. If you don't want her, you can't pout if she finds someone else to play with.

He hated when his inner voice was right.

****

Robert returned to his rooms torn. With the perspective of daylight and time apart, part of him wanted Beth to be gone to avoid temptation. Evan's use of the word "outrageous" made him nervous. But a big part—growing bigger as he neared the room—hoped she was still abed, where he could encourage her to stay and skip breakfast.

She was dressed and sifting through piles of leather accessories when he returned, a scenario he should have but hadn't envisioned.

"Robert, these are magnificent." She looked up as he clicked the door shut. "Are they all your design or are some by request?"

"One or two are from creative minds, but most are mine."

"How did you learn this?"

"By happenstance, really. My first year room at Oxford was not as fancy as Evan's and other heirs'. It was one of four rooms in a tanner's house, attached to his tannery. I watched him work when I needed a break from the endless books." He'd watch the man's arms flex as he forced tools and needles through the hide, fascinated with the convergence of craftsmanship, design, and strength.

"The couple did not have children; I suspect that is why they hosted students. They treated us as family. When I visited him at work, the house master always asked if my reading was complete before he allowed me to stay. One day, I picked up a scrap to try sewing, and he took it as an invitation to teach me the trade. 'It can never hurt,' he told me, 'to have a variety of ways to put food on the table. If only they taught you more business management at that fancy school, you'd be unstoppable.'"

Robert had chuckled at the man's words, but the idea had taken root.

He moved into a house with Evan for his last two years, because it was much easier to help one another sneak back in after an Evan-inspired escapade. But he visited the tannery at least once a week and kept a small project on the side at all times. The complexity of the items he made increased as he honed his skills.

What he did not tell Beth was that he did not need to sell these. Indeed, he could have given all the pieces away and not impair his net worth. He'd happily turned his entire quarterly allowance over to Evan while in university, and his friend had made them all bags and bags of money, earning him his nickname. Robert wasn't even sure he still received funds from his father, as the income from investments and his bank balance eclipsed those stipends. However, Robert had remembered the tanner's words and kept his skills honed, and designing and creating unique leather apparel and accessories quickly became a passion.

He needed something to occupy his days, anyway. He wasn't social enough or attractive enough to be a—

what was the male equivalent of a socialite?—a fop or dandy or rake. He just provided them with the tools they needed. The Merlin behind each would-be Arthur's throne, with Bags being the king of all kings in this particular world.

"That explains the leatherwork, but not the subject matter." She arched a brow.

"You've met our host, haven't you?" he asked with a sardonic grin.

She laughed.

"Inevitably, Evan's propensity for outrageousness led me astray as it so often does. I tried my hand at a few restraints for sexual games, and a secret, elite, lucrative business was born."

A servant knocked, delivering tea.

Beth gasped. "I hadn't realized the time. I must go check on Althea."

She pecked him on the cheek as she brushed by him, then he was alone.

Telling himself he was relieved, he went to check on the day's activities. The rain continued, so riding or walking the estate were not options. As those were the only things that might have tempted Robert, including a quick nip in to visit with Evan's mama, who he adored, he chose to continue his leatherwork in an attempt not to obsess on how and if he'd find a way to get Beth naked again without an audience.

Tying off the last stitch of another piece, he moved to place it on the pile of completed work. Frowning, he flipped through the pile, then the other piles, then gazed around the room in consternation. A garment was missing.

Understanding dawned. "Why, that little hellion.

'Outrageous' is right. So much for 'only the evenings.'"

52

Chapter Five

Beth took her time dressing for dinner.

When Robert had left that morning, she could not resist rummaging through the piles of leather cut in all widths and lengths that lay around the sitting room. Hoping he'd participate in that night's games with her, she wanted to ensure he'd search her out.

She could not decipher how to wear most of them.

I suppose there is not a wrong way, given that he employed two different configurations with me last night using only one set. I must admit, though, I am impressed. He might think about intimacy even more than I do. And he is certainly more creative.

She'd found an item that looked like drawers cut off at the crease of the thigh, leaving only the person's most private parts covered. They had a narrow channel around the waist for a drawstring, but there was no tie added yet.

What made these so exciting? Was it the feel of leather against one's nether regions or the tight fit, assuming they were specifically designed for women? Or were they simply very short drawers in a different fabric? It seemed rather tame.

Nevertheless, she wanted Robert to search her out again, and taking them had been a way of ensuring he did so.

Beth pulled them out of the drawer she'd tucked them into. Althea had already dressed for dinner and gone to take the meeting Beth had arranged with Evan regarding her store expansion.

Untying the wrapper she had slipped on after her bath, she removed its sash and ran that through the waistband of the leather garment, using a bent hair pin to lead it through.

Even before donning them, the thought of that rich smooth hide sliding between her legs had her pulse racing. As they slid up, there was less and less slack in the leather, and she worried they would not fit her bottom or even her thighs. When they glided up over her cheeks, she sighed in relief. The leg holes still had a finger's worth of room.

She shifted side to side for the pure pleasure of the animal skin against her own.

Oops.

There seemed to be a seam or fold of fabric that caught against her most sensitive spot. Frowning, she tugged them down a few inches to peer into the undergarment.

No seam. No fold of fabric. In fact, he'd taken care to ensure there was not a seam or hem near sensitive flesh, by adding a layer of leather inside. But—she prodded—there was a lump under that layer.

Ah, well, she'd tell him about the flaw when she saw him. She dragged them back up and tied them around her waist, layering a petticoat and a gown of a dark color, to ensure the black of the leather did not show through.

Her first strides into the hall were large and confident. Drawing a sharp breath when the lump brushed her folds, she shortened her gait and slowed. Stepping onto the first stair wrenched a gasp from her.

Oh my. She paused with one foot still on the floor of

the upper level, one foot on the step.

With one leg stretched and one bent, the bump caressed her growing protuberance through her parted nether lips.

Right, then. Not one to waste an opportunity, she took the stairs at a lingering pace, swinging her hips to test different angles. By the time she reached the main floor, the leather was slippery with her arousal. She was hungry for more than dinner and hoped Robert was sitting near her to plan for dessert.

Reaching the drawing room, she found everyone pairing to venture to dinner.

Desperate to find Robert, she returned Althea's nod and kept scanning the room. She sighed in relief when he stepped from the shadows to offer his arm.

"I believe you have something of mine," he hissed, leaning in and turning his mouth toward her ear so others would not overhear.

He mustn't be angry with me. Althea insisted I behave. I should not have done this, certainly not before she met with Cheltie. Contrite, she slid a look at him through her lashes.

"Are you wearing it?" he whispered, running his gaze over her.

"I beg your pardon. I should not have taken it without your leave, Robert. Truly, I am sorry."

"We shall discuss it after dinner."

A sharp thrill shot through her at the idea of being alone with him after dinner, as she had hoped.

They reached the dining room, and he pulled out a chair for her. "But are you wearing it?"

As she lowered herself, the leather garment stretched over her bottom and grew tighter between her legs. The bulge nestled directly against her already-swollen nub, exerting gentle pressure. Her breath caught.

"I shall take that as a yes." His smile was grim as he strode away and down the length of the table.

Beth shifted her weight from side to side, varying the position and pressure of the bulge.

'Tis like having a finger on my button as I sit here fully clothed. Delicious.

Robert reappeared across from her, seating himself with his gaze narrowed on her.

His surveillance stimulated her as much as the friction of the drawers. Of course, it helped that when he looked at his plate to eat, she'd circle her hips in a tiny wiggle on the chair. She was starting to wonder if it was deliberate rather than a flaw and was impressed with his foresight.

Watching Robert watch her also made her nervous. Without these, would he have spent more time with her? Should she simply return them and move on? After all, men and women seemed interested only until they'd bedded her, then they grew bored. Men in particular seemed to like the chase. And since she had not provided Robert with a challenge, in fact had pursued him, he was probably considering his next conquest.

She wished she hadn't taken these.

No, she shouldn't overthink. He intrigued her. Her parents would remind her it did not matter who pursued whom. What was important was whether the two people were compatible. And their interlude would end with the party. Putting aside her fears, she vowed to make his and her own evening entertaining.

Catching his eye, she took a bite of pigeon, swiveled her hips deliberately, then moaned.

"Stop that," he hissed, frowning.

"Oh, but this meal is so…pleasurable. Have you tasted the…meat?"

He narrowed his eyes.

She widened hers innocently.

Spearing a bite of pigeon, he popped it in his mouth, then choked on it at her next words.

"I think they marinated it in peach juice." She referenced his encouraging comment to her from the night before.

Coughing, he glared at her from behind his serviette. "I do not play in public."

She smirked. "I was simply enjoying my meal." Her voice was low to be heard underneath the buzz of others' conversations around them. "Look around. No one sees anything amiss."

He slid his eyes left and right without moving his head, his neck stiff.

Was he really that worried?

That made her nervous. She loved group settings, enjoyed flirting and more. She'd never cared whether the act itself was private, as her priority was always enjoyment for everyone involved. If someone did not want to see an activity she was engaged in, they could leave the room or the stable. If Robert was that stodgy, her actions would frustrate him quickly.

His jaw relaxed a fraction, and she nearly sighed with relief. The shift touched off sparks from the lump in her drawers, and her sigh became a sucked-in breath.

He tilted his head at her, seeming to concur with her assessment of their privacy. Slicing another bite, he brought it to his lips. Rather than chewing it, however, he sucked on it.

She held her breath.

"I believe you are correct. Peaches." There was just enough of a pause before the last word that no one else would know he was addressing her.

She swallowed audibly, her throat tight.

"Try another bite. I love hearing your enjoyment."

He's telling me to swivel. Godsakes, the man can control me without any tethers whatsoever.

She forked something off her plate and chewed on it, not tasting it. Her flesh pulsed against that leather finger without a single hip movement, simply from his gaze and this private-in-public game they were playing.

He arched a brow.

She circled her hips slower. While she'd played in public, she'd never orgasmed at the table during a formal dinner, without anyone touching her. The idea was titillating, but she felt suddenly shy.

Why am I shy? This is my type of play. Certainly, this particular crowd would be more likely to applaud than condemn her performance. But would Robert feel exposed? He'd said he did not enjoy public play.

He was still watching her, assessing her reaction from her expression. His gaze dipped.

She glanced to where he was looking. Her nipples stood hard and proud through her chemise and dress, pointing at him.

She looked at him through her upper lashes. "I find the potatoes a little firmer than normal, don't you, Mr. Orford?" she said with a grin.

"They taste perfect to me." He licked his lips.

She nearly orgasmed on the spot—no rotation needed.

"No more." He held her gaze. "You may not finish

at the table."

She bit her lip. That solved her dilemma about exploding during dinner, but she was not sure she could hold off.

Dessert was served, a small bowl of creamy custard with a slice of peach decorating the plate.

She groaned again and met his gaze.

His smile bloomed slowly. Dratted man.

"No more movements. Eat your dessert and I shall help you up after dinner."

She really hoped "up" referenced her pinnacle of pleasure. Watching him savor the custard, licking then sucking it off the spoon after quick glances to ensure no one observed his poor etiquette, nearly undid her. She was almost incoherent with desire, afraid to swivel any more for fear of creating a wet spot on her gown. When he bit into the peach slice with a grin, she had to clench to avoid going over. Closing her eyes, she panted.

Robert's hand gripping her upper arm brought her head around to him. Dinner was over, and the guests were standing and moving toward the doors, ready for the games to start.

She was beyond games, wanting only Robert. Here and now if he was amenable. She was ready to clear a few place settings out of the way or drop to her knees to suck him in supplication.

"You should have asked. What if those were a custom order for someone and I did not have the measurements with me to recreate them?" His voice was a gruff whisper, and he kept glancing around to check that no one could overhear them. He pulled her out of the path to the ballrooms where the crowd milled, discussing their options of games.

"Are they?" She peered up at him through her lashes, trying to judge his mood.

"No. They're a new design. At least now I can get feedback." The grin he shot her was quick but wide.

She opened her mouth to praise the garment.

He hastily raised his finger to her lips. "But not here, please."

"Right, then." She refrained from rolling her eyes at his prudishness. "Were you planning to participate in the games tonight?"

Belatedly, she realized her predicament. She'd been so focused on the slippery flesh sliding against the leather at the juncture of her thighs and the thought of moving again, she hadn't heard Cheltie's announcement. Remembering how many times he had teased her to the edge of orgasm then eased back, she feared his answer.

Please take me to your room. I cannot believe I don't want to play games, but I don't.

She held her breath, her eyes wide and pleading.

He shook his head. "I am not one for public play."

"Well, then. Where would you like to discuss this design?"

Chapter Six

Robert kept his expression neutral, unwilling to show his emotions to anyone he did not know well. His school years had taught him that people would use them against him. On the other hand, he was not sure he could even wait until his room to taste the peach he wished for. Dinner had been torturous. He hadn't experienced a cockstand for that long ever, even in his teenage years, and he was concerned that he had enough blood left in his legs to walk.

She referred to designs. Is she really interested in my leatherwork or simply what it can do for her? Thinking about it more, he wasn't sure those reasons were much different, given the purpose of the garments. *'Tis supposed to be about pleasure. Relax and enjoy the party. She'll be gone at the end of the week.*

Her curiosity also provided a unique opportunity. Beth was ideal for much of his work, because he designed with her shape in mind. Her body was ideal to him. He loved womanly curves. Of course, he tailored each piece to its buyer or their partner, as needed. After all, they paid his ridiculous prices for custom work.

He charged those prices because he could. However, his design of each new toy, garment, or tool was pictured on a buxom figure, with a waist that dipped in, flaring again to rounded hips, like Beth's.

"We can use the second drawing room." He gestured

toward the rear of the house, testing her interest in spending time with him beyond discussion. "It need only be a brief conversation. Bags plans to show my pieces tomorrow night."

Her initial parlay back at the London party had been toward Bags, and he didn't compare to his friend looks-wise. However, if she wanted a repeat of last night, given how attracted he was to her physically, he was willing to accept second place.

"Do you not want me to return these? I'd rather hoped to ask you about a few of the others."

He gaped, momentarily forgetting he had offered somewhere other than his room as a deliberate probe. Ladies in polite society did not push like this, and if they did, it was to men like Michael and Bags, never him.

Recovering, he stammered, "Uh, my rooms?"

"Yes." She nodded and linked her arm through his.

Robert's mind was already running through his inventory, deciding what he wanted to see on her most. The corset, the chair sling…

His cock stirred in his breeches as he led her to the stairs. He slid a glance sideways.

At the bottom of the stairs, she dawdled and gripped his arm tighter. Her impressive bosom heaved. Ah, the *kleis*—he'd borrowed the Greek word for key for the protrusion, as it was also part of *kleitoris*, the sensitive part of Beth's body it mimicked—must be extra interesting on the stairs. He smirked, tugging her forward.

As they ascended, he tucked his arm with her hand on it tighter against his side to support her. Not allowing her to linger, he kept a steady pace upward. By halfway, she was panting; by the last several steps she was twisting on each one, curling forward at the waist.

"How do you like my design? It seems to work as I intended, although I had not accounted for stairs."

"If you intended it as a torture device, 'tis certainly working as intended."

"Ah, foreplay, torture. A fine line, don't you think?" He shrugged, stifling a laugh.

She glared at him, still gasping for breath.

A grin formed despite his attempts to suppress his humor.

"I may need to change petticoats," she muttered.

He continued to smile as they gained the hallway, deeming this pattern a success. He'd bet that garment was wet with her juices and clinging to her, given her reaction to the stairs.

In his suite, Beth bounced in excitement as he began to open his trunk. Allowing it to snap closed, he gestured her back. "Oh, no. Use the bedroom to remove the garment you borrowed, then go sit in an armchair. I am not showing you everything tonight. I want to be sure I see you tomorrow as well."

Her responding smile was incandescent, and he blinked.

I shall have to do that more often. Just because she initiated doesn't mean I should sit back and not woo her. He frowned. *Wait. Woo her?* Wooing should not be a consideration. Their dalliance was only for the duration of the party.

But praise was chivalrous, and he was determined to offer her that, after she'd been so encouraging to him.

As she went to change, he brought out two sets of leather cuffs with lace ties, connected by an adjustable strap. The strap was two pieces, connected like a belt, with a series of holes, a buckle, and a keeper, a loop of leather beyond the holes for the length of the piece beyond the buckle.

Beth returned and sat, cocking her head at the bundle of leather. She looked curious, albeit faintly disappointed, as though she had expected something more elaborate.

He chuckled to himself. If only she knew how many ways he could use these.

"May I?" She sounded shy, at least compared to her usual tone, as she held her hand out.

He brought them to her, dropping them into her palm.

"I fear I am at a disadvantage," she said, glancing up at him. She licked her lips.

He enjoyed her nerves. Keeping a woman off-balance in his bedroom was his favorite thing. Usually, it happened when the leather was already on. Then again, that was because he chose women who had seen demonstrations of his pieces and were eager to try them. "How so?"

"Don't you usually display them on models or in use?"

"Yes, and Evan will do so tomorrow. You can enjoy the show then."

"But I asked for a private show." She was pouting again, and Robert found himself tempted to threaten punishment. This little hellion apparently required a strong hand.

"I don't have a model handy. What do you suggest?" He knew she'd led him there, but he sure as hell wasn't going to volunteer himself. This would also address agreement, the one thing he demanded from partners, given that bondage was involved with much of his leather work.

"I will model them. Then I can get the full experience, rather than simply watching a show."

Perfect. He suppressed another smile. "Excellent. These can be used without removing any clothes. 'Tis bad enough we are in here without your maid or someone. I don't want to harm your reputation."

She gave a snort that told him of her disregard for her standing in society. It was a timely reminder of why he should want the liaison to end with the party and forego wooing.

He attached one cuff to her left wrist, leaving the leather strip and the attached cuff trailing. Her right hand received one end of the other set of cuffs, with the laces wrapped around the outside of the cuff in opposing directions and tied off. He slid a finger under each cuff to ensure her blood flow was not restricted and stepped back.

She gave a small circle with a hand. "And? Where do the other ends go then?"

"You'll see."

Stepping forward and going to one knee by her side, he threaded the strap of one set through the opening below the carved wooden arm of the Hepplewhite chair. The arms were padded where her elbow naturally rested so he was not worried about her comfort. He then brought the leather around the outside of the chair leg and attached the cuff on the other end to her ankle, checking again for circulation.

"Hmm. I can still move quite freely." Beth tested that side, as Robert secured her other ankle similarly.

"Reach for me." He shifted back on his heels.

As her hands came forward, her feet were forced to lift, to give her range of motion.

"Now. Let's see how you like this." He leaned forward to one side again.

Unbuckling the strap, he drew the tongue further through the buckle, passing one, two, three holes.

Her ankle lifted. She gasped and tried to keep her thighs closed, as a lady would when sitting. But with the strap threaded around the arm of the chair, her ankle was drawn outward. She tried moving her arm from her lap to the pad, then over it to grasp the vertical wooden piece of the chair arm.

Robert grinned and absorbed the slack. Finally, after another two holes, he buckled the strap together.

Beth stared at him wide-eyed from behind her raised knee, her foot dangling just below her hand. "Oh."

"Not going to reach for me?" He chuckled and turned to do the same to her other side.

Beth squirmed. "This is terribly inappropriate, Mister Orford."

He grinned. "Which you knew when you asked to see these. The actuality of being restrained is quite different to the idea, is it not?"

She wiggled her bottom on the chair again, and her skirts, which had inched upward as her knees rose above her hands, fell toward her, exposing the tops of her stockings and garters.

"Oh!"

"Really, now, Miss Jenkins,"—if she was going to tease with formal address, then so could he—"for someone so verbose usually, I'd expected a wider vocabulary than 'oh'. But never mind." Raising one eyebrow, he removed his jacket, waistcoat, and cravat.

This was the one area of his life, his world, where he was confident. He knew exactly what he wanted to do with her this second demonstration and was happy to take command. *She can't very well, can she?* He grinned again.

Leaning in, he kissed her. She tasted sweet, and given her fondness for the hue and her skin tone, he nicknamed her "Peaches" there and then.

She melted under him. Her arched spine and muscles straining against her bonds went limp.

This, this was his goal with restraints. The moment the woman accepted being at his mercy, where he could do anything to her. This time, he'd go easy. But if she came back for more, all bets were off.

He pulled away from the kiss slowly, staying within a few inches, so her focus was on his face. He wanted to kiss her for hours, but the rest of her magnificent form called him. His control was razor thin for the first time since secondary school, shocking him. His taste of her the night before had loosened his restraint. His hands shook as they found her ankles and smoothed up her legs. Reaching her knees, they smoothed farther, downward to her core.

Her pupils dilated, and she gasped for breath, drawing his attention to her impressive breasts.

He straightened a little more, his hips almost against the seat edge, and folded her dress and petticoats farther back to expose her. Her womanly folds were right there on display, spread and glistening. He licked his lips, but his attention kept straying upwards.

His hands smoothed up, over her soft stomach, over the lusciousness of her décolletage, to the edge of her dress. He hooked his fingers in it and slid them between her skin and her chemise. And yanked downward hard.

"Oh!"

"Still with the one nonword, I see."

The neckline had held, taking the chemise with it to under her bosom, and now pushed her mounds up even higher. He caressed and fondled them for long moments, watching her face to see what she liked best. As he squeezed and pinched, then rolled her nipples between thumb and forefinger, he swallowed so he wouldn't drool.

Splendid. He could do this all night, although his cock was so hard that he worried his brain had enough blood to maintain restraint. His goal was always to keep partners coming back for more, and he'd never wanted that as much as he did with Beth.

Cupping her breasts, he flicked one nipple with a thumb and licked his lips to suck the other one into his mouth and press it against the roof of his mouth.

She moaned, her arms jerking as though she tried to clutch at him. And moaned again at the restriction.

Still sucking, he moved one hand to her mons, rubbing three fingers up and down gently, then pressing more firmly, bringing even more blood to the area.

As she swelled against him, he dipped one finger into her wetness, then smoothed it up to circle the hard kernel of flesh—her *kleitoris*, he thought with a grin— just above her opening.

He reared back to talk to her. "No 'oh'? You've realized that I can touch you anywhere, any way I like. And, make no mistake, Peaches, I like."

Her gaze went dreamy at the nickname, but she was still silent. Against his finger, her nub hardened further, and another rush of wetness coated his hand.

"If you were wearing less clothing, imagine where I could touch you. Or if I pulled you forward to the edge of that seat, I could fuck you, just like this. And you couldn't stop me."

"Oh…" She sighed with pleasure, drawing a half-smile from him at the repeated utterance.

"It doesn't appear you would want to stop me, though, does it?"

His finger circled faster.

She squinted her eyes closed and shook her head.

"Right, then. Think about this. This configuration? Even using the same chair, this is only one of several ways I could keep you at my mercy with just these cuffs."

"Oh, oh—"

He retracted his hand.

Her eyes flew open, and he saw realization dawn. She'd given over control of her pleasure to him, and like the previous night, he did not intend to give it back for some time, no matter how hard his cock thumped against the placket of his breeches.

Chapter Seven

Dratted man. She'd been so close to the pinnacle.

His one-sided smile said he knew that.

Godsakes, was he going to keep her on the edge for what felt like hours again? Then again, that might not be terrible. The previous night's orgasm had been the most explosive of her life.

And for me, that is quite the milestone.

She'd never slept better than after being wrung out by this talented and handsome man. The juxtaposition of his public shyness and his private vocal confidence intrigued her, to say nothing of seeing the rest of his trunk's contents. His creativity also added to his appeal. Or it had until he'd turned it to withholding pleasure.

Before she could complain or beg, his mouth was on her breast again. Setting his teeth to her nipple, he tugged gently. His fingers plucked her other hardened tip for a long moment before he switched breasts.

Beth wanted to clutch him to her, to move his hand where she needed it most, to open his breeches and grab his cock. Her hands grasped at air, their tethers too short to allow her farther than his shoulders.

His fingers feathered over the folds between her legs again.

She moaned and tried to thrust her hips forward despite her lack of leverage, hungering for a firmer touch like he'd used minutes earlier.

He swiped his finger once up her center, his teeth biting her breast.

"Oh." Belatedly, she realized she'd yet to formulate more than the same exclamation he'd teased her about. Never before had she been rendered monosyllabic. She hadn't even been coherent enough to express her delight at his nickname for her. No partner had stuck around long enough to bestow a nickname.

The dastardly man raised his head and grinned.

She rolled her eyes. 'Twas time to try a different tack, bound or not. She found her words. "How will you fuck me with these?"

He slid his hands along her thighs and yanked her forward. Her hands and feet did not move, only her bottom, but she had no leverage to gain more pressure, more pleasure.

He raised his brows with a smirk. "Should I return to what I was doing, or would you see any other configurations?"

"No, thank you. I mean, yes, please. Ack, you know what I mean."

"You did better with the simple 'oh.' Let me see if I can render you completely mute. Or better yet, I shall wait until you beg."

"I can beg. I can beg now. Please?" She batted her eyes at him hopefully.

He ignored her, however, and returned his mouth to her breast and his fingers to feathering light strokes over her most sensitive flesh.

"Robert, please."

A tiny bit more pressure.

She moaned in response. Her nub hardened, and her nether lips clenched on air, wishing to be breached.

He withdrew.

"Please. I need you. I need your cock."

"Ah, the lady has specific requests. And where do you want it?"

Her eyes flared. "In me. Please." No one had made her beg before, dratted man. Why did she like it so much? His control, with bonds and skill and words, was oil on the fire of her lust.

He pulled back again.

Noooo.

As she opened her mouth to beg in more detail, he unbuckled the straps through the chair arms. He held out a hand and, when she put hers in it, tugged her upright then swooped his arms around her back and legs and lifted her.

She clutched at him in alarm. "No, you'll hurt yourself!" No one had picked her up since she was a child.

"Ha. I fight with leather and tools all day. You are fine. Or do you doubt me?"

"No, no," she demurred, resting her head against his shoulder. But her muscles remained tense, ready to catch herself should the need arise.

He dropped her on the bed, and she fell back, breath gusting out in relief. He flipped her and unlaced her gown and her stays under it, fumbling under the layers until he located the tapes of her petticoats. Rolling her back over, he yanked at her garments until she was naked.

Dazed with pleasure and in awe of his forcefulness, so absent in public, she remained compliant. When her right wrist and ankle were tugged away from her side, she realized she was lying on the diagonal, and he was buckling one tether around the head post. He did the same with a footpost, and she was again at his mercy.

Robert stepped away to snuff all the candles and screen the fire. Only then did he return to stand near the footpost and stare up her length. In quick motions, he kicked off his shoes, then dropped his hand to his breeches and shucked them before shedding his shirt and climbing onto the bed between her legs.

She wished he hadn't dimmed the light in the room to near-darkness. His broad form looked delicious, and she desired to at least see her fill, given that she could not touch him.

"Now, you were saying? Or begging, as I recall?" His words distracted her from wishing for a better view, bringing her need rushing back to her hot, wet core.

"Fuck me, Robert. Please."

****

Thank heavens. He hadn't been sure how much longer he could hold out.

He'd been worried he would rip her clothes, he'd been in such a hurry to see her naked again.

Then she was spread for him, all her gorgeous peaches and cream barely visible in the dark but accessible for his pleasure as well as hers. She was at his mercy, and he had none.

Having undressed after dimming the room, he did not want her eyes to become accustomed to the darkness. Best that she not see his tree-trunk-like shape unclothed. Even the thought dimmed his pleasure for a moment, his shaft bobbing.

Her begged request to be fucked saved him from spiraling downward. He tugged on protection, then his cock was at her opening. He held it to her entrance, swirling it in her essence before inching inside.

Her inner muscles squeezed him, trying to pull him into her faster, harder.

He stifled a gasp. This was heaven. She was an angel—a slightly devilish one, mayhap, but an angel—sent for his rapture.

He blocked the sensations caused by the clasp of her channel, ignoring the pulses from his cock to his bollocks. On his knees, gaze on the shadows where they joined, he edged in an inch.

She thrashed. By bending her knees, she could create slack for her hands, but not enough to grab him and yank him to her. Raising her hips, she tried to impale herself on him, but he laughed and held her still.

Another thrill shot from his belly to the tip of his cock, making him shudder. He'd known she'd be as active a participant as he'd allow. He also suspected her eagerness in the past had prevented her from scaling the highest peak of pleasure, and he was determined to give her that.

Finally, he was buried to the hilt. He leaned over her, careful not to put his weight on her, and nipped her breast.

She moaned, and her hands opened and closed to gesture him closer. "Robert, I want to feel all of you."

He consented to lower to his elbows, dying for the brush of her breasts against him, but still wary of crushing her. Her nipples caught on his fur as he shifted in and out of her once, and they both sucked in ecstatic breaths.

He wanted to linger and take in every point of touch, every rub, and luxuriate in the pleasure each evoked. His cock leaped at the idea. Simultaneously, it demanded he pound her harder and faster. His bollocks tightened.

"Ehh. Stop. Faster. Please."

He chuckled. She did better with "oh." At least he was not the only one with muddled thoughts about making this last.

He withdrew, then drove into her. And again.

She was so sensitive after all the foreplay torture, she only needed a third thrust before everything contracted around him, her thighs and inner muscles locking tight and milking him. Her eyes squeezed shut, and he watched the pleasure wash over her.

The inferno that had been building in him tightened into a fireball in his belly before erupting outward, sending tingles of heat into her, outward to his fingers, toes, scalp.

"Robert!" Her yell was loud enough anyone in that wing might have heard.

He kissed her, swallowing her shout, and sighed into her mouth as he shuddered with the last of his release.

She lay limp as he clambered off the bed, taking care of the cock sheath and donning a nightshirt before he unbuckled her tethers and rolled her under the covers. He spooned behind her, drifting toward sleep.

I am quite sure this qualifies as keeping her entertained. If only I could find a reason to entertain her beyond this week. If only she'd be comfortable with just me for entertainment.

****

Beth woke, slitting her eyes against the daylight from the window she faced. She was still in Robert's bed, and the angle of the sun told her Althea would be looking for her.

She'd only gotten tantalizing flickers of his body in

the dark room last night.

But now it's daylight. She rolled over, ready to see more of the incredible strength she knew leatherwork—and lifting her—took.

Cold sheets and a flattened pillow were all that remained on the other half of the bed. *Drat.*

Throwing on her clothes, she stumbled back to the room she shared with Althea to freshen up. She found Althea's trunk by the door and Althea packing Beth's things.

Althea spared her only a quick glance. "I need to leave here."

What? No! There are more cuff configurations to explore. And I want to see Robert's cock, mayhap taste it.

"But I've heard the entertainment becomes more interesting each night." Voicing the quickest excuse she could think of, her voice rose to a whine even she recognized, before she stopped to wonder why Althea was suddenly so adamant about leaving early. "Wait, where did you go last night? Did you not play any games?"

"Oh, I played a game. And lost. Evan—Lord Cheltenham and I could not agree on terms. So I shall need to explore other options."

Hmm. 'Tis Evan now, is it? "Right, then. We shall go home and regroup." She could see her cousin was in a state, and Robert was only ever planned as an interlude for this week, anyway. Her cousin's need for support was more important, even without considering all Althea had done for her. However, she'd certainly be asking more questions about Althea's activities the previous evening.

"Thank you."

A thought occurred. "Can we please visit the dower house, though? I met Lady Cheltenham—Cheltie's mother—and she's lovely. I promised her I'd come back." *And promised Cheltie I'd find a new nurse for him.* Although she hoped she would not need to tell Althea that she'd bribed their host to listen to the business proposal.

"I suppose, if 'tis quick."

"Thank you, cuz. Come on, then."

"You don't want to change clothes?" Her cousin cocked her head and gestured at Beth's rumpled dress from the prior evening.

"To sit in a carriage much of the day? I'll have a bath at the inn we stay at on the way home."

On the road, Beth stared out the carriage window. Despondent at the prospect she might not see Robert for weeks or months, she in turn berated herself for the melancholy. She'd known him a mere two nights. Godsakes, she'd missed all but one night of Cheltie's imaginative games and a chance to further her acquaintance with Franklin the footman.

However, her thoughts continued to return to the quiet blond man. She only hoped Althea allowed Cheltie to aid in her business expansion and provide her opportunities to see Robert again.

****

Beth threw herself into interviewing nurses. She remembered one alumna of the charity school who had taken an unofficial apprenticeship with a physician forward-minded enough to allow a woman access to medical knowledge. Another graduate's sister had trained with their mother as a midwife and caregiver. Not satisfied with having only two choices, she put feelers out through her network of servants, others like herself who flirted with the edges of the aristocracy without their own titles, and the teachers at both schools.

Day after day, as she went about her tasks, Robert lingered in her thoughts. Her enthusiasm for finding a nurse might have been tinged with a hint of desperation that it would lead to more time with him.

Inevitably, Althea noticed her distraction.

As Beth lounged in Althea's office one afternoon while her cousin reviewed the store's ledgers, she fidgeted, ignoring the book in her lap.

Althea looked up from her desk. "Are you not enjoying your book?"

"'Tis fine, thank you."

"Then what has you distracted?"

Beth cast about for a reason. "I want to ensure I find the very best candidates for Lady Cheltenham. She is such a lovely woman, I wish her to have the best care possible."

"Hmm." Althea shook her head. "No, I don't think 'tis that. You never doubt yourself in that." She cocked her head, and Beth squirmed under her scrutiny. "I know this twitching. This twitching comes from interest in a sexual partner. You're not harassing the servants again, are you?"

"No!"

Althea shot her a sardonic glance for the vehemence, then asked, "Is this about Robert, perchance?"

"'Tis just—" Beth threw up her hands. "I did not get a chance to say good bye."

"I know. I am sorry." Althea pressed her lips together in chagrin. "Did you not want to say farewell, then? I rather assumed it was just another fling."

"No, no. It was. Well, if he wanted to continue… No, 'tis fine." Beth shut up as she wasn't making much sense.

"Ah. Without discussing it with him, you wonder if he'd like to see you again and how he'd manage that, because you are interested in continuing."

"Well, yes."

"I confess to surprise. You rarely get attached to a particular bed partner. Did you have time to get to know him that well?"

"No…yes…I don't know." Beth squirmed again. Her cousin would be shocked to know the details of Robert's bedroom skills or leather skills. How much could she share?

"Hmm."

"Stop humming at me. If you must know, at least part of my 'attachment,' as you say, is because 'twas the best sex of my life."

Althea's brows rose.

Bravo for her not showing shock, at least.

"Do tell," the older woman drawled.

"Hmm." Beth said with a grin, turning the phrase back at her cousin. "I do not think you're ready for the details." When Althea took a breath to argue, she added, "Nor am I ready to share. Not right now, cuz. I am trying to forget it, in any event."

"Goodness me, why?"

"Because men never want a long-term relationship with me."

"Only because they don't understand what an incredible person you are." Althea staunchly defended her, even to her.

Beth smiled. "Thank you, cuz. But as you have told

me in the past, if my body is so easily conquered, they often lose interest in the rest of me. Men are shallow and fickle." If only she could believe Robert was not, but his reserve throughout their clothed exchanges told her he would not pursue her further.

"Then they don't deserve you."

"I agree. I shan't pretend to be someone I am not to capture a man's interest. I'd rather be true to myself and end up as one of those aging spinsters with attractive young maids and footmen who I goose regularly and pay handsomely for their…services."

Althea chuckled.

"Are you in?" Beth asked through laughter.

"Mayhap. If for no other reason than the entertainment of watching you and hearing your stories. They might have to expand the service program at your School of Enlightenment to staff your needs."

But as the women giggled together, Beth could not help envisioning Althea and Evan and her and Robert at a table surrounded by sexy servants. Dratted man.

Chapter Eight

Robert had run out of leather. That was a new problem—a good problem, but a problem nonetheless. While he kept spare materials at Cheltie's, his home in London not only offered more choices but also easier purchases of additional goods as needed. He had not expected to finish the pieces he brought so quickly, but he'd worked at a mad pace to avoid dwelling on Beth's abrupt departure.

Sitting at meals, lying in bed, even while shaving, his thoughts conjured her curious expression as she fondled a leather item, her voice husky as she cajoled him for more pleasure. She'd called the first night the most intense experience of her life. What, then, had he done wrong on the second night?

He'd left her in bed that last morning, stepping out to check in with Evan. Unable to find his friend, he'd returned to an empty room. When their seats were empty at dinner and he asked after her, Evan informed him that the cousins had returned to London.

She left without even a message. Though why would she write a note? The liaison was only ever expected to last the length of the party. He debated asking Evan if they'd given a reason for their departure, but his default was to withdraw and protect his heart. Dispirited, he'd thrown himself into work.

Despite being unable to start new garments, he

waited for Evan to be ready to return to London. Evan's time with his mother was far more important than Robert's clients getting their goods a fortnight sooner. Robert loved Rose almost as much as Bags did, anyway. He visited her several times in between cutting, sewing, and pounding metal accessories into place.

Days later, the two men sat facing each other in Bags's well-appointed carriage, swaying their way to London. Robert was glad for the change of scenery, and thought he might gain information on Beth by asking about her cousin, given Evan's interest in her.

"Right, then. You've barely left your room these past ten days. How are the orders coming?"

"I've gotten through two-thirds of them. Your parties, both at Cheltenham and in London, sell more than I do all the other days of the year," Robert said, thankful again for Cheltie's investment guidance so he didn't need the money. He would not have been comfortable selling to a wider audience and risking ridicule for debauched appetites.

"Finally, we have time to discuss the wench you had in your room." Bags grinned at him. "I haven't forgotten, but I know how you get when you're working on a backlog of orders."

Robert frowned at the word "wench." He knew Bags employed it for even a duchess if she attended the party, but he didn't like it for Beth. "Why don't you tell me more about Lady Egerton, and we'll see?"

"Ah, you noticed. I like her, Ford. She's smarter than almost anyone I know. Hellfire, she had to be to make a go of a business. She won't let me invest in her expansion if I want an ownership interest because she doesn't want a man involved."

"So now what?"

"Ford, this is the first time in—gads, maybe ever— I have been interested enough to pursue a woman. As you so often like to point out, I've never needed to. This is unfamiliar territory. I've offered her advice, no investment needed. If she takes me up on it, 'twill likely mean a trip to Bath. I need you to come, too, and keep her petite cousin occupied again."

"Beth? I don't think she'll be amenable to that."

Evan narrowed his eyes in confusion. "What makes you say that?"

"You asked who was in my room. 'Twas Beth. Then they disappeared from the party without a word." He shrugged and looked away from his friend as he admitted, "I can only assume my performance was not up to snuff."

Evan barked a laugh. "Sadly, I think the issue was with mine. But gee, thanks for putting it that way." He shared his failed attempt to coax Althea into a bet or a dare. "My guess is that she asked Beth to leave. After all, you've never had any complaints; nor has Beth to my knowledge."

Robert frowned.

"Do not look at me like that." Evan raised a hand to placate him. "My knowledge is secondhand only."

Robert's brow cleared, and he pondered for a minute. Despite his fear of being the focus of gossip, he could not resist seeing the little baggage again. She'd also make a nice tester for his new designs, at least until she tired of him.

"Bath is ever so delightful this time of year," he said with a nod and a grin. "And with some additional attractions to enjoy in the evenings, I don't see why I couldn't join you. That is, if you don't drag me to a party every night we're in London, so I can finish these pieces."

"Every other?" Evan asked with a teasing grin.

Robert rolled his eyes, happy the Season was over and most of the Ton had deserted London for their country homes or one of the seaside resort towns in the south.

****

Sure enough, within three nights, Evan had pleaded and cajoled him into attending an off-Season gathering.

"There is a soirée hosted by one of Sarah's regulars tomorrow night." Evan described it. "Downstairs will be a proper ball, upstairs will be less rigid…or, should I say, more rigid?" He mock-pondered it for a moment with a head tilt and finger to his chin.

Robert rolled his eyes, but acquiesced when Evan told him that Michael was attending with his lovely bride Penelope. Given their newlywed status and Michael's family's concerns about obeying the proprieties, their attendance was not a given, and Robert welcomed the chance to see them.

As he dressed for the evening, he wondered whether Beth would attend. His neutral-colored apparel was designed to blend in—a dark jacket and breeches worn over a cream waistcoat and white shirt and cravat. With a chance to see his curvy peach again, he didn't hate Evan's constant party invitations for once, although he'd never admit it to his friend.

In the ballroom, he trailed Evan as his friend greeted allies, acquaintances, and sycophants. As they so often did, the latter groups included men who had been quick to ostracize the less-than-beautiful second son until Evan took him under his wing at school. Robert hovered silently, declining to engage with them, even when greeted cordially now.

While downstairs would have all the components of a Ton fête—dancing, a supper room, and a card room, upstairs was a different story. The homeowner, who Robert thought might be an earl, had drilled peepholes in most of the rooms on the upper floor. He shuddered at the idea of being a guest in the home. He'd never sleep knowing there might be eyes on him. And did the man's parents know?

Given the nature of the ball and the fact that it was off-Season, no one was announced. Robert appreciated the ability to come and go inconspicuously and was certain many of the titled Lords and Ladies here with someone other than their spouse did as well.

If the timing was not soon after Evan's house party and he'd had spare pieces, he might have arranged for his wares to be displayed for sale in an upstairs room. Instead, this was a rare occasion to mingle and crowd-watch.

Then Evan smirked and cocked his head, and Robert spied his new favorite form wearing her signature color bobbing behind her taller cousin's. Keeping his face neutral so Bags would not heckle him endlessly, he followed Evan toward Michael and Penelope. Althea and Beth met them there.

"Penelope!" Beth performed her signature hop on her toes. "'Tis lovely to see you. Tell us how this works if you will please, Cheltie." Her gaze slid past Evan to meet Robert's for a second, and her eyes widened.

"'Tis my understanding that downstairs is for the tame—ahem, I mean, Ton…" Evan joked.

Robert had attended parties hosted here before. He focused on Beth's reactions rather than Evan's words as his friend explained the arrangement.

Guests could use any unoccupied rooms if they liked to be watched while other guests were welcome to view the occupants' activities through the peep holes. If a door was open, people were encouraged to enter to enjoy the show from a closer vantage point.

Which side of the door would Beth prefer? She seemed to favor being part of the action when given a choice. Nothing could make him perform like a circus act for people to watch. Yet he dreaded the thought of her choosing someone else with whom to play. He could not watch that.

"As you can see," Beth said to Penelope as she gestured at Evan, "your entrée to Cheltie's house party was appreciated and put to good use. How are bakery plans coming?"

At that question, Robert turned to find Evan whispering with Althea and leading her away.

"Michael, are you and Penelope planning to enjoy the viewing options?" Robert waved a hand over their heads toward the upper level.

"Absolutely. Pen has not attended before and is exceedingly curious. What of you, Ford? I rather thought we'd have a spread of your work laid out in a room above stairs."

"Too many orders from Bags's Cheltenham fête. I ran out of leather this year." He shook his head.

Michael snorted a laugh. "Trust that crowd to continue to find excesses they must try, to outdo each other."

Robert slanted a sidelong look at Beth to gauge her

interest in that statement, but she was asking Penelope about staffing at the bakery.

Michael continued, "Bags and Lady Egerton, eh? I think they've disappeared upstairs already. D'you think it will last?"

"She is not his usual type. 'Twill be interesting to see who is swayed to whose view. She is much more private than Bags's reputation allows for."

"Did you spend much time with her and Beth, then? I've only met them a time or two. More often, the girls gather for tea and baked treats."

Robert shook his head but slid another glance to Beth.

"Hmm. I am guessing Bags asked you to entertain our little bundle of energy while he wooed Lady Egerton?"

A shrug. He told himself to remain noncommittal. *Although, mayhap Michael has knowledge that could help.*

Before he could ask, Michael gave him a perfect opening. "And Lady E is the opposite of her young cousin when it comes to…er, relationships."

Robert grunted. "What do you mean by that?"

"You've seen Beth. She has never met a stranger. 'Tis for people such as her that I hate Society's unequal rules. Bags and I, and even you, can do as we like with impunity. But she looks twice at a man or—God forbid—fans herself too many times while looking at him, and she's a harlot. Her parents taught her she should be able to do anything a man can do. And she should. Yet she cannot without receiving criticism. So she flaunts her differences, and it spirals. With the right opportunity, she'd be upstairs playing in a room in a heartbeat, reveling in an audience. With a man or a woman. For no other reason than 'tis fun."

Robert's eyes bulged. Michael had just voiced his worst fear. He could just hear the criticisms of his form, his face, his lack of a title if he joined her.

I knew she was too flamboyant for me, but I wanted her anyway. No more. Sarah vetted her clients and required confidentiality, but those who hosted their own soirées did not necessarily employ the same diligence. It did not matter. Even if he was willing to risk the Ton's viciousness, a quiet sedate man would not hold the interest of someone as vivacious as Peaches for long.

Michael did not notice. He shook his head. "She is misunderstood…or mayhap no one bothered to try to understand in the first place. From what Pen's said, she has the kindest heart of anyone I know."

The biggest, softest heart in the world could not compensate for someone's willingness to flaunt their strangeness to the Ton. He had spent years avoiding the limelight and would not risk it now, even for the tempting conundrum that was Beth.

He turned to watch Beth as she finished her conversation with Penelope and settled her gaze on his.

****

Beth had negotiated an agreement with Althea. She would not engage any of the house servants while Althea attempted to hire a few servants from the School of Enlightenment that would be more open to advances. In return, Althea would accompany her to a few soirées on the edge of polite society if the host and attendees were vetted enough for Althea's concerns.

She'd had high hopes of Robert attending this party and had dressed accordingly in a low-cut peach gown with a layer of chiffon over it that created varying shades and depth. When she spotted him, she'd bounced in anticipation, although she covered it with a greeting for her school chum.

After Cheltie had explained the nature of the party, Beth was impatient. She pictured Robert leading her upstairs, where they could check each peephole to each room, mayhap picturing themselves in the various scenes they found. Together, they might ponder which of his creations would work best for that position or design a new configuration.

Then she became engrossed in hearing about Penelope's plans for staffing the bakery.

"I have asked Mrs. Montague for suggestions for managers. The idea of giving working class girls a chance at roles other than courtesan appeals to me."

"I love it. Come to think of it, when you need more counter clerks, one or two girls finishing at the school here in Town might suit. What of the kitchen?"

"That is where I struggle the most to give up control. I can hardly bring myself to staff the kitchen." Penelope grinned. "Although if I can trust anyone, 'twould be someone you find. Send them on."

They discussed timing of hires for a moment before Penelope excused herself to greet someone she'd met through Michael, and Beth turned back to see Robert staring at her.

Tilting her head, she gave a short upward nod toward the stairs.

He frowned.

Mayhap he does not wish to be seen together, given his privacy issues.

She lifted a shoulder at him and turned to the stairs.

With one foot on the first step, she twisted her head to stare at him, raising a brow in challenge.

His mouth tightened, and he shook his head in the negative.

Crestfallen, she continued to watch him, as he turned to say something to Michael.

Owen—she still did not know his surname, as was common among the guests at Cheltie's house parties—appeared behind her. He reached for her hand and bowed.

"'Tis lovely to see you again, Owen." She cast a quick glance to see if Robert was paying attention, but he was still talking with Penelope's husband.

"If it isn't the delectable—" He glanced at the bountiful display of her bosom. "—Beth. May I interest you in some entertainment upstairs?" He grinned.

She had no doubt that he'd be fine with either side of the door, just as she had always been. Firming her lips, she was determined to have fun tonight, with or without the prude below. Any orgasm was better than none. Placing her hand on the crook of his offered arm, she nodded her assent.

Halfway up the staircase, she gave in to one last glance below.

Robert stood glaring at her with a muscle ticking in his cheek. When she met his gaze, he turned and strode toward the door. Dratted man.

After two doors, she was more frustrated than aroused. Self-directed anger surged. She could darn well do what she pleased. But no amount of staring at carnal acts through a hole in a door distracted her.

Owen led her to a third door, this one standing open.

She peered in, trying to picture herself with the man

inside. Or with Owen.

"Care to join in, my lovely?" Owen whispered in her ear, his hands skimming her sides and lingering along her breasts.

Always before, the very idea would have set her pulse racing, her nipples tightening. But her body did not respond as she'd expected. If anything, her stomach felt a little queasy. Had Robert ruined her for other men? That would be devastating. No man had expressed interest in her long term, and she was sure he was no different.

He's not here, the dratted man. I can play with whomever I like.

But neither her body nor her heart wished to, no matter what her head said. Disheartened, she excused herself, thanking Owen for his escort, and descended the stairs to the ballroom, finding Michael and Penelope starting upward.

"Have either of you seen Robert, please?"

Michael's and Penelope's eyes widened in tandem at her use of his first name. She could not bring herself to care or explain.

"He excused himself to home." Michael's voice was gentle. "Hold on, did he accompany you? We can see you home."

"No, although I appreciate the kind offer." Beth swallowed against the ball of hurt in her throat. "I came with Althea, and I think I spied her with Cheltie upstairs, so I shall give her a few minutes."

"Right, then. Shall we all fetch a drink?" Penelope asked, looking up at her husband.

"Certainly. I shall fetch. You two sit." They turned and descended back to the main level.

Michael had only been gone a few seconds when Althea swept down the stairs, her face flushed, and begged Beth to leave.

Happy to leave a party mayhap for the first time in her life, Beth agreed.

Chapter Nine

Beth had arrived home from volunteering at the charity school and had just ordered tea to the library when Althea entered and flopped into the chair across from her, throwing her feet on the delicate matching Hepplewhite footstool.

Beth tilted her head. "Cuz? Are you quite all right? You appear flushed."

"I've just had the most explosive sexual experience of my life in the back room of my shop. 'Tis no wonder I am flushed!"

Beth nearly fell off the settee. She never would have anticipated that response. "What? Do tell!" Beth sat forward. "With whom?"

Althea gave her a withering look.

"Ah. Cheltie does get around. It seems he lived up to his reputation. Come now. Share with your best friend and family member." Beth was impressed. The rakish earl never chased. But even if his popularity was well-earned, he'd need to work harder to scale her cousin's walls, to say nothing of the fact that last she knew, neither wanted to marry.

Silently, she admitted she was a tad bit jealous, given her frustrated state these past weeks. Unable to muster interest in a single stable hand, no matter how flash, she'd been further irked by her reaction to Owen and the ball. And pleasuring herself as she replayed her nights with Robert was unsatisfying.

"Only because I need advice. Please, you cannot breathe a word of this to anyone. The shop will suffer, never mind my reputation."

"I promise, I promise. Now spill." She focused on her cousin's puzzle, rather than her own confusion regarding one man who seemed ill-suited for her temperament and should have been a hazy memory as one of many.

Althea explained, then added, "But, cousin, I must also confess something. Part of the reason I sent you to the School of Enlightenment was because I stumbled across one of your, er, interludes in the stables."

"Oh, that," Beth scoffed. "I was actually hoping it would help convince you to try sex."

Althea's eyes bulged. "You saw me? Why did you never say anything?"

"Me? Why did *you* never say anything?" Beth laughed, arching a brow. "I glimpsed you hurrying away, is all. If you recall, I was rather busy at the time. Regardless, 'tis quite all right. I don't mind. The more, the merrier, and all that. And I know why you sent me away. If I had stuck to the stable hands, you might not have felt the need to find the school, but I am very grateful for my time there."

"Oh." Althea sagged against her chairback then straightened again. "Beth, there were two stable hands watching before I arrived. You say you don't care, but I still can't comprehend that."

Beth snorted. "Before Evan, you thought sex was for procreation, not pleasure. I see you're not trotting that tired argument out now."

Althea's cheeks warmed.

Beth continued. "Look at Aphrodite. She had many lovers, and she lounges around naked in most of her depictions. I'd wager her motto was the more the merrier, too."

I wonder what Robert would think of that attitude.

"It just feels wrong to watch others in an act specifically referred to as intimacy," Althea insisted.

"What if their definition of that is inviting anyone interested to participate, bringing people together in a different way?"

"I cannot fathom it."

"Well, then, let me ask this. If Evan had neglected to lock the door, and your employee had entered just before he took you over, would you have cared? Would you have even noticed?"

Althea lowered her gaze to her hands in her lap, silent.

"Is he as well-endowed as they claim?" Beth teased her cousin, relinquishing the debate and telling herself to stop worrying about what Robert would think when she was unlikely to spend more time with him.

Althea glanced up, asking, "Who are they, and— never mind. Beth, please. Now is not the time for idle gossip. What do I do, cousin?"

"Right, then. Sorry. You have nothing to lose by taking his advice, which he's already offered. However, he's come to you twice now." Beth raised a brow. "Cheltie never chases. He doesn't need to. You shall likely need to go to him."

Althea shook her head. "But now he is insisting on sexual favors in return."

Beth grinned. "'Tisn't the worst idea in the world, from the look of you. And they say he is a very generous lover."

"If by generous, you mean he has brought me over three times with not even a single opportunity for me to return the favor, then yes, he is very charitable. I might even be contrite if I didn't feel quite so…satisfied."

Beth giggled. *Three times!* Cheltie had been busier wooing than she'd thought. She'd congratulate her cousin if she didn't think it would earn another frown.

Of course, Robert managed that in two nights. Imagine what he could do—

Stop. She gritted her teeth. *This is about Althea's well-deserved pleasure and allaying her fears.*

"And please stop talking about they!" Althea frowned. "I cannot afford a scandal, however marginal I am in the Ton. My shop sales will suffer, and expanding to improve sales is the entire reason I am in this predicament."

Althea stood to pace.

Beth sat back and sipped tea from the tray a servant had brought in. "Cuz, apart from the risk of rumors, what do you want? A month ago, you'd have told me you had no interest in sex. But that is no longer the case, is it?"

Althea threw herself back into the chair. "Gah! No. Blasted man. And you!"

"Me? What did I do?"

"You described it to me, and that pushed me into making claims he felt forced to disprove. 'Tis all your fault!"

Beth snorted.

Althea snorted.

Then the two of them burst into giggles and laughed until they were crying.

Finally, wiping the tears from under her eyes, Althea

straightened in her chair again, reaching for her lukewarm cup of tea. "Here, I'll give you the words I know you are slavering for. You. Were. Right." She stuck her tongue out at her younger cousin.

"Oh my, I've been rubbing off on you. Or Evan has—literally." Beth snorted. She took a deep breath and sent Althea a level gaze. Her cousin would not relish her advice. "Look, you have the upper hand at the moment. He has come round twice, so even though you must go to him, 'tis clear he wants you and will flex on the terms. Use his negotiating tactics. If your biggest concern is rumors, trade sex for advice. Just make sure he agrees to keeping it secret."

Two days later, they climbed into Althea's carriage to go see Evan.

They found him readying to depart for Greenborough Park with one of the nurses she had arranged for him to interview. He suggested Althea meet him in Bath to look at locations and competitors, with Beth accompanying her.

Beth refused to ask if Robert planned to accompany him, or acknowledge that her heart rate sped up at the thought. As she still could not fathom intimacy with anyone else, it promised to be a few more frustrating sennights in a lonely bed.

****

"Ouch. Holy hell." Robert tried to push the needle through the pre-drilled holes in the bustier he was sewing. Even with the holes created beforehand, pushing a needle through leather was work, and Robert hated thimbles. He needed to feel the animal skin.

Sucking his thumb, he threw the project down. He'd worked for long hours every day since he'd returned to

Greenborough Park, in an effort to not brood over Beth. Beth in each of the creations he finished. Beth spread on a bed with someone pounding into her and him watching. No. He'd quickly moved on from that view to being the one pistoning into her. Despite his timidness about women seeing his body, he wished he'd had more candles lit when he'd fucked her in this room. He wanted more details for his memories.

Pacing around, he grumbled, "Damnation. Now what shall I do?"

His callus on his thumb, built from pushing the needle through each stitch, had torn off yesterday from working too long. The spot was tender new skin and hurt more with every stitch.

For the millionth time, he wondered if Evan was lingering in London to woo Lady Egerton. Should he see if Evan's steward had heard from him? He could meander back to London and drop Evan a note that he needed to look for a blacksmith.

"Ha." His bark made him jump in the quiet room. Turning for another lap, he continued aloud, "You're not fooling anyone, idiot. You don't need to move locations. You haven't left this suite for the most part. You are lusting after that voluptuous creature, and she is a bad bet." He sliced a hand down. "Stop it."

Now he was talking to himself. Great. Mayhap he really did need a change of scenery. He'd walk to the dower house to see if Rose was up to a visit, even if her dementia might not allow her to recognize him. At least reading to her would not hurt his thumb, and he'd be talking to someone other than himself.

Two hours later as Robert finished punching a last hole for stitches with the sharp stitching awl and put the bundle of leather in his lap aside, Evan knocked and entered.

"Bags. You look tired." He looked as though he'd been crying. Robert guessed he'd already visited his mother.

"Just worried. I brought the new nurse back with me, but mama gets out of sorts at changes in routine." He shrugged.

Robert poured them each a drink and hummed in commiseration.

"Her focus was on ensuring I lived as full a life as possible, as I was liable to have it curtailed. And to remind me she would always love me. But how—" Evan choked up again and gulped a fortifying swallow of whisky. "—can she love me when she doesn't recognize me?"

Robert shook his head. "I don't think it works like that, Bags. Love underlies it all for a parent. She did everything she could to prepare you for this time out of that love. And said that to mitigate your pain when it got hard."

"Well, it did no such thing. And I cannot imagine doing that to a wife or child."

"How did you find a new nurse so quickly? You've been gone less than a month."

"Didn't I tell you? Beth had agreed to help me find Lucy's replacement. It was how she got Althea her audience with me. That and her friendship with Penelope."

"Ah. I wondered what brought about that interest in an apothecary, beyond the attractive owner. You usually seduce the owner but decline the investment. That girl is wily. And she is close to Penelope. Interesting."

"The girl knows everyone. Her network rivals Charlotte's, mayhap even mine." Evan referenced the Dowager Duchess of Peterborough, one of his closest friends who competed with him in finding the best investments.

"Really? Why does she need such a network?"

"She excels at bringing people together who need each other. Or one who needs something with one who has the exact thing the other needs. It seems to be a passion, like your leatherwork. She ferreted out my need for a new nurse for my mother and offered to find one for me. I suspect she loves doing it because she enjoys finding people's place to fit in this world. Mayhap because she hasn't found her own."

"Hmph. Well, mayhap I should hire her. Whilst I've restocked leather, I am short on buckles and other accessories. And my blacksmith is getting older and has been talking of going to live with his daughter and son-in-law to spend more time with his grandchildren."

"Just say the word. She'll likely have you three candidates in a fortnight."

A tempting excuse to spend time with her again. Damn. He tried changing the subject. "How was the rest of your time in Town?" He wondered if Evan had managed to seduce Althea yet.

"Frustrating. Slow. But, finally productive, I think."

"So she invited you to invest?"

"Not exactly. Care for a trip to Bath?"

Yes! I thought you'd never ask. Robert managed a casual shrug. "Why not?"

****

As their carriage entered the outskirts of Bath, Beth sat forward. Another adventure awaited, a new city, new experiences. Cheltie had praised all three candidates for a nurse, which was satisfying. And after he got Nancy settled, he'd meet her and Althea at a guesthouse he'd specified. Would Robert be with him?

The dratted man had hied off to Cheltenham after his abbreviated appearance at the last ball. She was furious at him. She hadn't gotten to see his latest designs. However, her real issue was the explosive elongated orgasms he had gifted her at the house party. She relived them every night in bed—alone. Hence the fury.

After Owen failed to interest her, she'd attempted to engage a stable hand. But again, looking at his lean, muscular form left her cold. Despite that, she'd kissed him, then had to excuse herself, an embarrassment for which she also blamed Robert.

Knowing Cheltie, he'd drag Robert along. Cheltie could make everything a party. She also hoped he'd want Robert to entertain her, so he could garner more time with Althea.

Sure enough, there were four rooms reserved at the small but luxurious guesthouse near the river, a short walk north of the city center. The men's rooms were on the first floor, above the public rooms, and the ladies' rooms were above them. Smaller and less opulent than the guest room they'd shared at Greenborough Park, the rooms were nevertheless well-appointed. A small desk, wardrobe and bedframe all matched, and the neutral creams and golds of the linens and upholstery were a pleasing contrast to the dark wood. Beth noted the posts on the bedframes, in case Robert had strap configurations that would benefit from them.

Or rather that I would benefit from.

The men had arrived and already ventured back out.

Althea always preferred to unpack immediately to hang her gowns. Beth took only a minute to decide to wait for Robert in his room, hoping to provoke him into a quick tumble before the evening meal. She could not recall the last time she'd gone this long without a bedmate.

After stripping off her warmer gown and petticoat, she donned one thin petticoat and a blush-colored silk gown. She contemplated dampening it, but the wind off the river was sharpening as the afternoon wore on, and they'd likely walk to supper.

Running down one flight, she found one door locked and the other unlocked and hoped for the best.

Her nipples peaked with the hope of Robert's hands on them, and her thighs rubbed together to assuage the ache between them. She contemplated the bed, the chair—oh, memories of him and chairs—and the window. Unsure of her welcome, she decided the light from the window filtering through her gown to show her figure would overcome any resistance from him.

From her vantage point, her gaze roamed the room for new projects, items she might test for Robert.

Hearing footsteps in the hall, she arched her back to thrust her best feature out. The door opened.

"Rob— Oh, Cheltie. Lovely to see you." She gave a shallow curtsy. "I beg your pardon. I thought this was my room but had just realized my mistake. I believe I stopped one floor too early. If you'll excuse me, I shall correct that immediately."

Robert followed his friend into the room, quirking an eyebrow at her.

Cheltie smirked and caught her arm as she skittered around him. "My dear Beth. Entering a man's bedchamber is naughty. I believe you should be punished, don't you?"

Beth gasped and slid her eyes to Robert, a plea in them. Once she might have jumped at the chance to have Cheltie's hands on her, but now Robert was her sole focus.

Robert turned away.

Disappointment lanced through her. He did not care if his friend touched her.

At Evan's repeated question, she answered, "Yes, my lord." Trying in vain to live up to her reputation, she gave a half-hearted flutter of her lashes.

"Excellent. I agree," Cheltie went on. "Unfortunately, I need to speak with Althea before supper, but Ford here"—Robert whipped back around with a glare—"is quite good at correcting naughty girls' bad behavior. He may even have some toys—ahem, tools, which could help manage that behavior through the meal?"

Robert nodded thoughtfully.

Ohh. Yes, please.

"Right, then. You two work out the specifics. Althea is coming to this room in a few minutes, and we shall await you downstairs."

Robert beckoned her to follow him, and she did so with alacrity.

Reaching his now-unlocked room, he hustled over to a trunk and dug through it, muttering, "Right. With that gown, our options are limited."

"I can change." Beth sighed with happiness at his enthusiastic contemplation of choices for her punishment, as she knew she'd enjoy it by the end of the night. However, she remained wary given his easy capitulation to Cheltie a few minutes ago.

"No. You will go out like that, my peach. You wanted to show off your assets. You will do so. Our choices may be limited, but I have something perfect for the occasion."

He pulled out a corset with holes in the bosom area and a strap hanging from the bottom of the front panel. It was the palest of tans, almost the color of butter.

"My supplier found this hue and held it for me. I bought the entire length and asked for more. I think 'twill be perfect for any apparel I make for under lighter colored gowns." He smirked at her pale peach-pink gown and circled a finger in the air. "It appears tonight is an excellent opportunity to test it. Turn, please, let's not keep our friends waiting."

He undid her gown and tugged it downward for her to step out. Without a chemise, she hoped she'd convince him that Althea and Evan could wait.

But the prince of delayed gratification ignored her very obvious assets, reaching around to pass the corset in front of her, then drawing the laces through the first several eyelets at the base of her spine.

She twisted an inch from side to side, feeling the leather warm to her skin. Not as smooth as silk, but certainly not as rough as muslin.

Oh, but the cutouts. The holes in the cups lined up almost perfectly with her nipples, allowing them to rub against the silk of her gown, mayhap even be visible through the pale fabric.

The thought made her rub her thighs together as a spurt of heat surged through her. Her nipples tightened, poking through the holes.

As though he read her mind, Robert turned her toward him with the corset half-laced and stepped back to admire the front.

She preened, arching her back an inch.

"Hmm. I was off by a hairsbreadth." His finger circled the opening of the leather around each nipple. "I am glad I cut them larger than they needed to be."

"Off? You made this for me?" Godsakes his finger was distracting. Had she heard his comment correctly?

"You seemed determined to try every piece on. I thought you should have your own. I cannot adjust the placement here though."

He expected to see me again. Dare I hope the thought pleased him? Or did he only consider our shared friends circle?

He lifted his finger, allowing another more urgent thought to enter.

"Robert, what if my nipples show through my gown?"

"Mayhap it will help you remember a chemise next time. I'm more interested in what the slide of silk will do to you throughout supper."

She moaned in anticipation. She could hardly reconcile this confidence with his reticence when Evan seemed about to punish her.

He scooped her breasts to ensure they were fully in the cups of the corset top, making her moan again, then turned her to finish lacing it.

"Robert?" She bit her lip. It was easier to ask without looking at him. "Would you really have let Cheltie punish me?"

Chapter Ten

Robert had been so eager to see Beth in another of his creations that once he received the go-ahead from Evan, he'd surged into artistic rumination.

Beth's question took him by surprise and made him frown.

Caught off-guard, he answered without thinking. "Given the choice, women prefer Bags. Far be it from me to stand in the way of what a woman wants."

Beth turned and glowered at him.

That did not sound as bad in my head.

"Do you not think the woman should have a say in that? Did you not see the pleading look I sent you?"

"I thought you wanted me to accede." He spread his hands and shrugged.

"What about the fact that Cheltie is here for Althea?"

"Admittedly, he seems to fancy her, but it has never stopped him in the past."

"Right, then. Let me make this clear. I do not want Cheltie. I'm quite sure Cheltie does not desire me. But I do crave you. Enough that I'm furious with you for abandoning me over a fortnight ago, and I'm annoyed at not having seen you unclothed yet, when you've had me naked in positions that exposed parts of me I swear no one has seen since I was a babe."

She wants me? That idea was so appealing, he was

tempted to take a page from her book and bounce. But when the rest of her words sank in, he realized she still wanted to see him without clothes. His ardor cooled, and he swallowed back a shiver of fear. His naked form would not invoke passion. Quite the opposite, in fact. He should have known the little termagant would continue her demands to see more of him. He'd hoped she would drop the subject. "I told you, you're prettier to look at. I am not."

"And I told you, I shall judge that for myself. Now, can we please get through supper so I can take your punishment then see to your pleasure?" She arched a brow at him.

"Certainly." He tugged at the laces to ensure snugness.

She shivered and gasped.

"Too snug?"

"No." Her voice was breathy.

Wait until you have the final piece in place.

Her breath caught as he unlaced her petticoat tapes and it dropped away. He smoothed his hand up the inside of her leg and grasped the hanging strip of leather to pull it toward him, then upward.

"Oh no. Does this have another of those lumps that look like an innocent mistake but are actually a torture device?"

"A *kleis*? No." Robert answered through a chuckle. "You need to be able to walk in this."

Unlike the configuration she'd tried at Greenborough Park, this was one strap, thicker for the front half, then narrowing. Robert snugged it against her flesh, centered along her lips and the seam of her bottom. Then he slackened it a fraction and attached it to the base of the corset back.

He slid a finger along the inside, checking for the gap between her and the strap. When she walked, it would tantalize, but when she sat… He grunted another laugh at the thought.

Beth took a shallow gasp of air as his finger brushed her nether lips.

"Walk across the room for me, so I know I set it to the correct length, please."

She moved carefully at first, then closer to a normal pace.

"Mmphf."

"Yes, my peach?"

"It, ah, brushes against me as I walk."

He grinned, snickering with pleasure. She needed to spend every evening with him for the foreseeable future. Her boldness allowed her to give detailed feedback without stammering and blushing, and he had all sorts of designs. Her figure was inspiring.

"Robert, please…" Her voice bordered on a whine. "Can we skip eating?"

"You do recall this is a punishment, right?" He chuckled. "Keeping that in perspective, what was your question?"

"Never mind," she mumbled, lowering her gaze.

He knew she'd noticed the thick bulge in the front of his trousers when she licked her lips. Cupping himself, he said, "This? You only get access to this if you behave at supper."

"That shan't be a problem," she scoffed.

He suspected she thought that once she was sitting still, the brushing would not bother her. *Ha.*

He suppressed his laugh and caught her arm to meet

Evan and Althea for supper.

****

Beth lowered herself to her chair in the private dining room Cheltie had secured for them and shot straight back to standing.

Cheltie studiously ignored her while Robert, behind her to hold her chair, chuckled under his breath.

Althea looked over. "Beth? Sit, please. I am hungry." Her gaze slid towards Cheltie and did not see Beth's grimace at the prospect of sitting again.

The dratted strap had tightened as she sat, pressing in against her wet puffy folds and riding up between her bottom cheeks to rest against her bumhole. How was she to eat with that?

"Robert—" She turned to beg.

"Ah." He wagged a finger at her. "Punishment, Peaches. Remember the reward for good behavior."

She whined and inched downward to the chair seat at a snail's pace. Once sitting, she daren't move. Every inch of the strap lit nerve endings as it slid against her. Tingles raced from her bottom forward to where her flesh swelled against the leather. Her arousal enlarged her lips, and they escaped the confines of the strap, allowing the strap to nestle in against her hard little nub. Every twitch of her hips rubbed her heightened nerve endings front and back against the strap.

Her nipples were diamond-hard, poking through her dress.

Cheltie cast one look at them and grinned at Robert with a nod.

Robert returned his grin before returning his gaze to her. She hoped her breasts distracted him from his meal as much as his strap drew her attention from food. Her hunger was not for a meal. The desperate worry that a wet spot would mar her gown when she rose should have cooled her ardor, but it didn't. Instead, it added to the sexual tension humming through her body. An internal whisper insisted this was exactly what she'd missed so much, but she could not find that detachment through the sensations coursing up and down her body.

Sure enough, by supper's end, Beth's thighs were slippery with anticipation.

Robert brought her back to his room, drawing out of his bag the same set of cuffs he'd used in Greenborough Park.

After stripping her of clothes and leather corset, he placed her on the bed and turned to fiddle with the leather strips of the cuffs. Placing one cuff around her left wrist, he drew the lead around the headpost of the bed, pulling her wrist up near her shoulder.

She noticed the length was as short as when he'd tightened it in the chair. When his hand circled her knee, her eyes widened. If he drew her knee to where her wrist was and locked her other side similarly, she'd be bent almost in double.

Stiffening, she resisted his tug on her leg.

The room was brighter than the country estate had been, with ambient light from businesses along the street reaching their first-floor room. Beth was happy with herself and knew how to make the most of her assets. But she also knew part of her attraction was her personality and how she framed those assets in clothes. This setting left her no armor, no pretense. Would her curves presented so lewdly repulse him?

He glanced up and stopped tugging her leg. "Beth?"

She frowned, then shook off her concern. Her

parents' voices in her head told her she was beautiful. If he didn't accept her as she was, he could go hang.

Releasing her leg, he skimmed his hand up her center to cup her chin.

"If you do not want this, you need only say the word. I will take them off. Are you worried about comfort? I promise I'll loosen them if you need me to. I want you in them for"—he wiggled his brows and grinned—"some time, so we will find a length that you can maintain. But I'm dying to see you like this. In my bed, your lush beauty on display and available for me to touch, to lick, to pet…mayhap to tease."

See? He wants these curves on display. A grateful smile spread across her face. She relaxed her muscles to allow him to manipulate her as he liked.

"So few Ton ladies have your figure," he went on. "Some are gawky or flat-chested or heavy-bottomed. I could not be Bags's friend without finding something to admire in each of them. But always, when I've designed, from the very beginning, 'tis been for someone perfectly proportioned. A round arse and luscious breasts. A soft belly that flares to womanly hips. And in the center, a lovely blushing mound." He stroked each part of her as he referenced it. "Always, the goal of cuffing someone is to rearrange their limbs to access whichever part of them one wants to reach at that moment. Tonight, I wish to see both sets of plump delicious lips, with your gorgeous face framed in the vee of your legs." His hand cupped her chin again.

Beth blinked back tears. Lud, he'd said everything she'd ever wanted to hear from a man. She might be half in love with him already, between that and the orgasms. She, who was supposed to be all about fun, never serious.

Uh oh. What am I supposed to do now?

He touched her ankle again, quirking a brow.

She nodded. She'd worry about her heart later, the rest of her needed satisfaction right now.

Robert took his time drawing her leg up, his gaze on hers.

Whether he was checking for emotional or physical discomfort, she didn't know, but she appreciated it.

After cuffing her leg just above her knee so it hung next to her wrist, he sat back, his gaze eager.

She experimented. Straightening her leg tugged her wrist upward, the smooth leather shifting easily around the bedpost. Next, she straightened her arm along her side.

Oops. Her leg drew higher on the bed, almost lifting her bottom off the bed.

His words about her face being framed by her legs made sense. She squirmed from a mix of self-consciousness and eagerness. He could do whatever he wanted for however long he wished…again.

As she tested various angles of her arm with her leg moving accordingly, Robert climbed onto the bed and secured her other hand and ankle. Kneeling back with his arse on his heels, he sucked in an admiring breath.

She squirmed under his regard.

"You are gorgeous. And mine to do with as I'd like." When her gaze locked with his again, he continued, "Stop thinking. Just feel. You aren't in control here, so relax and enjoy."

She sucked in a deep breath as his words calmed her, drawing his gaze to the mounds of her breasts.

"Will you remove your shirt?" she asked.

He shuddered, and replied with a quick, "No."

"Why not?" She frowned in confusion and frustration.

"We've established that I see you as beautiful and me as not, and I am in charge here."

"But—"

"No."

Dratted man.

"'Tis not fair," she grumbled. "I am trussed up for you, with all my—" She searched for the words. "—parts on display, and you will not even lay bare your shoulders?"

He ran a finger through her folds, distracting her from her petulance as she mentally pushed his finger to the throbbing kernel that needed it most. But he avoided that spot, instead pinching and petting and fondling her swollen lips as he knelt fully clothed above her. "I see the corset did its job. Mayhap you can provide me with critical feedback later."

Contemplating the pros and cons of the corset and particularly the strap, her mind drifted for a moment.

Robert was quick to remedy that. Lowering to taste each breast, he paid homage to both before sliding farther to stare at her weeping center. His breath gusted over her sensitive flesh.

All thoughts of the corset fled as her core clenched, wanting his fingers, mouth, or cock. She writhed, making small thrusting motions with her hips toward his face.

"The more you move, the longer I will take."

What? No.

As she was about to beg, he parted her feminine lips and flicked his tongue up her center. Her arms yanked against her bonds in an involuntary reflex, shifting her legs up. The lick was exactly what she had wished for and yet still not enough. She found her voice. "Unh, please."

"Please, what?" She could feel his lips curl in a smile against her inner thighs, the evil man.

"Please touch me."

"Oh, I will. Indeed I am. Mayhap not the way you'd like, though. Did you think the punishment was over, Peaches?" He smiled up at her.

She jerked her legs, testing her bonds, and blinked as the extent of her vulnerability sank in.

He rubbed his cheek on her leg, holding her hips with his hands. "I won't hurt you, just torture you for a time."

She relaxed, then thrashed again when he restarted his light, slow licking.

"You want me to take longer, then?"

"Wha— Oh, no." Her hips stilled, but her whole body remained tense, as she struggled to restrain herself from pushing at him.

He added a finger, spiraling it in and out of her tight channel in slow repetitions. She was wet enough that the movement was audible, and moisture slid down between her bottom cheeks. His tongue drove her mad with its speed and lack of pressure, but his finger curled in just the right angle to brush a particularly sensitive spot on her inner walls.

Yes, yes, she chanted silently. She could almost see the crest, everything in her tightening, gripping his fingers and mounding her stomach as she reached for the pinnacle. Just one more lick would get her there. Her hips made one uncontrolled thrust.

He withdrew and moved up to suck her taut, needy nipples.

After endless minutes and her third peak, she thought her punishment was surely finished. Convinced he'd allow her to go over, she shoved toward his licks as best she could. When he drew away again, tears seeped from her eyes.

"I trust you'll behave better next time, Peaches?"

"Yes. Yes, Robert. Please," she gasped.

Rising to his knees, he ripped off his jacket, waistcoat, and cravat.

She held her breath, hoping he'd remove his shirt as well, but when he scrabbled at his trouser buttons, she had no regrets. She needed his cock.

In his haste, he shoved them down to his hips rather than remove them before donning protection and shoving into her.

Beth squeaked, her back arching, the tide of her climax rushing toward her.

Yes, this. One more pump and I'm there.

****

Robert had been worried when she'd pushed again for him to remove his clothes. He wasn't ready to lose her yet.

Knowing exactly how to distract her best, he'd set about his favorite method of punishment.

By the time he sank into her, he was worried he'd find his own release before he ensured Beth experienced hers. Then her squeak concerned him and took the edge off. He stilled, knowing this angle allowed for deeper penetration, worried that he'd hurt her.

"Robert!"

His cock throbbed at hearing his name whispered so harshly. All the practice at controlling his pleasure to direct hers flew out the window. He wanted to rut, to pound her exposed flesh, to bury himself in her over and over.

"You. Are. So. Deep," Beth gasped.

"Does it hurt?"

"Lud, no. 'Tis delicious." Her breasts shook with each breath, and he struggled to bring his gaze back to her face to check for a frown or pinch of pain.

Seeing none, he returned his fingers to where they joined and tweaked her tight bundle of nerves.

Beth ground her head into the pillow and screamed. Her internal muscles squeezed him.

Swallowing her scream with a punishing kiss, he plunged in and out of her, groaning at the slippery, tight grip. He drove into her, the smack of his sweat-slickened hips hitting home each time ratcheting his pleasure. Lightning shot down his spine, his bollocks tightening, and he roared the thunder as the storm of ecstasy broke over him.

Beth's arms and legs yanked against her bonds, her breasts quivering, and her nipples hard peaks. Her inner walls contracted around his cock over and over, milking every drop from him as he pounded into her.

As her orgasm waned, he slowed his movements. Curling over her, his head hung as he shuddered with sensation.

She lay spent as he withdrew, disposed of the sheath, then snuffed the candles before moving around the bed to undo the restraints. He rubbed the circulation back into her arms and legs.

She hummed in thanks. "May I stay?"

He frowned in the darkness. He should not want her in his bed all night, but he could not imagine letting her leave.

Grunting, he slid into bed and wrapped his arms around her. Unwilling to admit more, his answer was simple. "Yes."

Chapter Eleven

Beth woke feeling sated but wrung out. Robert repeatedly bringing her to the edge of orgasm only to deny her the fall into ecstasy had resulted in her longest orgasm ever, a new best. He really was addicting, the dratted man. She renewed her determination to see his full form unadorned.

Stretching under the covers, she reveled at how warm she was. Rolling over, she recognized her source of heat—Robert. Feeling a twinge of stiffness in her limbs from resisting her tethers, she stifled a grunt of discomfort.

He still wore his shirt. She peeked beneath the duvet. No other clothes were hidden under there. *Why the shirt?*

Rising, she wandered naked to the two chairs with a small table between them in front of the fireplace. As she stoked the fire to life again, papers on the table caught her eye.

Robert had sketched her, presumably while they'd been apart. He'd drawn her in his designs.

Recalling his words of her beauty, she saw it in the pencil marks. He'd captured her expression of rapture and had highlighted her eyes, lips, nipples, and weeping folds with shading, drawing the viewer's attention there rather than her middle.

Ever curious about his designs, she shuffled the remaining pages, but they were empty. Moving over to the small open trunk from which he'd extracted the cuffs, she peered inside. There were several leather pieces of varying shapes and sizes, but many lacked hardware.

Robert stirred, sitting up and running his hands through his hair.

She straightened.

"I'd be annoyed at you poking through my things, but I was enjoying the show too much." He grinned.

"Thank you. Shall I join you again then? Mayhap with another design to test?" She gestured to the trunk.

"Unfortunately, that shall have to wait." He leaned over to grab his trousers, then slid across the bed to the opposite side from where she stood. Dropping his feet to the floor, he shuffled into his clothes as he stood.

Beth recalled his comments about their respective beauty.

Is he shy? Or ashamed of his body or even scarred? Is that why the room is always dimmed, and why he kept his shirt on? Is that why he declines to play in public?

After all his lovely praise of her, she hoped she could return the favor and reassure him. "Why must it wait? I assume Cheltie asked you to entertain me today whilst they take care of business." She gave him her practiced coquettish moue.

"Yes. I have a few appointments. If you care to accompany me, I can show you a bit of Bath at the same time."

"I'd enjoy that. Shall we meet downstairs for breakfast in thirty minutes?"

He nodded again.

Forty minutes later, Beth sailed into the breakfast room of the guesthouse.

Robert had a teacup waiting for her and poured a cup

from the pot on the table as she sat.

"Care to tell me about your appointments?"

"Blacksmiths."

"Is that why you have half-finished pieces with you?" Beth asked, undeterred by his one-word answer. She was already pondering how to help him solve this, and who she might know to ask.

"Yes."

"Where have you been getting the hardware for your designs until now?"

"I have an excellent blacksmith, but he is getting older and finds the more detailed work difficult during the cold dark winter months. He also has a grandchild he wants to see more often."

"So, you are looking to replace him?"

Robert nodded, his lips twisting. "Over time, anyway."

"What do you look for in a blacksmith? How do you judge quality?"

"Much of what I need is on a smaller scale than many smiths' usual work. The ones that supply horse outfitters know what is needed for leather attachments. On the other hand, furniture requires more detail and finesse with the metal. Unfortunately, I rarely find a smith who works with both."

Beth nodded. He still hadn't answered her question, though.

"Sometimes, I can evaluate their work if they have pieces in progress. Otherwise, I carry a few samples and get their reaction to them. If they think they could recreate them, I will give them one, and offer a small fee for them to duplicate it."

"What of availability? I presume these men already

have enough work to feed their families."

"Ah, yes. That will be more difficult to judge. When I found Burke, my business was smaller. One saving grace is that I have the luxury of being able to order the fasteners I use most in bulk and maintaining inventory."

That means he is doing enough business to afford such a thing. Good for him. Beth was impressed. She'd never cared how a man supported himself because her affairs were short term. But the more she discovered about Robert, the more he fascinated her.

"I am surprised Cheltie could not find one for you."

"He does better on the investing end and hasn't funded anyone's smithy business."

"Ah. Right, then. Shall we begin?"

****

By the end of the day, they'd talked with several smiths and one apprentice. None of them did indoor work, as they called it. When Robert produced his samples, two of them shook their heads.

"Not worth my time," said one.

"D'you know of another smith who might be interested?" he asked.

"Not here in Bath."

Beth chimed in, asking where belts were made, and they shrugged and guessed, "London?"

As the day went on, Robert talked less and less. She picked up on his detailed questions after the first stop, and was so bubbly and charming, the smiths preferred to talk to her, so he stepped back and watched.

She had a knack for honing in on the aspects of his work that differed from others' and tailoring her questions about the skills needed without offending the blacksmiths. It was easy to attribute it to her outgoing nature and inquisitiveness, but he perceived the sharp intellect simmering below her seemingly carefree surface and was awed.

They strolled back to the guesthouse to change for the evening meal. Thoughts swirled as Beth chattered about what she'd liked about each smith's work.

I could so easily fall in love with her. That sharp wit, her creative ideas, her caring nature.

She clearly wanted nothing more than to see people around her happy, despite how Bags and Michael said the Ton treated her. Her conspicuousness and outlandishness were challenges, however. Her star shone too brightly. While he did not wish to dim it, neither did he want to stand in its light. He preferred the shadows. He attended the parties because Evan dragged him and for inspiration, but he hated imagining what might happen if the Ton learned he was the designer of those pieces they loved so much.

No matter. She will quickly tire of me—the quiet outcast, the second son, the frumpy friend. His lips twisted.

He would enjoy this time in Bath, away from the Season and the Ton. Not because she was helping him, although that was a nice benefit. Rather, he could bask in her light safely and enjoy the warm glow of her *joie de vivre.*

They turned onto the block for the guesthouse. As though she read his last thought, she slid him a look. "I think I should see a few more examples of what you need."

He grunted, playing at noncommittal.

I want her in every last piece, but I am afraid if I put them on her, I'll never part with them, even the commissioned ones.

Always before, he had paid little attention to the person in his contraptions, instead focusing on the design. Would it be comfortable for a half hour? An hour? Would it work for various body types and sizes, for men and women?

Last night, though, the possibilities of the woman rather than the leather enthralled him. He'd scrutinized every expression, wanting to ensure she experienced the utmost pleasure possible. He'd watched every physical response, more so than he'd ever done. His years since university had been spent learning women's bodies and how to read them, and last night he'd applied every ounce of skill. The cuffs had merely been a means to an end.

Taking his silence as uncertainty, Beth prodded, "I think I deserve a reward for my help today." In the foyer of the guest house, she turned toward him and drew a line down his waistcoat buttons with one finger. "Don't you?"

Grabbing her hand, Robert tugged her upstairs. "I do want to show you a few pieces. Some will require more delicate metalwork than others. Smaller buckles, more decorative fastenings, and the like."

"Excellent." Beth was out of breath.

He'd like to think it was at the prospect of seeing more of his work.

In his room, he knelt at the trunk and picked out a few items. Laying a pile on the bed, he held one item up. It was a set of cuffs with a long lead to a collar.

"Here, look at the clips and rings. I want some smaller than this and some larger."

"Why?"

He smiled. "The larger, as you saw at Cheltie's house, are for men, as they are stronger than women. The smaller are to attach cuffs to different places. For instance, you don't want two big rings on either side of a collar on a woman. It would not look appealing. However, I want her partner to be able to cuff her wrists to that collar to keep them out of his or her way."

"Oh." Definitely breathy again.

He smiled.

Putting that aside, he picked up the corset she'd worn the previous evening.

Poking at one of the breast holes, he glanced up to catch her gaze. "These are simply cut at the moment. The circular shape does not allow stitching around it, so I'd like to add a ring to smooth and hold the edge of the leather and press into the areola. It might also add an element of cold."

She shivered.

He grinned again.

"W—with your current blacksmith…" Beth seemed to struggle to form the question. "Do you tell him the purpose of the pieces you're requesting or simply provide specifications of what you want?"

"I tell him. Often the smith will have better ideas on how to mesh the metalwork with the leatherwork. It requires trust, but I also pay well for his discretion."

She nodded, gulping, her eyes still on the corset. "How do you judge what size cups a woman needs?"

"Usually she'll provide a set of stays or measurements from her modiste. Or I can judge for myself." With her obvious arousal, he needed no further permission to reach out and cup her delectable breasts.

Her weight shifted, pressing into his hands, and she

grabbed him for support. "Do you mayhap need someone to help you test items before you offer them for sale?"

Was she volunteering? He hoped but had to make sure he understood. "Are you volunteering to help me find someone?" He punctuated the question with a swipe of his thumbs across the pointed tips of her breasts.

"No! I meant me."

He smiled with satisfaction. "Right, then. After eating, we'll test a few things."

****

Robert was glad Beth's behavior did not warrant punishment tonight, as neither of them would have made it through supper.

He watched her from the corner of his eye, seated at a right angle to him. She shifted every few minutes. Licked her lips. Smoothed her skirts. And was uncharacteristically quiet.

He wanted to perform lewd acts on her right there under the table.

But, of course, he couldn't. Even as distracted as Evan was with Althea, he'd have noticed. He might not have cared, but he'd have noticed, and Althea surely would have cared.

Instead, he recalled the dinner at Greenborough Park. Private play in public he could do. Turning when the other pair were laughing at something from their outing that day, he whispered his fantasy in her ear. "Imagine, as I talk to Evan, I draw your skirt up, dragging your petticoats with it. I find you soaking."

She grabbed his arm, gasping and undulating in her chair.

"I slide a finger through your folds, right into you, curling just a touch against your most sensitive spot.

Then I leave it there and continue my conversation, forcing you to sit still. Maybe I'd even ask you a question or two to ensure you join the discussion."

"Robert, please," she whispered.

He doubted she was sure what she was pleading for—him to follow his words with actions or to desist. In lieu of either, they declined dessert and left Evan and Althea in the private room at the restaurant. Robert hoped his jacket and cloak hid his tented trousers as they returned to his room.

He laid out the new cuffs he wanted to test. These were simpler to make and would have a lower price point. He thought he could still market them to his regular crowd as more portable, therefore worth purchasing as a second set. In a simple X, four five-inch leather straps were stitched around a center ring, with no buckles to adjust their length. The leather cuffs at each point of the X were plain with simple buckles and no padding.

When he turned to face Beth, she was already pushing her dress and petticoat over her hips.

"Unlace me, please, Robert." She turned to present the laces of her stays to him. Once they were loosened, she shoved them to the floor and whipped her chemise over her head.

He reached a hand to hold her from turning back to him, and rubbed her back, trying to ease the impressions from the stays.

She rolled her shoulders forward, pressing her spine backward into his touch, and moaned in pleasure. "How do you know to do that?"

He shrugged. "It seemed like something I would appreciate."

She turned. "Thank you."

With every intention of doing the same over her ribs, his gaze caught on her impressive bosom, and his hands skimmed right past her ribs to cup the gorgeous mounds. He could not get enough of these. His breath quickened, his cock growing harder against the placket of his trousers.

She rolled her eyes. "So easily distracted, even when doing good deeds."

"Can you blame me? These are magnificent. I've seen many breasts in my work…" He trailed off, realizing that sounded terrible. Then he made it worse, trying to correct it. "I mean, not as many as Bags…" He huffed. "Oh never mind. I beg your pardon, Beth. Please forgive me and allow me to enjoy these most lovely of breasts in silence."

Her chest was shaking with muffled laughter, making the bountiful globes jiggle in his hands, exciting him further.

Her fingers feathered over one wrist, not stopping him.

He looked up.

"I, too, have seen quite a lot of breasts, and I do agree mine are rather nice. 'Tis all right, Robert." She leaned in and kissed him.

He sighed. *Luscious. Forgiving. Likes breasts too.* He was in trouble.

She leaned over and picked up the restraints. "Where do you want me?"

"For these, on the bed." Tonight, he wanted to enjoy the rear view of her beauty.

She lay down, and he paused to admire her front curves before flipping her over.

"Robert, when do I get to see you unclothed? I get so distracted playing with your toys, then realize I missed my chance each time."

"Hmph. You're not missing much," he muttered.

"Wait." She came up on her elbows. "Why would you think that? Has no one told you how attractive you are? Surely they must have."

He blushed and turned his head away. *Damnation, she is too perceptive by half.* His cockstand flagged at the change in topic.

Beth rose to sit. "You know not everyone wants Cheltie, right?"

"Ha. You did. Do you not recall the party when Michael requested Penelope's hand?"

She blushed. "Honestly? 'Twas habit." She plucked at the bedcover by her hip. "You have likely heard—how do they say it?—I am not the most discriminating. I would argue that I am simply more open-minded than much of the Ton but still discerning."

"What do you mean?"

"I do not only enjoy blonds or tall men or large-breasted women." She winked, and he grinned, feeling his shoulders drop away from his ears.

She continued. "I like many shapes and sizes. In part, because I look beyond the physical, even for a casual encounter. I prefer to spend time with kind, generous, thoughtful people. After all, as you demonstrate here"—she swept her hand from the restraints on the bed to the open trunk—"smarter people offer more interesting ways to be intimate."

His cheeks warmed. "Oh." He was at a loss for words, unsure if anyone had called him smart before her. His parents had focused on his older brother, the heir.

And Bags's intelligence had eclipsed anyone else's prowess.

"But let me be clear. I want you for your physique as well. Your broad shoulders and muscular arms make me feel petite in ways I don't normally." She gestured to where her belly mounded in her lap, her bottom and thighs spreading beneath her on the bed.

She is *petite; she's perfect*. He appreciated her verbalization of her attraction, though. His cock had re-engaged, thinking of manhandling her and showing her how dainty he found her.

"Your bulk comes from strength, from wielding tools and a fabric most can't work with, and calls to mind your creativity. Then your rough hands scrape just so against my skin, and I am wet within minutes of you walking into a room."

"Really?" His voice went high at the end, his head leaning forward. He wanted to believe her but hardly dared.

"Really. Now, please, at least remove your coat and shirt? Then show me how you want to test these before I attack you and put them on you?"

He laughed but shook his head "no" at her. Making quick work of his coat, waistcoat and cravat, he slowed when he got to his shirt.

"Shall I redress then? It seems only fair." She pouted.

After extinguishing a few candles, he tugged off his shirt.

"Wait there, please. Let me look at you."

"No." He came toward her.

Sticking her lower lip out again, she scanned his broad chest and thick arms. "Delicious. I told you I would form my own opinion. I've decided. You are simply delicious."

"Thank you." Robert blushed, ducking his head and hurrying the last few steps to the bed. Taking the X from her, he distracted her by testing the cuffs in several ways before draping her face down over a pillow so her hips were raised. He knelt behind her and took in her arse. More than two handfuls, it was a dimpled ripe peach, soft to squeeze and pale with a seam down it. His mouth watered for a bite.

First, though, the restraints. Laying the X on her back, he pulled one hand behind her, then the other.

Her shoulders pulled tight.

He knew he could not keep her here long, but neither of them could handle much more foreplay. He spread her knees on the bed and drew each ankle up to restrain all four limbs behind and above her.

Again, he sat back on his heels to peruse. That seam of her peach widened to show the red center at the heart of her. Glistening in the candlelight, it too begged for a bite.

Taking a moment to indulge his appetite, he put his mouth to one raised cheek.

She gasped.

He bit.

She squealed.

Lowering farther, he licked a path to her weeping center and blew a breath.

She twitched, trying to squeeze her legs together. Mayhap to clutch him to her, mayhap to find her own friction, but his design and their positions restricted her movements.

He smiled, then put his teeth to one of her nether lips

and closed them to tug.

Her back arched another inch, despite the pillow under her hips.

He rose. Smacking her once on each bottom cheek, he grabbed a protective sheath and aligned. Holding his cock, he rubbed once, twice.

She writhed and moaned.

Shoving in, he drove all the way to the hilt, and she undulated under him. Lava swirled in his bollocks. Her *kleitoris* and the tuft of hair around it teased the fire higher. He set his jaw, determined to ensure she reached ecstasy first.

Voice muffled by her head sideways against the bed, she begged, "Please, move!"

He barked a laugh before he complied. Withdrawing, he shoved in hard again, then repeated the motion at a steady pace. She tightened around him, but he did not increase his speed. Besides trying to keep her on the edge, he feared if he moved any faster he'd come without her.

Instead, he leaned forward and slid a hand under a breast. "'Tis the only part of this position I don't like," he muttered. And squeezed, then pinched her nipple.

Her undulations lost any semblance of rhythm.

His thrusts smacked his testicles against her, giving him a pleasant jolt. More, she flinched in reaction and keened with each slap.

He pinched again, and she shrieked. Her core rippled up and down his shaft, on and on. He gave one last hard thrust and held himself there, cushioned by her generous arse, still pinching her nipple, as the volcano of his orgasm erupted. His hips made miniature piston motions against her, and she squirmed, her back arching and her fists clenching and unclenching in their manacles.

He shuddered in and over her with the last of the orgasm, holding himself off her with outstretched arms.

She grumbled into the pillow. "Another reason to dislike this position… I still have yet to see you fully naked."

He swatted her behind again as he knelt back to undo her cuffs and rub her shoulders.

Keeping my clothes on won't protect me from being hurt. Might as well go all in next time.

Because there would be a next time. He could not give up this woman. He'd just be grateful for his time with her when she inevitably walked away from him, as they all did.

Chapter Twelve

Their last three days in Bath flew by. The four of them explored the city. While Althea and Evan sniffed candles and soaps and tested pens and inks, Beth helped Robert interview a few more blacksmiths, then circle back to retrieve two samples he'd purchased.

She knew without him saying anything that he was not satisfied with any of the workmen he'd met, and her mind raced at how to find a blacksmith. 'Twas not an occupation she had worked with before.

In between, the two couples met to guzzle tea and ices and pastries and review their adventures. They excused the pastries as research for Penelope, should she ever want to open a bakery here, then laughed at themselves when they could not find criticism of any of the sweets.

Twice, Robert had her wear his contraptions under her clothing for short outings, making sure they were not visible. One made her bounce more frequently until he quelled her movements with a hand pressed to her shoulder, and one caused her to become near-silent. Each time, he did not allow her to reach the pinnacle until after they were in his room for the night and she'd provided feedback on the item.

Althea and Evan were too focused on her business and their budding relationship to notice, and in the evenings produced foolscap and pencils to discuss boring things like inventory trades and partnership parameters to propose to local apothecaries.

So in addition to considering metal sourcing, Beth offered criticism and praise for Robert's designs, particularly those she tested. Tentative at first, she grew bolder when he asked follow-up questions and even solicited her thoughts on new design sketches.

"Could you make the X configuration we tested the other night adjustable? If it were modified to be kinder to people's shoulders who are not as bendable, you might broaden your audience to older people who still enjoy a creative sex life."

He agreed, grinning.

She pondered out loud, "What if you sold the X without the cuffs to clients who already have them?"

"Oh. I was going to sell it as a travel accessory—" He broke off when she laughed. "To existing clients. You're right. Most already own a set of cuffs."

"And you could sell the cuffs alone, and different length straps alone. Again, by having more affordable options, you'd expand your client base."

He nodded, albeit not as enthusiastically as she'd expected. Why did he want her help if not for more sales?

"Basically, for those who need it, you can offer items separately so they can build their own adventure. If you're comfortable offering two different grades of leather or different colors, you can tick up the price for those, and it may appeal to the less adventurous but still curious nobs, as well."

"Won't it detract from my other sales?" he asked with a frown

"Maybe. But you said you sell mostly through private parties, with demonstrations by the host or hostess of the party? The acting would be done with products in sets sold as such." She thought further. "With the individual items, you might broaden your audience to those who do not attend the parties. Maybe you sell those through the Sc—" She broke off.

"The what?"

"Uh, nothing. I want to look into another channel before I propose it." Beth could not believe she had nearly blurted out the name of the school. She'd enjoyed helping Robert so much. He was much better at the design, but she brought a woman's perspective. Her real strength, though, was in her network. Bringing people together to help them both. Or in this case, providing people with a way to spice up their love life while helping Robert. But the school was sacrosanct. She would never threaten the secrecy of the program; it helped too many young women and had proved invaluable to Beth herself.

On the other hand, nothing was stopping her from speaking to the headmistress about opportunities to sell Robert's products.

He had changed the subject. "Beth, when we return to London…"

"Yes?" When he looked awkward and his voice trailed into silence, she braced herself to hear that London would mean the end of their dalliance.

"You know I value my privacy, so we must keep it quiet, but I should like to see you again."

Yay! She nodded. "I should like to spend more time with you as well."

"I shall send a note 'round when Bags and I return from Cheltenham, then?"

"Yes, please." In the meantime, she'd write to Helen

Montague, the headmistress of the School of Enlightenment.

****

Back in London, Althea rushed to check on her store and her inventories, having convinced an apothecary owner in Bath to partner with her. Beth was sure there'd be unending amounts of paperwork and other drudgery on which her cousin thrived.

She visited the charity school to re-start volunteering and to see if there were older students searching for their next step in life. She acted as a second counselor for them, after their teachers and the headmistress. While she did not have the same training as the instructors, Beth's network and her experience of bouncing between three homes allowed her to relate to the students and envision suitable paths for them to consider.

After she'd finished at the School of Enlightenment, Beth had returned to Althea's home. Understandably, given her past transgression with a fellow clerk, Althea was reluctant to have her help in the store again. So Althea had asked the Enlightened Salon for ideas to fill Beth's time with something other than mischief. One lady had suggested volunteer work.

Beth took to the charity school like a duck to water, and Althea sighed in relief. When Beth found the first student she'd thought would excel at the School of Enlightenment, she'd written to the headmistress. Helen Montague had sent a recruiter to visit with Beth, then interview the student, and the woman had agreed. Helen also raised the idea of Beth helping to place graduates of the school. Beth preened and soon found coordinating with the school the most rewarding element of pairing people with opportunities.

After seeing Robert's products, she saw an opportunity to add another layer to that networking. The school and its network of alumnae were an excellent untapped audience for his leatherwork.

Dear Mrs. Montague,
She'd not yet been able to bring herself to think of the headmistress as Helen, despite invitations by the older woman.

I have encountered a man—she scribbled over *man* and wrote *person—who creates leather pieces to enhance intimate activities. Bondage, apparel, and beyond. This individual values anonymity. Thus, I am wondering about a way to sell to the school and mayhap a few select sponsors and alumnae.*

Do you believe this might be possible? If so, how? I am loath to raise it with my new friend until I get your thoughts on the matter, particularly your permission to discuss information about the school even vaguely.

Sincerely,

Beth Jenkins, exemplary student extraordinaire— her standard tongue-in-cheek signature to her former headmistress, as she had been wild even as a student.

The list of names of people associated with the school was a closely held secret. Thus, while she could be a conduit for his sales, they'd need a method to market the goods. There were too many pieces to make a sample set, and the audience was spread far and wide across the country.

Mayhap a catalogue? They could hire an artist to sketch the pieces. Should they use models?

Her blood surged at the idea of modeling for sketches. She'd get to try all the pieces again.

She straightened abruptly.

They wouldn't do anything. He could use any model he wanted.

There is no we. This is Robert's business, and our time together is only a lighthearted romp to him.

Why did the idea of their end, of him touching someone else hurt so much? 'Twas stupid to give someone so much control over her emotions.

****

No matter how long Robert would want to play with her, and how much she'd get to interject into what was essentially his business, Beth was not one to mope. Instead, she decided to enjoy her time with Robert for however long it lasted.

She'd help him because she liked him and because that is what she did. And she'd enjoy their time together, leather or no, while it lasted. The rest she'd worry about later.

Unsure what Robert would think of selling to the school and the method he'd prefer, she was anxious to hear back from Helen Montague. She daren't share any information about the program or alumnae without permission.

Upon arriving home Tuesday, she found Althea in the bath with news that the men had returned. She pivoted and raced for the front hall and the pile of mail. Sure enough, a note from Robert awaited her with his address and an invitation to visit after supper. She would not hear from Helen for at least another fortnight, but she was eager to talk to Robert about selling through Sarah Potter's club with a catalogue.

Chasing back upstairs, Beth borrowed Althea's bath, ensured her cousin was dressed appropriately to entertain her man, and returned below stairs to borrow a maid's dress. There was no one her same shape, so she nabbed a dress that was a tad small, knowing the tightness would accent Robert's favorite aspect of her anatomy. She traded the girl one of her simpler gowns that was hardly worn, knowing most of the maids sewed and someone could tailor it for her.

Changing her dress, she grabbed her borrowed servant's cloak and hood and waited for the hour to be late enough. Pacing the library, she kept checking out the window for darkness, then for Cheltie. When she heard him on the stairs, she darted out, shrugging on her cloak as she exited the back door he had just entered.

Robert had told her where he lived when they were in Bath, as she wondered where he had storage space for his work. She'd been surprised that he owned a townhouse in the City, not far from Mayfair, the most elegant and expensive neighborhood.

Knocking on the kitchen door as a servant would, she gave her name to the servant who answered.

They were back within a minute, out of breath, and gestured her inside. "Please, miss, this way."

"Thank you. I am sorry to disturb you so late."

"Not at all. Mister Orford only arrived home from his club a short while ago."

Beth wondered which club he'd been at, Sarah's or White's. Jealousy stabbed behind her ribs when she thought of him at Sarah's. But she had no right to be jealous. She reminded herself to take what fun she could from him and not worry about the rest.

And then he was there, sitting with a half-stitched

leather strap in his hands, frowning. His eyes ran down then up her, and he spat, "What on earth are you wearing?"

"I borrowed a simpler gown and cloak to ensure I did not draw attention to myself on the way here. 'Tis why I knocked at the servant's entrance. You ought to give me a key, Robert." When in doubt, Beth tried to bluster her way through a situation.

He raised his brows. "I ought, oughtn't I?"

"Is that even a word? But yes. Yes, you ought, and here is why. I have had some excellent ideas to get you more sales. How did you plan for me to arrive? Shall I knock on the front door next time? You said you wanted to keep things quiet."

"You are, as always, outlandish." He approached and caught her hand, pulling her into his arms. The garment he'd been working on slapped gently against her back. Slanting his mouth across hers, he caressed her lips with his, teasing and nibbling in an extended welcome kiss.

She'd be outlandish any day if she received such caring soft kisses that she knew would lead to rougher, more dominant play. Her eyes drifted shut, and she leaned against his comforting strength.

He pulled away from the kiss, loosening his arms around her, and asked, "You're here now. Do you want a drink?"

"Oh, yes, please. Do you have sherry or champagne, or mayhap port? Spirits will make me groggy at this hour, I confess." *Or groggier than his kiss already has.*

Shaking her head once to clear it, she scanned the room. It looked much like his workshop at Greenborough Park—lumps of unidentifiable furniture under half-finished leather garments, with one chair and a settee mostly clear. The walls were a neutral cream with dark wood wainscoting below the chair rail.

"Hmm. I wonder if I might not enjoy you being calmer or groggier once in a while," he grumbled, but he rummaged in the cabinet and produced an only slightly dusty bottle of port. Uncapping it, he sniffed it before pouring a measure into a glass for her.

She grinned at him. "Now then. What are you making?"

Chapter Thirteen

Robert glanced at the item he still held. It was an order for a customer, not a new design. Whilst the girls at Sarah's were always ready to try new experiences, none of them had Beth's gorgeous curves or her sharp intellect in evaluating his work.

Beyond enjoying the willing test subject, he could not imagine returning to Sarah's girls when Beth inevitably moved on to someone less shy, less grumpy, less *him*.

Half the time, he wanted to strangle her for her flagrant disregard of society's rules. The disregard he could live with. It was the publicness that bothered him. The other half, he wanted to strip her and buckle her to his bed and torture her for hours or mayhap days. He couldn't decide which was the better path. Likely neither.

Admit you're happy with her interest in you and your work.

Always before now, he'd preferred to work and live alone. At Greenborough Park, Evan only expected him at the evening meal. Even when not busy with the earldom or his mother, Evan knew Robert liked his own space. However, more and more, he enjoyed Beth's assistance with his work.

Beyond that, her willingness to try all sorts of new toys and positions fitted his creativity to perfection, and—this he still marveled at—she said she found him attractive. He was still working on believing her, but the possibility added to her allure.

If only I could keep her. He still doubted her interest beyond the novelty of his designs, but oh, how he wished she could care for him, as he found himself increasingly smitten with every interaction.

A shiver went through him as he feared heartbreak in his future, and he shook it off. She'd said something when she first arrived about increasing his sales. He should probably pursue that, if for no other reason than to forestall further efforts from her to widen his clientele.

"I am not working on anything new right now. Pray do not get distracted. You've come so far to share these fascinating concerns regarding my sales; do tell."

Her grin did not flag in the slightest. "Where were you earlier? The servant who let me in said you'd come from your club?" Her brows lifted in question.

"White's, with Michael and Bags, of course."

"Not 'of course.' I know you three—well, Michael may not any longer—also have memberships at Sarah Potter's Club."

He blinked, freezing his expression at neutral.

"Do you care to confirm that? No? Right, then, I shall continue. Do you sell your goods to her?"

He blinked again.

"Come now, Robert." She wagged a finger at him. "You do remember I have quite a lot of friends, do you not?"

"Yes."

"Yes, what exactly?"

"Yes, I sell to Mrs. Potter for her establishment." He ignored her snicker.

"Do you sell to her other clientele?"

He glared at her continued playful jabs. "Not directly. But her private parties sometimes include a selection and/or a demonstration of my wares by her girls, without my direct involvement."

"I thought of a way to do that beyond the balls."

He shook his head. "Too many men are protective of their memberships. They don't even want to meet others' eyes in the waiting room, much less hold conversations or discuss their preferences in toys."

"I thought as much. But what if you created a catalogue? It could be left in that waiting room. Or mayhap in Sarah's office."

He gave her a sharp glance at her use of Sarah's first name.

Does she know Sarah? She did say she has a lot of friends. And Bags said her network rivaled his. Ugh, I don't want my worlds to be this entwined.

"Clients—and the employees, for that matter—could select their choices and place orders with her. They'd remain confidential because you'd get them anonymously and Sarah would handle all exchanges, for a commission."

He considered the setup. "What about items that need personal measurements?"

"Oh, right. I hadn't thought of that. Mayhap those are in a section that stipulates a meeting with the designer? Then they won't know you unless they share their identity."

He wasn't sure he was comfortable with that unless he had right of refusal. What if one of those bullies from school wanted something until he found out Robert was the designer? However, he also wasn't ready to share those fears with Beth. He suspected she'd scoff at them, given her fearless approach to life.

"Do you really think this sort of thing would sell from a catalogue?" he asked instead.

"I think if you offer sketches as well as descriptions, it could. Especially if the sketches included a model. Think of the various positions you showed me for the first set of cuffs. You needn't show them all, but a few to spark someone's imagination would likely improve sales."

"Who would—" Seeing her grin, he shook his head. He should have guessed. "You? You want to model?"

"And get to play with all those lovely wares of yours? Yes, please."

He had to admit, the idea held merit. He tilted his head, mind racing at the challenge. Evan's party created more work than he'd prefer, but that was only once a year. The rest of the year, he could certainly handle more volume. His need for a new blacksmith suddenly felt more pressing.

Do I dare? Will this expose me? Or someone else?

He'd worked so hard to fit in and stay in the shadows. He dreaded exposure and being shunned again like in school. Was it worth the risk when he didn't need the money? He perused Beth's face again, her eagerness evident in the glint in her eyes, her bouncing leg. He was not sure he had the heart to tell her no.

"Let me consider it. You may return tomorrow night, and we shall discuss it then. In the meantime…" He stepped to his trunk by his bedroom door and dug through its contents. She'd brought up the spanking club. He had two items that might prove a mild deterrent for her boldness. Of course, he did not wish to punish her too much, as the goal of his designs was always fun.

Finding them, he produced the two items he'd been searching for—a narrow paddle and a leather strap with the end split into two narrower strips and held them up for Beth to see.

Beth's eyes widened.

"Since you brought up Sarah's club, I should like to test both of these. This," he wiggled the paddle, "is narrower than I usually make a paddle. Stiffer than a strap but because of its width, whippier than a normal paddle. The other is something a friend informed me of after he visited Scotland."

She watched silently.

"Any objections?" Concerned that her silence meant fear, he needed assent. "Have you tried any of this before? Do you know what to expect?"

"No, no, and no."

Alarmed, he dropped his hands. "Right. I can put these away."

"No!" She stepped forward and grabbed the tawse he'd made from his friend's description. "I was simply answering your questions. No, I haven't experimented with spanking so I do not know what 'tis like. But also, no objections." She smiled, tugging against his hold on the object.

"Oh." He let out a breath. "You had me concerned that I upset you."

"Thank you, Robert. I am not anxious. Mayhap a little nervous. Certainly excited."

Stepping into her, he forced her back through the doorway toward the bed, making her breath shorten.

I should have known she'd be open to almost anything, but my insecurities interfere all too often. Not tonight.

Sighing with relief, he put his hand against her sternum, just above her cleavage, and shoved.

As she bounced, some parts more than others, he bared his teeth in an anticipatory grin.

She was in for a long night of testing.

****

Beth woke confused. She was lying on her stomach when she never slept in that position. She rolled over and realized why. Her bottom was sore.

The tawse had been too painful, so Robert switched to the narrow paddle. She'd tolerated it well enough, but even light smacks did not excite her much.

After a few, Robert requested feedback.

"It offers a wide variety of sensation, from tingles to pain, quite easily."

"Shall I continue?"

She lifted a shoulder in a half-shrug. "If you'd like. You are the one with the spanking club membership, after all." She glanced over her shoulder at him. "Does it please you to spank me?"

"Only if you enjoy it as well." He set the implement aside. "My membership is for testing such as this, not out of any need to hurt a woman."

At his aggravated tone, she quickly replied, "I did not mean to infer that. I simply wanted to know what you like, just as you asked me. But I'm sure I can apologize more thoroughly."

"Oh?"

She slid to her knees and used her mouth to beg forgiveness without words. Sadly, she had to return home after, in order to avoid being seen leaving his house. He'd sent a servant with her for protection.

Lounging on her side in the morning light, Beth considered their history. She'd approached him more often than not, but he'd been in charge of their play. Between school and her enjoyment of physical intimacy, she'd tried just about everything two—and three—people could do together. But always before, she'd been in control and, in fact, most often led the party.

For all his shyness in public, Robert was wondrously dominant in private. Submitting to his wishes was like drinking an extra glass of port. She felt a little off-kilter, dizzy, but also exhilarated.

She considered his blacksmith dilemma, listing her acquaintances in her head. *Penelope.* Why had she not considered her female friends? Penelope's stepfather was a blacksmith.

Sending a note 'round to her friend, she asked when they could call. She apologized for her boldness, although she knew Penelope would laugh at her apology, expecting nothing less from her.

When she received the expected invitation, she made arrangements with another instructor at the charity school to switch days. Two afternoons later, on one of Althea's days off, they knocked on Penelope's door.

Penelope ushered them into her drawing room as the middle-aged housekeeper, Mrs. Thorpe, bustled in with tea and pastries. Beth greeted the older lady and asked after her husband, who also worked for Penelope.

After Mrs. Thorpe assured her he was well and left, Beth turned to Penelope. "How have you been?"

"Good. Busy. The bakery is coming along, and I spend time with Barbara, Michael's mother as often as possible. She continues to offer countessing and Ton tips."

"How to suck your husband's cock whilst wearing his coronet?" Beth snarked.

Penelope looked shocked.

"Pen, you really ought to be used to me by now."

"Oh, I am—but, but he'll have a coronet?"

The two of them laughed so loud and long they were holding their sides and wiping tears away as Althea gazed on questioningly, not having caught their exchange.

"Right, then. Enough about the *many* things I have to learn." Penelope ignored Beth's snicker at her emphasis. "Althea, what is happening with your shop?"

Althea explained Evan's idea and Charlotte's willingness to invest.

"Oh!" Penelope bounced in her seat, and Beth stifled a grin at the unconscious action. "Lady Peterborough is also funding my bakery. I am so glad she agreed to help you as well. 'Tis almost as though we are keeping it in the family."

Charlotte's husband had died last winter, leaving his younger brother, Edward, as the earl. Pen's closest childhood friend, Sophia, had married the new Earl of Peterborough earlier this year and, in the process, reunited with Penelope.

Beth chuckled at how small a community the aristocracy was. 'Twas a bit incestuous, even beyond the men knowing each other from a spanking club.

Althea had met Sophia's cousin in the Enlightened Salon, made up of graduates and investors in the School of Enlightenment, and had been pointed to the school for Beth's education. Then Beth had met Sophia in the introductory course, just after Sophia's marriage. Then she'd met Penelope in the advanced course. *And oh, I still shiver in pleasure when I remember that one night.*

All of that happened before Sophia and Penelope rediscovered their childhood friendship after six years apart.

And now, she'd dragged Althea into the friendships she'd formed. Her cousin seemed to enjoy it well enough, thankfully. Her name pulled her out of her thoughts.

"Beth, what have you been doing?" Pen asked.

"At least 'tis no longer a question of who," Althea interjected, only half under her breath.

Beth shot her an annoyed look.

Pen's brows shot up. "Really? Do tell." She leaned forward, folding her hands in her lap in an eager pose.

"'Tis nothing serious. I've been helping Robert."

"Ford? With his cock?" Pen asked. Then, as the other two hooted, she blushed and apologized. "I swear, Beth, you bring out the worst in me. Or rather, the dirty. My apologies. Please continue."

"He doesn't need any help with that, I must say."

"*Really*?" Pen goggled. "Still waters run deep. I would not have thunk it of Ford. He is always so reserved. We shall return to that in a moment. First, what are you assisting him with, then?"

"Are you familiar with his trade?"

"Only vaguely, I'm afraid. He works with leather, I believe?"

"Oh yes." It gusted out on a sigh of pleasure.

"Explain, please."

"He creates leather cuffs, often attached, sometimes in shapes which make for very interesting sexual positions. Some are incredibly adaptable to whatever piece of furniture he wants to put to use. And corsets and cock and bollocks corset thingies and…"

Penelope sat back, gusting out a breath. "I shall say it again. Still waters run deep. Oh my. I am not certain I can ever look at him the same way again."

Before Beth could respond, Althea interjected, "Come now, Pen. That is not very fair, is it? None of Michael's friends look questioningly at you, despite how your relationship began."

Pen blushed and lowered her gaze to her hands. "You are right, Althea. You have my apologies. As does Ford. I did not mean it as critical, more that I shall feel awkward thinking of his creations. But that is no excuse."

In the ensuing silence, Beth smiled at Althea and squeezed her hand, grateful for her cousin's leap to her defense.

Penelope took a breath and turned back to Beth. "Mayhap the three of us should have a viewing party of Ford's work one day soon."

"We can have a private party at some point. He also takes them to the demi-monde parties at Sarah's for sales, but he does so anonymously," she warned.

"Excellent. I shall be on the lookout for one of those."

Beth recalled Penelope's stepfather's business. Despite Robert's lukewarm response to her attempt to help his sales, her passion for helping find people whose needs meshed was dimmed rather than doused. Mayhap he could afford to spurn potential sources of income. However, there was a blacksmith somewhere who needed to put food on the table for his family, and she had an opportunity to ensure they could.

"I have a question for you, please. Robert's work

needs small, intricate metal pieces. Buckles, other fastenings, and adornments. The blacksmith he works with is older and may retire soon. He is also already struggling to keep up with demand. Might your stepfather know someone who could help, please? Oh, and 'twould need to be someone very discreet. And ideally someone closer than Peterborough."

"Ah. Of course. I shouldn't think discreet will be an issue, but he may not know other smiths beyond the Peterborough area. I shall write and ask him. He has an apprentice now. He'd once thought Matthew would follow in his footsteps, but Michael has said he wants to send Matthew to university if he's interested. And David will make sure he's interested, as he wants Matthew to have an easier life than he's had. So he brought in a younger man to train to take over the business. I shall ask how he found him, as well as other ideas for you."

"David will be open-minded about the specifics?"

"Oh yes. Michael and I came clean to him after our betrothal. He was surprised but not shocked, given my friendship with the four ladies at the end of town. It was also easier for him to accept with the happy outcome."

"Robert is adamant about confidentiality. He'd likely hate that I told even you."

"I will outline the idea for David without names, to see what he thinks."

"Wait." Beth's mind was two steps ahead. What if she could convince Robert to go to Peterborough—with her? "Mayhap it would be best to speak in person, as I don't know what questions Robert will have. Could you word the note to introduce that idea as well, please?"

"Certainly. He met both of you at the wedding breakfast, and I know he'd be happy to speak with anyone interested in his profession."

Her new scheme distracted her as the women snacked and caught up. A trip would be perfect. 'Twas out of the public eye of the Ton. They could discuss designs and have daytime as well as nights together, like they had in Bath. Assuming he'd agree to the catalogue—and why wouldn't he—they could determine the number of pieces to include and positions for each sketch. Should it be comprehensive or a sample?

As she replayed the night before in her thoughts, Beth frowned.

Why hadn't Robert reacted to her catalogue idea more enthusiastically? She could not fathom what his concerns might be. Mayhap he thought she was interfering or was too proud to accept help.

Mayhap you're just convenient for testing his products and using for sex. After all, that has been every other man's view.

Beth's good mood, her default to start each day, deflated. While she was secure in her networking skills and eschewed the Ton's strictures, her confidence in herself as a long-term partner to anyone was fragile. Should she even ask to accompany him to Peterborough?

You *often choose sexual partners for convenience or physical attraction. Why is he not allowed?*

She gritted her teeth. Her conscience sounded a lot like Althea. Despite that, 'twas a good question. He gave her the best orgasms of her life. She had an outlet for her creativity and possibly her people-matching skills. And he found her beautiful.

She could not bear it if that was smoke and mirrors to pacify her into remaining in his bed longer. While she found she reveled in giving up control in the bedroom,

she refused to do that with her heart.
  What if 'tis too late?

Chapter Fourteen

The next evening, Robert did not go to his club. *Clubs. As the little minx knew.*

He'd spent the entire day contemplating the risks and rewards of expanding his business with a catalogue and the additional trade-offs of doing so with Beth as a model. She'd be outraged if he used her idea without her modeling.

He worried about her coming to his house alone. Her dress may have been innocuous, but there were still dangers to an unaccompanied woman, especially at night. Mayhap even more for someone who appeared to be working class. To his chagrin, he feared someone seeing and recognizing her almost as much as her safety. She had a network beyond the Ton, and the servants gossiped like Society matrons. However, he doubted he could prevent her, and 'twas more her risk of being seen, especially if she had a key to the back door. Besides, did he really want her to stop?

He kept running into the same concern about her visits and the business venture. *She is too high profile for my comfort.*

But he'd argued with himself throughout the day again, a habit becoming more frequent the longer he knew Beth. *If her face is not included and my name is not on the catalogue, 'tis an excellent idea.*

It was silly to risk exposure for more sales; he didn't

need the money. His pride in his work argued with the logic against the risk. He also dithered over the question that bothered him the most. If her repeated visits were focused on the novelty of his wares, was he willing to risk ending her visits by declining her help?

He liked Beth. Indeed, he kept finding more aspects to admire about her. In turn, she'd said she liked his strength and form, and he believed her. But just as he objected to her inattention to Ton gossip, would she not lose patience with his desire to avoid it? Someone with her energy and network deserved someone able to move in the same circles and support her, just as she had supported his work. He was not that person.

Despite the threat of exposure, he was willing to risk being hurt. If he could keep their relationship to the dark hours of the night, he could enjoy it until her interest waned.

With that in mind, he foraged through his office to produce a spare key and requested a cold supper to be served in his workroom. He picked at it, keeping some aside to have food on hand for her visit. The same servant who answered her knock the night before was asked to direct her upstairs.

Unable to focus on the intricacies of cutting and stitching such an unforgiving material, he paced until days or hours or minutes later, he heard a tap on the sitting room door.

Beth entered, shedding the same servant's cloak she'd worn the previous night.

Robert stepped in front of her, reaching for her hand. But instead of bowing over it, he tugged her closer and leaned in to kiss her cheek.

"Oh! I am happy to see you as well, Robert." She

beamed.

I love making her smile.

He led her to a seat near the fire and offered her a plate to fill from the supper tray. "Port? Or I had them bring sherry up, although I confess my valet thought I was mad when I asked him for it."

A laugh burst out of her, her bosom jiggling. "Sherry would be lovely, thank you."

Robert dragged his eyes away from her neckline to pour them each a drink then sat across from her. He reached for a pile of rough sketches to hand her.

"Robert, I have a lead on a new blacksmith." Her words stopped him as his hand met the sketches, and he left them in place. "Well, rather 'tis a lead on finding a blacksmith, but still."

"Really? How?"

"I am actually surprised you didn't think of it. I learned yesterday that Penelope's stepfather, David Hunter, hired an apprentice, and I asked her to provide an entrée with him."

"What?" he near-yelled, standing. This was one of his fears, that she did not respect his privacy.

"Stay calm. I would never give your name out without your permission." Beth gestured toward his chair, and he lowered himself, still frowning. "But think, Robert. If we go to him, we are two days from London. He knows how Penelope and Michael met, so his discretion is proven. And he's hired an apprentice, so he can speak to how he found him." She cocked her head.

Dammit. *She has a point. 'Twould be like Bath, almost a holiday with no disapproving Ton to worry about.*

She kept inching him toward the edge of discomfort

and just beyond. He knew she'd continue to prod at him the more he acceded to her requests. Despite that certainty, he was unable to decline the opportunity for more private time with her away from the Ton.

"I assume your presence is required?" he asked, cocking his head.

"Yes, to facilitate the interview. You liked my help in Bath."

He smiled. Her voice was pleading, almost as much as when he held back her ecstasy.

"Right, then. I can be ready to leave tomorrow, if that suits you?"

Her eyes widened in surprise then narrowed, leaving no doubt she was formulating a negotiation. "Your word as a gentleman?"

He nodded.

"I am afraid I can only join you on one condition." She folded her arms under her prodigious chest, drawing his attention to it as he was sure she intended.

"Let's hear it, then."

"I must see you naked before the end of the trip. Now is acceptable, too."

Ugh. After a barmaid in his university days had complained about him crushing her with his weight, no one had seen him naked in close to a decade. He reviewed his choices. He wanted that time together, away from prying eyes. She'd said she found what she'd seen attractive. He was also less nervous about the prospect of stripping for her than he'd expected to be. He trusted her, at least in private. Gathering his courage, he nodded.

"Really?" Beth bounced on the chair cushion in glee, and he licked his lips as her breasts jiggled.

"On the trip." Courage was fine, but it did not preclude procrastination.

"Thank you, Robert! Thank you so much! I can be ready at whatever time you want." She noticed where his gaze had focused and ran her finger around the plain gown's neckline before leaning forward to place a cushion on the floor near his feet. "May I express my gratitude in another way, sir?"

His burning gaze lifted to hers, and he sat forward, unbuttoning his trousers. "Why, yes, my little housemaid, you may."

****

In the carriage the next day, Robert extracted the pile of sketches from the small travel bag he'd placed by his feet.

"Might you have thoughts on these?" He handed them to Beth, hoping that any tremble in his hand was attributed to the bouncing ride rather than nerves. Eager to know her opinion, he also wished to impress her with his creativity when he'd never cared what his friends thought of his work. "Those aren't good enough for a catalogue yet, but I hoped you could offer suggestions for improvement."

Her eyes widened, and she glanced at the stack before focusing on him again. "Does that mean…" She jounced on the seat.

The distraction allayed his nerves.

"Yes, 'tis an excellent idea, and you have my gratitude." Her expression told him he'd made the right choice. "I should very much like your help in finding a discreet sketch artist we can trust, and we shall have to decide how to bind them into a catalogue."

"And I may model?" She tilted her head.

"I hope you will. You have the perfect figure for it, and I trust you." And he did, he realized. That was part of why he'd allowed himself to care for her.

Beth squeaked and hopped in place on her seat again, drawing Robert's eyes to the bounciest part of her. "Oh Robert, you shan't be sorry. I am so excited. I shall work on sourcing an artist as soon as we return." She turned to the drawings. "For now, will you show me these and share your thoughts about them?"

He laid them out, pointing out features and answering questions. Her enthusiasm was contagious, and he pictured men in Sarah's drawing room, flipping pages and discussing pieces while they waited for their requested hostess to arrive.

Sitting back, he watched Beth. She was in her element, her mind racing. He imagined doing this in a year, two years, mayhap in five years after the children were abed. Shaking his head, he snuffed that thought.

Women have made it clear you're not marriage material. At least wait until she's seen all of you. And be sure you're willing to have a public relationship.

By the time they arrived at the first night's inn, she'd demanded a pencil nub and a scrap of paper to make notes.

They paid for the room under the married name of Thorpe as Penelope had suggested—she and Michael had borrowed that name from her housekeeper and husband when they'd traveled to Peterborough the prior year.

After requesting a cold supper in their room, they retired straight away. Beth showed him her notes. She had drawn a line bisecting the length of the paper. On one side, she referenced positions to prioritize for each item. On the other, she recorded new metal pieces he would need, he supposed for her ongoing search for a blacksmith.

Smart and beautiful. No wonder I lo-care for her. He swallowed the other thought, the dangerous one. He'd ride this horse until it dropped. Hmm, speaking of riding… He took the papers from her hands and tugged her to her feet. "Enough designing for now. I'll show you more configurations for sketches of the existing sets."

Beth licked her lips.

"You'll need to be naked, however," he said, grinning.

"As will you in the next few days, Mr. Orford." But she acquiesced and unlaced her dress.

He'd brought the cuffs they'd used their second night in Bath and a few times since. The trip was a perfect opportunity to test how easy they were to use when traveling, no matter what furniture was available.

When she was naked, he produced the cuffs set. "Let's try the low table here, shall we?" He gestured to the table where their supper tray still sat. Stepping around her, he moved the dishes to a side table, then knelt and thread the long straps beneath the table, end to end.

"Face down or face up?" she asked, her eyes bright.

Damnation, she was magnificent. He'd already planned a "private in public" play for the next day's ride. Mayhap he could even face the bullies if he got to keep her.

****

The second day of travel was shorter.

Beth sat swaying in the carriage across from Robert, watching him from the corner of her eye. She wanted to bounce on her seat for the whole ride, she was so happy. Not only had he agreed to the catalogue, he'd asked for her input in designs.

After an hour, her excitement waned, and she was bored. Yesterday's ride had flown by looking at designs. If only she enjoyed needlepoint or could read in moving vehicles without feeling nauseous. Shifting again, she drew Robert's attention.

"Is something the matter, Peaches?"

"Will you tell me more about your childhood, Robert? You know I struggle to sit still."

"Hmm. I can do better. I shall give you a real contest to remain still. If you master it, you shall get a lovely reward in Peterborough. If you keep fidgeting, you shall earn a punishment." His eyes glinted and his tone was bedroom-commanding.

Beth's body awakened, warmth spurting in her belly with interest at what he had planned. Her mind, however, remained wary. "What is the game?"

He shook his head.

"Could you give me a hint of the reward at least? Please?"

"No hints."

"Could we not simply converse?"

"'Tis too early to beg." He laughed.

The dratted man was not giving her many options other than acceptance.

"Well?" He folded his arms across his chest. He always knew when she struggled to acquiesce to his demands.

"Right, then. I accept your challenge." She lifted her chin in defiance.

His grin was evil as he dropped his arms to gesture.

"Feet on my seat, one outside each of my knees."

The pose was vulgar, but no one had ever accused her of being overly ladylike. Besides, no one could see them. That was the whole point of this trip.

She bent her knees and set her feet on the edge of his carriage bench, splaying herself open. Her breath caught. In the tight confines of the carriage, every part of her was accessible to him. How did Robert imagine these stances? His creativity shone through his work, but she had yet to unpeel the layers of his mind to understand what drove him and how his ideas developed. Knowing that would not prepare her for these titillating games, but it would allow her to find the best fit possible in a smith.

Her thoughts scattered when he smoothed his hands up her legs, taking her dress and petticoats along. He flipped the front of her skirts back toward her waist, so it fell away from her raised knees to puddle on the seat around her, baring her lower half.

She glanced at the open curtains on the window.

He arched a brow at her. "Anyone could ride by. I seem to recall you're not averse to an audience."

A shiver ran through her. In a dimly lit stable or a room at night was one thing, but this was the bright light of day. Still, the risk, however minimal, excited her further.

Nothing held her still except self-discipline. She would be the first to admit that particular trait was not one of her strengths. The dilemma kept her on the razor's edge of torture and rapture.

His hands skirted up her arms, around her neck to brush her nape, then down to cup her breasts.

She shuffled her hands where they braced her from sliding forward on the seat by her sides.

"I haven't even begun the contest," Robert said. "Be still, so I may enjoy this delicious view."

He must have seen her arms move, as her wrists and hands were hidden under her tossed-up skirts. Grateful for his reassurance that he liked what he saw, she sighed and tried to relax and await what he had in store for her.

For long minutes, he repeated the path of his hands—up her legs, sometimes inside, sometimes outside, then skipping to her arms before he got to the good parts. Up to her shoulders, then cupping her breasts through her dress.

I can sit still forever for his petting.

As though he had heard her thoughts, he changed course, rubbing a few strokes back and forth along the crease where her thighs met her belly. Then he withdrew one hand and dug into the traveling bag on the floor by his feet. A small handkerchief-wrapped ball was in his hand when it emerged. He opened it to unveil a small vial with a viscous light-yellow liquid.

"What's that?"

"'Tis an oil Michael gave me."

"What for?"

"It is infused with ginger. He was inspired by Penelope's love of that spice." He smirked. "Michael uses it for punishments."

"What? How?"

"I shall show you."

"But-but I wasn't aware I had earned a punishment."

"No, I hope it won't be a punishment. 'Tis more that I thought you'd appreciate the challenge. Remember, the goal is to sit still to gain a reward in—" He checked outside. "—less than an hour."

"That seems doable." But her tone was dubious as

she stared at the vial. *'Tis oil. How hard can this be? Will it make me slip on the seat or something?* She also wasn't entirely sure that she wouldn't fall out of position if someone did ride by.

Robert rotated the vial then uncapped it. The stopper was coated in the oil.

Beth sniffed and the delicious sweet-spicy scent of ginger filled her nose.

He held the open vial between his knees and placed the fingers of his free hand on the swollen folds between her legs.

She caught her breath, hopeful for more stroking.

The vial stopper spread oil over her protruding nub.

'Twas the first he'd touched it that day, and the contrast of the hard glass stopper and the smooth oil sliding against her made her want to arch into it. No, winning this game meant sitting still.

He slid the cap just inside her hungry lips and swirled it, as though he was coating the entrance to her channel.

Her nails dug into her palms on the carriage seat as she restrained herself from following his movements with her hips. She watched him carefully, hopefully.

He wiped the stopper, returned it to the container, and tilted it to coat the end again. Removing the plug, he reached toward her.

Where was he putting it now?

His free hand tugged her hips forward on the seat so she slouched, her knees higher on either side of him now.

Whoa. The stopper touched her bottom hole. He'd never touched her there before.

He's not actually touching me there now. Gah, semantics—something is!

As he dipped it inside her and swirled, she tried to process how it felt. It did not hurt. It felt strange but not unpleasant. Tingly, mayhap.

Oh no. 'Twas not his movements that felt tingly.

Her eyes widened as he wiped the plug and closed the vial, re-wrapping it and placing it back in his bag.

He chuckled at her expression, watching her intently.

'Twas the oil. No wonder Michael used it as punishment. Her whole front and back were on fire. She needed to move, to wipe it off, or swirl her bottom against the seat to soothe the burn, or something.

Can't move. Mustn't move. Her hands clenched. This was the challenge.

You can't say you're bored now. She rolled her eyes at her inner voice.

"Robert, oh you dratted man." She couldn't believe she called him that out loud. "Please, make it stop."

"It doesn't hurt, does it?" He frowned, even managing to sound concerned, although she doubted he had any compunction about his actions. "I used an inordinately small amount."

"Small! It burns!"

"Take a breath, Peaches. Does it hurt? Or is it simply uncomfortable?"

"I don't care," she wailed, but she was very careful not to fidget. She would win this contest of wills, even if he had tricks of torture. Instead, she bared her teeth.

"Ah, sweeting." He stroked up her legs again. "You're doing very well. Your reward will be grand, I promise you."

"Please, help. Distract me?"

"Shh. I am. Focus on my hands." They resumed

tracing her limbs.

The soothing motion was countered by the strange pulsing heat from the oil inside both her holes and on her little nub. The discomfort edged toward desire. She wanted nothing more than his finger on that hard protrusion, circling in the oil to soothe her, distract her, take her over. 'Twas good he did not attempt to entertain her with words, as she could not have focused to save her life.

Never, in all her vast and varied experiences, could she have imagined such a sensation. 'Twas pleasure and misery combined, and her inner muscles spasmed, begging for him to insert a finger, tongue, or cock. Anything. As her muscles twitched and the burn flared again, she had the sudden wish that her reward was drenching his cock in the oil and seeing how he liked it. Although then she would not want him inside her.

Robert focused on her breasts, massaging them, tweaking her nipples through her dress. "How does this feel?"

"I am struggling to focus on the pleasure given the burn." Mayhap an exaggeration, but she wanted to encourage his nicer play.

"Ah, but I know you enjoy an element of slight pain to heighten the pleasure. Like this." He tweaked her nipples hard.

"Hmph." She started to arch into him but caught herself.

"Good girl." He soothed her with words and with gentle fingers.

"Is the burn stimulating? Does it make you want more? Does it arouse you?"

"Is this research?" she asked, panting. She also was

loath to admit she might want more, might enjoy riding that edge.

He blushed. "Well, I procured it to experiment with you, but as we have some time left in our ride, I thought I'd ask. I have not yet seen how it affects leather, though. If it works well enough for short periods without damaging the fabric, I see possibilities."

She rolled her eyes.

"Now, Peaches," he admonished.

"You said no movements, not eye gestures." She pouted.

He leaned in and gently bit her jutting lower lip. "You're beautiful even when you are disgruntled."

She melted, despite the ongoing burn in her bottom hole making her want to squirm.

Her front passage, though, knew what it wanted. Soothing fingers or lips would go a long way to easing her ache.

If only she could believe there was a chance of that happening before they arrived in Peterborough.

Chapter Fifteen

Robert had tested the oil on his lips and had felt a light sting. He was relatively sure Beth would enjoy the experience, even if not at first, and he was quite certain she'd tell him if it was not pleasurable.

As she had not, he'd gotten to stroke her limbs and breasts for a half hour, his cock thickening in his pants. Then, when he could see the start of the city sprawl, houses and small shops emerging along the road, he switched to giving her the strokes he knew she'd craved for the past half hour. Spreading the oil around her swollen *kleitoris*, he kept his motions slow enough to excite but not tip her over into orgasm.

Her nipples beaded against her dress. She panted quick breaths that told him how close she was, at which point he'd slow or stop, or insert his finger into her dripping channel ever so slowly.

Swirling his finger inside her seemed to reignite the oil; her muscles clenched and she bit her lip as her breath caught.

He was almost as on edge as she was and tried not to think about what he would do with her as soon as they gained their room. As they ventured closer to the city center, he dipped lower and swirled his finger in her back hole.

She gasped again, and she jerked once, but otherwise remained still. As he had not forbidden talking, he waited for her to protest. When she did not, his curiosity was piqued. He wondered if she'd ever been penetrated there. His cock jerked in his trousers as he envisioned oiling himself, spreading the seam of her gorgeous arse, and easing past that tight ring of muscle. He would not restrain her, at least the first time. His cock throbbed again, and he pressed it with the heel of his free hand.

The leather harness with a cock-shaped attachment that a male couple requested might be useful as training for her in a smaller size. The couple had said they wanted it for use under clothes as titillation and foreplay, and he'd since sold several others. Tilting his head, he considered adding a second phallus to it for Peaches.

He thrust his finger in and out twice more. Her eyes shuttered, and she moaned, her muscles clenching around him.

He smiled in anticipation both at her reaction and his thoughts and withdrew, cleaning his finger on his handkerchief before touching her ankles. "We are entering Peterborough, Peaches. You prevailed. Well done."

She grinned back as she straightened, then winced as the remnants of the oil made themselves known with every change in position.

"You'll get your reward in our room," he added before she could ask.

"Soon?" she begged.

He nodded as he handed her down in front of the inn and laughed under his breath as she gasped with each step.

Once in their room, he twirled her to face away and started undoing her gown. "I fancy a taste of ginger."

"Oh!" She hastened to help him and was quickly naked.

"On the bed. Lie still." He knew the effects of the ginger were waning, and her body was likely flushing it out of her. Nonetheless, he wiped her front and back with a damp cloth he warmed by the fire, and then settled on his knees at the end of the bed.

Tugging her closer to have her legs hang off by his shoulders, he set out to soothe the burn. By the time he rose, unbuttoned his trousers, and sheathed himself to plunge into her, he was relatively sure she'd forgotten the sting of the ginger.

They rested, drifting side by side, for a quarter hour before he rose and tugged her to stand.

"Ugh, where are we off to now?"

"I thought we'd walk part of the main road to see the town Penelope's talked about so much and then have supper. An early night will make us fresh for tomorrow to talk to Hunter."

At supper, he was distracted, jittery with nerves. Beth may have thought their afternoon interlude was her reward, but he needed to make good on his promise. Her reward was to see and touch him to her heart's content after the meal.

Is it better or worse that 'twill be in a city far from home and she cannot leave if she is disappointed?

He reminded himself for the thousandth time that she admired his form. If their relationship was to continue, he had to trust her. Certainly, he trusted her with all aspects of his business. This was the next step.

By the time they arrived back to their room, he was silent, his jaw muscles aching from clenching his teeth. He wanted nothing so much as a large glass—no, a bottle—of whisky.

"Robert? Are you feeling all right?" Beth's concern melted over him.

"Quite all right, thank you. Shall I call for sherry?" And whisky.

"No, thank you. Strange, isn't it, how we can be this tired from sitting in a carriage most of the day?"

"Well, I'd venture to say that particular carriage ride might have been more taxing than average, Peaches." He managed a weak grin.

"It was worth it. My reward was magnificent, thank you."

It was now or never. "That was not your reward."

"Oh?" She perked up. "What is it, then?"

He swept his hand along himself.

She cocked her head in question.

Ugh, I'm still clothed, no wonder she did not understand. He removed his jacket.

She watched.

He removed his shoes and waistcoat.

Her eyebrows rose.

He undid his cravat and tossed it aside. Hands back at his collar, he scanned the room for candles to snuff.

But Beth had caught on. She settled on the bed. "A show." A clap of her hands. "All candles shall stay lit, thank you."

He sighed in defeat and undid his shirt. As he was tugging it off, the fabric muffled his words. "Not just a show."

He made short order of the rest of his clothes and strode to the bed. He'd thought standing in front of her would be fraught with tension and wanted to lie down, but hovering by the bed while she perused him, he realized her proximity gave her the opportunity to see more flaws. His hands fluttered. How embarrassing, on top of everything else.

Gathering his courage, he lay next to her. "'Tis an interactive reward," he grumbled, closing his eyes in fear of what he might find in her expression.

"Oh, Robert!" Her voice was breathy.

With fear?

"Thank you. Thank you, thank you, thank you." She peppered kisses over his face.

Well, that was both gratifying and disappointing. He realized he'd been looking forward to her lips on his skin. He wanted his own reward for doing this.

Happy kisses of gratitude were nothing to sneeze at, however. He dared a peek.

Beth was grinning from ear to ear, running her gaze over the length of him.

His cock stirred, preening.

Her hand hovered over him, then came to rest lightly on his furred chest.

"You are magnificent." She gave him the words he needed. "All these muscles from wrestling leather tools. These broad shoulders ready to hold me up or pin me down. This extra masculinity—" she rubbed chest hairs between her finger and thumb.

"You're laying it on a bit thick." His face heated.

"Hush. I told you when we first met that I preferred to form my own opinion. And I find you magnificent. Now, let's see if you are as delicious everywhere as your cock is."

Yes, please.

Nerves forgotten, he relaxed and lay still as she stripped and then straddled him. He focused on her gorgeous breasts so he needn't look at her expression if it turned to distaste.

She ran her hands over every limb, humming under her breath. Her breasts dangled over him as she leaned to stroke each shoulder and he reached a hand toward them.

Slapping it down, she wagged a finger at him. "My turn."

He smirked at her, promising payback later for that slap.

"I want to sink my teeth into these muscles." She squeezed his biceps, then prodded at the slabs of muscle on his chest.

His waist did not narrow as the fops' did, and he tensed as she smoothed her fingers downward.

She petted the trail of hair from the cluster across his sternum to his groin. "I adore your breadth and strength. The dandies always leave me cold. You are hard but not rigid. Unyielding yet tensile. Firm to my softness. I always feel safe from the evils of our world with you."

Robert whooshed a breath out, her words the reassurance her fingers could not fully provide.

Those fingers stole lower, taking his cock in a firm grip. Her tone mischievous, she added, "Mmm. The same could be said for this part of you."

He jerked in her grip, his hands reaching for her again.

She shifted back, however, hovering over his legs on her knees. Kneading his thigh muscles, she watched her fingers constrict and release, muttering, "We really must try a wall one of these days."

Grinning, he released the last of his fears and contracted his stomach muscles to sit up, drawing her attention.

"Nooo," she whined. "I need more time with all this deliciousness. I haven't tasted any of it yet."

"I have just the place you can start. But after. Right now, I need you. All this teasing and touching is torture, I don't know how you bear it."

She mock gasped at his audacity, and he laughed as he tugged her hips toward his. Holding her still with one hand, he skimmed protection on, then released her as she rose to impale herself on him.

Giving himself over to the ride, he had one last thought.

She might just be my soulmate.

****

They walked from the inn to David Hunter's forge north up Broadway. Beth pointed out Penelope's favorite pub and a bakery that once sold her experimental pastries.

Hunter's apprentice worked in a covered area open to customers in the front. Robert stiffened as Beth perused the young man. He was closer to Beth's age than Robert was and had far less bulk. Instead, his lean muscles were visible where his shirt clung to him as he swung his hammer. His taut buttocks flexed when he leaned over to check something on the piece he held in his tongs. How could Beth find that attractive and then want him?

She turned to him. "Not bad, eh? One day he'll grow as strong as you," she said with a fond smile, squeezing his bicep.

Oh. Robert could not find words. He blinked, gratitude and affection burning at the back of his eyes. All he could manage was to reach up to cover her hand with his and return her squeeze.

"Can I help ye?" The young man had turned. A shock of dark hair hung in his eyes, and he flipped it back with a forearm.

"Hullo. We hoped to speak with David Hunter, please." Beth stepped forward.

As usual, the man's gaze dropped to her breasts for a second before flicking to Robert's frown, then back to her face. Robert worried he might not have teeth left if their relationship lasted a year, as he'd grind them to dust at those looks.

"'E's in the back." The man nodded at a door in the rear wall. "Ye can go on in."

They picked their way around the forge area and knocked on the back door. Laughter behind them made them turn.

"Yer from London by the looks of ye. We're a wee bit more casual here. Go on in." He shooed at them.

Robert opened the door, calling, "Hunter? Robert Orford and Miss Beth Jenkins to see you."

David came forward. "Beth! I received Penelope's letter only yesterday. I am so happy to see you again." He kissed her on both cheeks. "And Mr. Orford, I remember you as well."

"Thank you. 'Tis Robert, please. I confess I only have a vague recollection of you, sir." He gave a shallow bow. "I was very focused on Michael's happiness that day—and Penelope's, of course. She was so excited you could make the journey."

"Ha. Michael would not take no for an answer, even if I had considered declining. Please, call me David. Penelope's note said you're looking for a smith?"

"Yes. More, I need this conversation to remain confidential, and any smith I work with must be circumspect about the goods and the relationship."

"Hmm, so she said in her note. I am intrigued. May I offer you tea in my small home?" At their acceptance, David led them out the back door and a few steps away to a separate small hut. Two rooms, it had a bedroom in the rear and an alcove with a smaller bed in it that Robert assumed was for Penelope's half-brother Matthew, and a kitchen and living area on either side of the fireplace.

Gesturing to the kitchen table, David put the kettle on and set up the teapot, placing sugar and milk on the table.

Robert began as David moved around. "Before I start, Michael knows what I do, but I'm not sure if Penelope is aware." He shot a look at Beth, but she shrugged.

"Right, then. Let's have it. You can talk as I get the tea. We're an informal lot here."

Robert and Beth shared a smile at David's repetition of the apprentice's sentiment.

"I make leather goods." Robert said, and David's head nodded in acknowledgement as he poured the boiling water over the tea leaves in the waiting pot. "Leather apparel."

"Oh." The kettle set down with a clank. Apparently, David knew enough of Evan's reputation to guess what type of apparel Robert meant.

"Yes. And other leather pieces to be used with or in lieu of the leather apparel."

"'Tis always the quiet ones that are the most dangerous. Evan made sense, but I did not see this coming," David said with a chuckle as he poured tea into three mugs and pushed one toward each of them.

Beth grinned. "Right?"

"I can buy in batches, as I can keep inventory in my workspace. The trick is finding someone with the skills for the finer work who does not already have a full client list."

David was nodding with a pensive frown as he listened to Robert's concerns.

"Robert, would you show David a few items that you use regularly, please?" Beth asked. As he bent to extract them from the satchel he'd carried, she turned to David. "Robert typically works in London or at Evan's home in Cheltenham. So I was thinking someone in that corridor would be ideal. But location is less important than skill and discretion. Penelope told me you brought an apprentice on recently."

"Yes. Adam has been a godsend. I am planning to spend Christmas at Mansfield House now."

"How did you find him?"

"I visited a few forges last time I was in London visiting Penelope and Michael. I can give you their direction if you'd like, although"—he smiled at Robert—"I suspect you have your own network there. The smiths I met knew who in Town had someone training, and I visited those shops. I watched the boys work, and then made an offer if I felt the quality warranted it."

"And Adam accepted?" Beth asked.

"Well, the first few offers were rejected. Many did not wish to come this far north when their whole family is in London. It took me three tries to learn that lesson." David chuckled.

"Michael was kind enough to loan me a carriage. I took the long way home, stopping in Luton and Cambridge once I had fine-tuned my research process.

Adam was in Cambridge."

"I bet Edward likes that part," Beth said, grinning, referring to Sophia's husband, the Earl of Peterborough.

"Ah, those boys and their school rivalry. Yes, his lordship took a strange pride in the fact that Michael's father-in-law is sourcing his employees from Cambridge rather than Oxford." He rolled his eyes. "'Twas the city, not the university. Sheesh."

"Well, I shan't hold it against him, if he can help me find my apprentice," Robert commented with a straight face, before they all broke out into laughter.

David picked up the corset hooks and one of the more intricate cuff connectors. "Frankly, I don't know if Adam has this skill or not, but we can ask him if he knows someone who does."

"Mayhap without showing him the leather pieces they're for?" Beth suggested.

"Ah yes, secrecy."

Robert breathed a sigh of relief. He'd have spoken up if she hadn't, but he was reassured that she respected his need for privacy and ensured it was top of mind for people they interviewed.

David put his hands flat on the table to push up to standing, but then dropped his shoulders and leaned back in his chair.

"Wait. One smith I spoke to in London said something that might help about an associate's apprentice. I'm trying to remember what it was." He frowned, staring at his empty teacup.

"'Twasn't that the young man's work was poor?" Beth seemed to be trying to prompt David's memories and Robert sat back to watch her skills.

"No. I don't want to misstate it, but I think he

recommended avoiding the lad, as he was making strange items in his spare time."

"With metal taken from the shop?" Beth sounded outraged, making Robert smile.

"Oh no, that is how the smith knew about it. The boy bought the metal fair and square, then made his goods and…there was something about testing…" David shook his head again.

He looked up at Beth and his face flushed, then he turned to Robert. "I think the items were for sexual play." He glanced back at Beth. "Sorry, dear. It seems like it might be an excellent fit for your friend here, or I'd never have said that."

She patted his hand. "David, love. You do remember I attended—" She slid a glance at Robert that he couldn't interpret. "—school with Penelope, don't you? 'Tis quite all right."

"Yes, well. Be that as it may, 'tis not something I'd normally say in the company of a good girl such as yourself."

"Aw." She wove around the table to hug their host as they all stood.

"David, you are right. That sounds like an excellent starting place. Even if that apprentice does not work, London is the right spot to begin. All things strange seem to herald from there, including me." Robert smiled and held his hand out.

David shook it, then grabbed a piece of paper to mark the address and the name of the smith who had referred him elsewhere. "Keep me informed of how you do? I should like to come down and meet whoever you find."

"I will, thank you." Robert swore he was floating a

foot off the ground as they exited the house and skirted the forge.

Beth was bouncing as well. "We did it. This is an excellent lead. I can hardly wait to return to London."

"You did it. I'd never have thought to ask David. And who would have believed that Peterborough, two days' ride from London, would lead us to pinpoint an excellent candidate back in London. Only you." He stopped in the middle of the road and turned to her. "You are magnificent. Beautiful, creative, smart, and"—he gestured back toward the forge—"well connected."

And mine, he wanted to shout. He faced the truth. He was in love with Peaches, and he was going to get hurt.

Chapter Sixteen

A few days later, Beth lounged on Robert's bed in his London home. They were back to late night forays while he finished the last of the orders from Evan's party.

Lying on her stomach, head propped on elbows and knees bent with feet swaying above her, she had thrown the sketches she was reviewing aside to watch him. She loved to watch him work, muscles bulging in his shirt sleeves, shoulders straining. She understood his obsession with her breasts, as she had one with his arms and shoulders.

Hating that the objects of her lust were far less visible than his, she pouted. More than that, though, his creativity, his thoughtful approach to keeping intimacy interesting for couples, his mastery of her body, and his care for her person were captivating. She was more sure every day that her fixation had edged into an emotion that would hurt when he ended their relationship.

And he would. She needed to be honest about her past. Cheltie might have shared some of it with Robert, but she needed to see his face when she shared her escapades. She was the girl men enjoyed sexual experimentation with before they settled down, married, and sired children.

Her lips twisted.

Robert looked up and tilted his head in question.

"Have you spoken to Cheltie today?" she asked.

"Yes." He arched a brow.

"So you know he escorted Althea to a soirée with investors for her to meet, then was mean to her. They aren't speaking. Or sexing."

"That does not sound like Bags." He straightened from his hunch over the work in his lap, and lowered his brows. "Even when he dismisses them or declines the many invitations he receives, he is always kind to women."

Beth rolled and sat up, swinging her legs to hang off the side of the high bed. "Ah, but he never cared for any of them."

He narrowed his eyes in thought, then nodded once.

"But then we met with the Dowager Countess of Peterborough, and she was lovely. She is going to fund our—Althea's—venture in Bath." She bounced once on the bed to punctuate her news.

Robert grinned. "And how is the lovely Charlotte?"

Beth stared at him without blinking.

How does he know Charlotte by her first name? Of course, he'd have met her through Cheltie's friendship with her. But to call her by her given name? There must be more to that story.

She peered around the room at the leather pieces in process and wondered again where he kept his records of sales. She'd love to see who bought what, but she knew better than to ask. Robert was as careful of his network as she was of hers.

"She is well, thank you. If I had known you were acquainted, I could have passed along your regards," she said with a wink. She'd heard whispers of the countess's relationship with her husband—very quiet, unsubstantiated rumors, but talk nonetheless. She decided to test those, as well as her theory of how he knew Lady Peterborough.

Trailing a hand along the bedcovers as she stood, Beth wandered past him, skimming his shoulders with her fingers before she swooped to pick up the X-shaped restraints. "Do you ever allow someone else to try these on you?"

"No," he responded with a shudder, his voice sharp.

Hmm. That response was disproportionate to the lightness of her question. The Dowager Countess of Peterborough was forgotten as Beth pursued the oddity. "Not even testing size and length and strength for male clients?"

"No."

"Mayhap I could—" She made as though to cinch a cuff around his wrist.

He snapped to standing. "I said no."

"Right, then. I understand. Why are you so adamant, though? You've never been critical of men who choose to be restrained."

"I do not critique men's or women's choices, no matter what they are. In turn, I should be allowed to make my own choices without censure."

"I did not mean disapproval, Robert." Still surprised at his reaction, his leap to assuming her comment was disparaging made her lower lip quiver.

"I am sorry, Peaches." His shoulders dropped. "At some point, I will share more of my past with you. However, it might ruin the mood so I'd prefer to do that another night if 'tis all right with you?" He stepped in to hug her. "Suffice it to say, I might have a teeny tiny issue giving up control."

"Fair enough." She nodded and let the subject and

the cuffs drop to return his hug. "Happily, I do not have that concern. Feel free to take control."

****

As usual, Beth leaped out of bed the next morning. As she helped Althea tally what samples she wanted to send to Bath with the note that confirmed the funding of the expansion, her mind drifted to Robert's comment about his past.

His unique designs had centered many of their conversations on his work. He'd also made it clear privacy was important to him. But why? And what of his family? His vague reference to his history had sparked her interest. She knew from her sources that he was the second son of an earl. If his trade was his sole source of income, her help might be more important than she'd realized. The idea of the catalogue improving his day-to-day comfort delighted her.

She lost count of the scented soaps she was gathering. Swearing under her breath, she started over.

Her lack of knowledge about his youth was one thing. His ignorance of hers was quite another. She'd mentioned her reputation in passing but had not explained the reasons for it further. As much as she wished to continue seeing him, even if only in the dark of night, he deserved to know more about her.

Her childhood had been so outside the norm and colored her view of the world, it affected others in her life, as Althea had learned. So she preferred to be fair to someone she cared for. She also would rather he left sooner if he was going to leave her for that reason before she fell any further in love with him.

She gasped, clutching a random bar of prettily wrapped soap so hard she smelled lavender.

I am in love with him. Drat.

For a time, she'd been able to pretend it was simple lust, respect for the unparalleled ecstasy he provided. But his work ethic, his artistry, and his unique admiration of her had forced her to admit her feelings were stronger.

When she found herself picking at her supper, she decided enough was enough. The uncertainty was worse than knowing his reaction. And nothing and no one stood between her and her enjoyment of a meal, darn it.

As she changed into the plain dress, she played with different approaches. What would make her past more palatable? A wave of anger rolled over her. Why did it have to be smoothed over? Hadn't Cheltie been intimate with far more people than she had? And he remained Robert's closest friend.

Her fists clenched, and her heart panged at the thought of losing Robert as she walked the dark streets to his townhouse. She burst into his workshop, formerly known as a sitting room.

He looked up at the force of her entrance. "Hullo. Happy to see me, are you?"

She smiled, bending to kiss his cheek. "Yes. But more than that. I need to speak with you."

"And so you are." He smirked.

He has been spending too much time with Cheltie. She rolled her eyes. Gesturing to the piece he was working on in his lap, she said, "I should like your undivided attention for this, please."

His eyes widened, but he said nothing as he put the pile of partially cut leather aside, along with his shears.

Crossing one ankle over the other knee, he folded his hands, the epitome of patience.

Beth sat across from him and took a deep breath.

"I've told you a little about how I came to live with Althea. I—" Her throat closed with emotion, and she swallowed before trying again. "It is in both our best interests that I share a few more details."

He nodded. "Right, then. I am listening."

"My parents thought a lady should be able to do whatever a man could and raised me to believe that. Unfortunately, society does not hold the same view."

"Society be damned. I agree with your parents."

She gave him a steady stare. "I believe you think you do." When he frowned, she hastened to add, "Please, hear me out."

Show time. They could debate all sorts of freedoms that men had but women did not. However, the one at the core of society's issue with her was one particular freedom. It was also likely what would cause him to walk away. She sucked in another deep breath then sighed it out and gave in to the inevitable. "As you know, I enjoy physical intimacy. Sexual play can be fun and lighthearted, just as it can be passionate and intense. And-I've-done-it-all-many-times-with-many people."

He blinked, as if assimilating her words that had gusted out in one string. Finally, he nodded. "I had some understanding of that from you and Bags."

She gaped at him. That was the extent of his reaction? She tested it further. "I've been with men and women."

He chuckled. "Did you think I was untouched when you bullied your way into my room at Greenborough Park?"

"Hmm, no." She smiled and tilted her head. "My tawdry past does not offend you?" She ignored her mother's imagined appalled gasp at her choice of words.

She'd rather push the subject now and test his sensitivity to the idea.

He shrugged. "It pales in comparison with Bags. Wait, were you concerned about my reaction?"

She jumped up to go sit on his lap. "A little. You know there is a double standard, but I confess I had the same thought. Then again, Cheltie is in a class unto himself."

He wrapped one arm around her back, the other clutching her legs to pull her more fully onto his lap before sliding up to grip her hip.

She nestled her head on his shoulder.

"I realized today we don't know much about one another, and I was worried my upbringing would repulse you."

"Not at all. I do have one question, though. Do you prefer men or women?"

Beth laughed. "Remember when I told you I liked many shapes and sizes because much of my attraction to someone is based on their intelligence?" At his nod, she continued. "So no, no preference. For me, 'tis about the individual and how we fit together in outlook, humor, and of course physically."

"So you don't miss being with women?"

Why is he asking? Dare I hope… She squashed the thought. This was temporary; they all were.

"Robert. You know me. If I missed something, I'd be frank with you and act on it. I want to be here with you. Because I enjoy spending time with you, and I respect your intelligence, your creativity, and your physical appearance. Shall I demonstrate?" She arched a brow at him, hoping to change the subject.

"I am learning so much. As you said, we do not

know enough about one another, in part due to your kind offers. Why don't we talk tonight and skip the leatherwork?" He looked almost crestfallen as he said it.

She giggled and his eyes dropped to her bosom. When she glanced down, she realized how close it was to his mouth, and her eyes gleamed.

He poked her side, and she gusted out an exhale.

"None of that now. You shan't tempt me with your magnificent assets until we've talked more." Contrary to his words, his eyes strayed downward before flicking back to her face.

"Right, then." She started to slide off his lap.

"No. Stay here. Can you reach your sherry?"

"Yes, thank you."

"You've told me something of your childhood. I shall share a bit about mine. We can take turns." It was his turn to sigh.

****

"I am a second son," Robert started. "You likely know what that means. Less governance, less attention, less training forced on me at a young age for running an earldom. My father's focus was on my older brother, and my mother's was on grooming my sister to make a good marriage."

"Hmm. It sounds like less love," Beth muttered.

His eyes flashed to hers for a moment. How did she perceive that so quickly? It had taken him years to understand how his family life affected him.

He continued, "They sent me to boarding school, but without motivation, I confess I was not diligent in my lessons. Nor was I particularly athletic. My lack of grace and my build is why I prefer to remain clothed when permitted."

She smirked at his sardonic glance.

"With all that, and lacking a title or endless funds, I was—" He swallowed, glancing away before continuing. "—unpopular."

Beth nodded her understanding. He could only guess that her unusual childhood helped her relate to his ostracization, even without him sharing the extent of it.

"Then a tall gangly golden boy who walked and talked like he owned the world sat next to me in the dining hall and nattered at me for an hour. Suddenly, everyone wanted to be my friend." He sighed at the memory, as always torn between gratitude and affection for Evan and disgust at how shallow boys and even men could be. If the right person spoke highly of someone, they'd assume that person was worth befriending, rather than taking the time and effort to judge for themselves. It was how Evan's house parties remained so coveted, as unconventional as they were.

"Ah, Cheltie." Beth's voice brought him back to the room.

He nodded.

"You had a new set of friends, then?" she asked.

"Not really. I preferred to lurk in Evan's shadows. Given his outrageousness, 'twas best anyway, as he could charm his way out of trouble with the headmaster."

She laughed.

"I am sure you can understand that I also found the other boys' friendship lacking, as it was based on my friendship with Evan rather than on my own merit. 'Tis much of the reason I crave anonymity."

Beth sobered, reaching to squeeze his hand as she nodded.

"Then I found leather work whilst at Oxford, and

Evan took over managing my small quarterly allowance from my father, and the rest is history."

"When did you meet Michael?"

"Also Oxford. He was mayhap even more sheltered than I had been." He shook his head. "No, he simply had more expectations pressed upon him, given he was heir to a title."

"Ah, yes. The mantle of responsibility. Yet, you all still had more freedoms than any girls your age."

"I am sure we did, although I never gave it much thought."

Her lips twisted.

He took a deep breath. He had considered her suggestion of a catalogue ad nauseam and continued to worry over exposure. Given her elaboration on her reputation, alarm bells were ringing in his head. On the other hand, he was not willing to walk away from Beth. Finally, he'd built a compromise that would give him a modicum of peace of mind and still move forward with creating a sales book.

"Look," he said, dropping his foot back to the floor and leaning forward. "I told you this so you understand my concerns regarding the catalogue."

"What?" Beth frowned.

Oh, no. This was going to be more difficult than he'd hoped. "I said I desire you as a model, and I do. However, I want more than one model in the publication, and sketches shall be from the neck down, no faces."

Beth's shoulders sagged, and her lips became a moue of hurt.

"I am not willing to have my name known as the creator of these. I've gone to great pains to keep the circle of people who know my identity small." He flung out a hand. "And if someone recognizes you in the sketches…"

He shuddered, unable to voice what might happen.

She may say she does not care, but it would affect her social standing even further, and I know she is hurt when Ton ladies rebuff her.

For himself, it would mean more bullying, this time about products of his imagination and skill. Or possibly worse, the need for Evan to save his reputation, even as a grown man nearing thirty.

He couldn't bear seeing her hurt or the embarrassment for himself.

"With no faces and different body types, buyers can more easily picture themselves or their partner in the pose." 'Twas a sound marketing strategy, and he was proud of it, despite having conjured it up as an excuse for keeping Beth's image obscured.

****

Beth could not focus beyond the word "concerns." He'd seemed to accept her idea wholeheartedly in the carriage to Peterborough. She'd hoped that signified an openness to her outlook on life, a willingness to ignore society's decrees, especially as they both lived on the periphery of the aristocracy.

The Ton needed her matchmaking skills to procure and retain servants, tutors, and even advantageous marriages. They needed Robert for his creative leather designs, whether for in their homes or their lovers'. Why should he care if people knew he was the infamous tanner? He should be proud of his ingenuity.

"But I—I—" she started.

It was my idea!

They're his products.

I asked to be his model, and I'm not certain I can bear him fitting another woman, arranging her for sketches, touching her at all. She started there. "I wanted to be your model. You said the items were made with my figure in mind."

"And you shall be."

"I dislike being one of many, Robert." Were they still speaking of the catalogue? They'd never discussed exclusivity. The subject had never occurred to her in the past.

"I know. I see that in your behavior. My reputation is at stake here also, however."

"What is that supposed to mean? Are you saying I don't care about my image?"

"Mayhap careless is a better word than not caring." He grimaced. "You said yourself that your parents taught you to disregard society's rules. I can understand and appreciate that. It does not mean I must choose it for myself."

"Really?" Her brows rose with her voice in challenge. "So 'tis good enough an approach for me, but not for you? That does not feel like acceptance, Robert. I am not at all sure it even represents tolerance."

"Come now, Peaches. I have the utmost respect for you and your decisions. 'Tis your life. Just as I should be able to make choices about my life. Your way is not for me. I've tried to compromise, like the carriage ride, with a modicum of risk of exposure. This is another such balance."

"What of us?"

"What do you mean?" His expression went blank.

"Are you expecting me to sneak over here in servants' clothes forever? Or are you willing to dance with me at a party? Be seen with me on the street?"

He stared at her for a long beat. "I—" He choked and ducked his head. "I hadn't figured that out."

Why, oh why did I not see this coming? But she had. It was the same as always. She was acceptable for fun behind closed doors, but not for a relationship or even a partnership for his designs. So much for his lovely words about admiring her intellect.

"We can discuss all that. I just explained to you why I prefer to keep a low profile. Surely you can see…" His voice was pleading. "The catalogue is an intriguing idea. I'm willing to try it, but only on my terms."

"Willing? I thought you were eager, that you valued my input. I was trying to help you." Beth stood to pace. "Instead, you act like you are pandering to me, offering me crumbs, whilst you decry my whole philosophy on life." She snatched up her cloak and headed for the door.

Robert stood. "Beth…"

She looked back at him, but he did not ask her to stay. His outstretched hand fell limply to his side.

"I'm sorry," he said, bowing his head.

"Not as sorry as I am." She slammed the door behind her.

Chapter Seventeen

Beth was despondent, angry, exhausted, and frustrated. Still upset by Robert's reaction, she was in turn furious at herself for pining for a man who did not share her beliefs. He'd sent her a one-line note saying Evan had requested his company in Cheltenham. He gave no indication of whether he'd inform her of his return, nor did he request her patience.

She was glad for the distractions that Althea's business expansion needed. They spent the next fortnight rearranging the store to make space for new products, estimating the increase in orders from suppliers for the products they'd stock in both locations, and made another quick trip to Bath with their first delivery and paperwork.

Still, she hadn't gone this long without a sexual partner since the introductory course at school. Which of course led her back to misery over Robert. All of which fed her irritation. She'd never let a lover interfere in her enjoyment of life this much, and her realization that she was in love with Robert was ill-timed and unhelpful, given his anxiety regarding exposure. While she'd understood his reasons, living in fear was something she could never do.

Beth did not have anywhere to be, and her cousin spent Fridays at the store. Determined to alleviate her sexual frustration, she'd eyed the servants upstairs and down, inside and out, and even the tradesmen who came to the back door with deliveries. No one appealed. Her fingers were going to cramp if she had to take care of herself much longer.

Desperate to distract herself, she unearthed an embroidery project she'd started after being banned from the shop.

Looking at the piece, she could see why she'd abandoned it. It really needed to be unpicked. However, she doubted she could do any better now. Shrugging, she started from where she'd left off…or thought she'd left off.

Jabbing the needle through the fabric, she envisioned Robert sewing leather. Under her breath, she swore at him with each stab. "Dratted man. 'Twas my idea. If he doesn't need the additional business, why does he care so much about what the biddies think. And other models. Hmph."

Her cousin's voice at the door almost didn't register. "Beth? What is amiss?"

She wondered why Althea was home, but not enough to stop puncturing this piece of linen. She poked the needle through again, then yelped and brought her wounded finger out from beneath the dratted needlework that would never hang on a dratted wall and sucked it into her mouth.

Althea perched on the edge of a chair facing her. "Talk to me."

"I like to have fun. With other people. Naked fun. And now. That man." She shook her head and returned her gaze to the needlework in her lap. Althea rescued it and tucked it beside her hip on the chair.

"What man? Ford?"

Beth growled, frowning.

"So does this mean you and Ford did not…ahem, were not intimate after the house party?"

"Ha!" What a silly question.

"You were?"

She nodded once.

"And now…are not?"

Beth nodded again, crossing her arms.

"Ah…and you are frustrated?"

"Yes, damn him! Always before now, I'd have simply replaced him with my next bedmate. But not a single footman, maid, or stable boy appeals." She wanted to stamp her foot.

"That is a relief, in any event," Althea muttered.

Beth glared. That was her response?

"My apologies, go on."

"I can't stand it." She dropped her arms and stared at her cousin. "Cuz, I tried to help him with sales. My ability to pair people and opportunities is the most valuable aspect of my admittedly shallow life. But he didn't appreciate it. He rejected it. More, he rejected me. He liked my input and my body, but not the rest of me." Her eyes burned and one tear escaped.

Althea took her hand.

"He and Cheltie disappeared to Cheltenham," she whined, "with only a one-sentence note to inform me. Mayhap I should not have interfered, but I really thought I was helping." She snorted a bitter laugh. "'Tis the story of my life, is it not?"

Her cousin shook her head. "Absolutely not. You help so many people. Look at your conversation with Penelope before our trip south. Through your incredible network, you were assisting Ford. When Evan needed a new nurse for his mother, you found one for him. You connect so many people, and they trust you."

Beth was shocked into silence. Althea sounded as though she truly valued Beth's skills, something they'd never had a reason to discuss.

She swallowed thickly, and said, "Thank you, cuz. I needed that."

Althea's tilted her head. "So…'tis not only sexual frustration by the sound of it?"

"Ahh. Don't get me started on that part again. 'Tis not as though he forbade me from relations with anyone else. We did not speak of it."

She shook her head, unwilling to mention any more of Robert's concerns about her flaunting of conventions, as his reasons were not hers to share.

Knowing her next statement would reveal the depths of her emotions, she said it anyway. "I just do not want to risk disappointing him, so I cannot bring myself to…play. Besides which, he may have ruined me for anyone else." She sighed.

Althea's brows rose in surprise. She squeezed Beth's hand again, and her mouth twitched up in a sly grin. Her voice held a laugh as she peered at the pile of fabric next to her and said, "I can't imagine why you thought making, ahem, use of a needle and thread would help. I think a girl's day out is much more the thing, don't you? Come on, we'll wander a few shops and then get pastries."

"'Tis raining. Again."

"We'll take the carriage. 'Twill be fun, you'll see. Go on, fetch a wrap."

Beth grumbled but did as instructed. Althea was likely looking for a distraction as well, as she'd been less enthusiastic about her expansion since her falling out with Cheltie.

When they ended the day with Penelope and Charlotte and pastries, Penelope offered them theatre tickets in Michael's owner's box.

Beth shrugged, wishing she had a better substitute for Robert's prolonged ministrations of pleasure. Still smarting over his rejection, part of her also worried about appearing in public. She wanted wine and comfy clothing, not getting dressed and interacting with strangers who would judge her.

Althea ignored her apathetic gesture and accepted for both of them. "Come now. It will do you good to see people for something other than charity work. I'm accepting, and you're accompanying me."

Right, then. Wine tonight, at least. Tomorrow, I shall don my armor and sally forth, so to speak. Robert be damned.

****

Her mood savage, Beth chose a particularly low-cut gown for the theatre and convinced Althea to choose a ballgown that highlighted her creamy skin and dark hair. It was most important that a woman feel pretty when a man had spurned her company, and that applied to both of them at the moment.

They arrived early and were shown to the box she'd occupied only once before, with Penelope and Althea for a girls' night out.

Sitting in the front row, she watched the other boxes fill, the ladies' necks glittering with jewels, their gloved hands sparkling with rings, as they leaned perfectly coiffed heads toward one another to trade gossip. Curling her lip, she sighed and looked away. Any other time, she would have lingered in the lobby, chatting with those she knew, ignoring skeptical looks sent her way in order to gather knowledge to add to her networking skills. Tonight, she simply could not summon the energy. Using the excuse that Althea hated mingling, she allowed her cousin to pull her straight up to settle into the dark box.

The bells rang through the halls, and the theatre quieted in readiness for Act One.

But as the curtain rose, there was noise at the entry of their box. Thinking Penelope and Michael's plans had changed, she turned. And saw two tall male forms backlit from the hall sconces. One was long and lean, the other bulkier and familiar.

Her traitorous heart leapt. *Robert.*

As Cheltie bowed and turned to close the curtains behind them, the light caught his visage. He wore a scowl. A fleeting second of worry for her cousin was all she had before Robert rose from his bow and moved to stand before her.

Leaning down, he whispered, "I missed you. We need to talk."

Hmph. Yes, they should talk, but even more than reconciliation, she needed him to manhandle her body as expertly as he did his leather pieces. Nevertheless, she should stand firm.

Althea stood, offering Robert her seat and moving back two rows. Beth spared a glance at Evan lowering himself into the seat next to Althea stiffly before Robert became her focus.

"I think we have done all the talking I can stand." She sniffed for good measure. "Talking has not done us much good."

"Please, Peaches. I want to be with you. I want to

find an approach to the catalogue that will work for both of us. *Please*?" he repeated.

"I shall think about it." She turned to stare blindly at the stage, trying to ignore her body's demands to accept his apology and see what they might think of for private play in public right there, immediately if not sooner.

His fingers crept to her thigh, tugging on her wrist until she gave him her hand to hold. After a gentle squeeze, he smiled before focusing on the stage. "Will you talk with me after the play?"

Beth frowned, her thoughts muddled. Her body, however, had no such concerns. Her heart throbbed in her chest, and her blood sang in her veins. Every muscle was an instrument attuned to the maestro beside her. Who needed the orchestra below when she felt the song of a symphony in this box?

She squeezed her thighs together as heat bloomed low in her belly. Fidgeting in her seat, she sucked in a breath when her breast rubbed against his arm. She repeated the movement.

Robert hummed under his breath. "I see we need to do more than talk. Shall we start there, then?"

Her pride demanded that she refuse. After all, would that not simply repeat the pattern she'd always fallen into? Yet again, she was an easy conquest, good for intimacies but not for partnership. Her lips firmed as she remembered him saying she was careless, and she yanked at her hand.

But his hand, still resting on her thigh, tightened around hers. Then he released her and tugged her skirt upward.

She stifled a gasp. Her body stopped listening to her pride. Never one for self-denial, she was tired of the unfulfilled ache. They could talk later. Unwilling to acquiesce aloud, she slid a few inches lower in her chair and spread her legs to accommodate further exploration.

He knows me so well. If only I wasn't in love with him, so he could not hurt me. Or if he were…

Her gown and petticoat hem were at her knee, and she abandoned wishing for impossible things to focus on the pleasure he could strum from her.

"Watch the show." He chastised her with a grin.

She turned blind eyes toward the stage as his hand met the bare flesh just above her knee. It slid inward, toward the part of her she wanted him to strum like a harp, play like a flute, or just plain bang like a drum. It paused mid-thigh to squeeze her leg. His grip reminded her of the restraints he often used to hold her immobile. She daren't move, unwilling to dispel the aura of anticipated pleasure only this man could give her.

Then his fingers were exactly where she needed them. They skimmed her lips, feeling the moisture already seeping from her from a mere brush of his arm and touch of his fingers.

She felt as much as heard his repeated hum of satisfaction.

Every finger movement twitched muscles in his arm where it rested against her breast. She heaved a sigh, loving the added friction against his thick, hard arm. Then he curled his fingers, thrusting two inside her suddenly.

"Mmph," she bit back her cry, sinking her teeth into her lip to remain still and silent.

"Shh. What do you think of the play so far?"

"Robert," she gasped, clutching his arm, hoping to force him to move those inert fingers that were both tease and torture.

"Oh no. You shall need to tell me something of the plot at intermission, before you are allowed more."

What? Plot? The man was dastardly. Why had she missed him again? He was a mean bastard when he did this. But godsakes, he knew how to build her excitement.

Finally, the curtain shut for the first intermission. Beth turned, to be met by Robert's direct gaze.

"It seems you missed me, too, Peaches." He twitched his fingers, and her eyes nearly crossed.

But he slid them out of her as sconces were lit, causing her lower lip to jut in a pout.

"Well?" He stuck his fingers in his mouth with another hum. "Have you seen this play before? How do you feel this performance compares?"

"Robert, be serious. I can't concentrate on anything but you when your hands are on me." She was ready to beg.

"Come now. We were both fully clothed. You forget, I've seen you evaluate harnesses even as I strap you into one."

****

Robert heard Althea and Evan talking behind them, and someone left the box, but his entire focus was on Beth. He wanted this woman back in his bed—in his life. Gulping at that thought, he put it aside. He needed every bit of his skill as a lover to get past their disagreement, but he was confident he'd win her back.

"Beth, I meant what I said. I have missed you, and I want to talk, but I know you. You need to be pleasured in order to focus. It seems my trip to Cheltenham was rough on you. Allow me to make it up to you."

"Yes! Please. But please, no quizzes." She pouted as

she begged. "I can't focus. I haven't been able to focus for days."

Oh, really? He was pleased to hear that, despite not having a clear vision of a future together. She was a bright star while he preferred the darkness of the shadows.

They had leaned toward each other to talk, and she clutched his arm. He used their proximity to reach across and tweak her nipple through her dress.

She gripped tighter.

The orchestra played a note signaling the end of the intermission. He dragged her onto his lap so they both faced the stage. It had the added benefit of hiding him from the boxes across the theatre, who would see only Beth. He hoped she recognized the compromise in his actions. He'd never have played even this much, this hidden, publicly before her.

The move had caused her skirts to drop, and he drew them back up to her lap. With a quick sideways check, he ascertained Evan had closed the curtains on either side of the box to give them privacy from adjacent boxes. As Evan and he had shared women and discussed leather pieces as they were modeled, Robert had no concerns about privacy from his friend. He slid his hand under her arm to cup her breast discreetly.

She squirmed, thrusting her bottom toward his cock.

"Should I bare you? Tug this dress down that last inch and show the audience your beauty? Pluck your nipple as the violinists pluck their instruments?" They were empty threats, but he knew the image would excite her.

"No. I want to be yours, not theirs."

He blinked at the unexpected response. He'd think

about its meaning later.

She squeezed her hand between them to grip his cock through his breeches.

"No, you don't get that yet. In fact, you'll need to stay very still so the other theatre-goers do not know what I'm doing." His hand slid from her breast to her inner thigh, bare above her stocking. He did not linger this time, instead aiming for her hot wet center immediately. He wished he could taste it, strapping her down for an hour or two of luxurious exploration before giving in to her begging. This would have to do for the moment.

She slid her legs to the outside of his, offering herself without hesitation. Her skirts, while above her knees, rested on the leg she straddled. And his lap was below the front half-wall of their box.

He thrust his two middle fingers into her, holding her lips even wider with his forefinger and little finger. His thumb unerringly found her swollen bundle of nerves and began tapping.

Beth jerked once, but then held still. She moaned in the back of her throat.

"Shh," he whispered in her ear, blowing a breath into the pink shell after that solicited a shiver. Her sudden movement had made his cock twitch against her arse, and it was all he could do to silence his own groan.

Her hand gripped his arm that held her in place across her stomach. Her breasts strained in her bodice with her ragged breathing, and he hid his grin. She was his harp, and he would play her with every ounce of expertise he had.

As the action on the stage accelerated toward the end of Act Two, and the orchestra reached a crescendo, he slipped his hand into her bodice and pinched her nipple.

She cried out, thankfully unheard by anyone other than him under the music, and the curtain dropped.

Withdrawing both hands, he held her tight. He set his teeth against the need to unfasten his breeches and drive into her right then and there. No. This must be about control, both to demonstrate his forgiveness and to prolong their ecstasy as he knew she loved.

He'd heard enough noise behind them to know Althea would want privacy for the next few moments. Beth moved as though to regain her own seat, and he clamped her in place.

"Stay still." He slid his hand back to cup her mound, and she froze, panting.

"Robert," her plea came from behind clenched teeth. "I need—"

"I know what you need. But you are not ready yet. I haven't heard nearly enough begging."

They remained motionless until the orchestra struck a note, and the curtain lifted. Robert relaxed his arms around her, and before he knew it, she was off his lap.

Slithering to the floor in front of him, she faced him on her knees. "My most effective form of begging does not involve words."

Humming in pleasure, he shifted his hips forward an inch and undid the fall of his breeches. "Well, then. By all means, beg away."

Their separation had been too long for him as well. Her lips barely closed around his cock, and his bollocks drew up, wanting release. He loved controlling his release as well as others', but he feared he was beyond that. Closing his eyes, he rested one hand on her head and enjoyed.

The hot wet heat of her mouth surrounded his shaft, her firm lips yielding to her tongue undulating against his sensitive vein and then the tightness of her throat muscles working against him.

Gah. Her hand splayed against his pelvis at the base of his cock, her nose hitting it on each thrust of her head.

This girl, this young woman, for all her flashiness and spurning of society's rules, was the most caring human he'd met, with more to lose by giving of herself than his friends or family.

He had reveled in having her on her knees before him, but he realized he should simply be grateful for her attention.

She glanced up, and he swore he saw hope and affection in her eyes before they glossed over with sensual bliss.

Oh, she was rubbing her breast against his leg, and one of her hands was…

"No touching yourself." He tugged on her hair. "Those sweet folds are mine to please."

She grumbled around him, even as her pace increased. She took him deep with each stroke, her tongue flicking the underside of his head as she withdrew each time. Her hand now held his base, following her mouth up and down, keeping the grip of her mouth and hands tight along his length continually.

Sweat broke out under his arms, and his skin became sensitive to the brush of his shirt against his nipples, his open breeches against his bollocks. His orgasm boiled at the base of his spine, building as though toward a crescendo of its own.

"Ah, ah." His voice was a harsh whisper, and he plucked at her hair again to warn her. He opened his eyes, finding her gaze on his face. Her mouth stretched around him was his undoing as she slammed down on the length of him again and held there, her tongue pressing against his length. Shuddering, he released control, his cock leaping and jerking in her as hot jets erupted from him for long moments. Her swallow of his ejaculate contracted her throat around him and milked more from him, extending his ecstasy for an extra few pulses.

Finally, he slumped in his chair, his hand idly fondling her hair. Focusing on her, he gestured. "Your turn, Peaches. Come back up here."

She bounced up eagerly.

He chuckled, and she giggled in return.

"Thank you. That was indeed some of your best begging. You have earned your reward."

He dragged her skirts up again, and feathered his hand over her damp folds.

She clutched his arm.

"No more teasing. I promise." He sank his two fingers in, and his thumb flicked her hard *kleitoris* from side to side, which he knew would take her over the fastest. Besides having teased her for two acts, he knew the performance was almost over, having seen the play before.

She held onto his arm, her nails digging through his jacket and shirt as he manipulated her pleasure.

"I shall sleep well tonight after that magnificent performance," he whispered in her ear. A new rush of liquid hit his fingers as they pistoned in and out of her. "I wish my teeth were on your delicious breasts, toying with you. Or mayhap where my thumb is now."

She bit her lip, her hips making tiny thrusts she probably was not even aware of.

"Imagine my cock thrusting into you instead of my fingers. Just as your mouth was a substitute for your sweet channel moments ago, I want to feel your muscles milk my fingers, your little bud harden and convulse against my thumb like I trembled on your tongue. Come for me, Peaches."

She let out a keening moan under her breath, and her chin dropped, her hands clenching and unclenching on his arm as her internal muscles did the same to his fingers. Her nub hardened even further and spasmed under his thumb as he rubbed it.

Finally, he slowed his movements, and her hands released him. "I shall see you tomorrow, then? Do you prefer to come to me or me to you?"

She giggled. "Both, obviously."

As he withdrew his hand, he pinched her thigh.

"Ouch. I'll come to you, Robert."

If only tomorrow goes as well as tonight.

Chapter Eighteen

No. I want to be yours, not theirs.

Her words had shocked her. Robert had taken them in stride, and at the time, they'd stoked the fires of lust higher. Then she'd gone home, expecting to enjoy the sleep of sexual satisfaction, only to toss and turn as her reply and her body's response to the idea of being his echoed in her head.

Always before, she'd enjoyed playing with any and all who wished to participate—or watch, as the case may be. She still believed all of those to be perfectly acceptable ways to have fun. However, she no longer wanted that for herself.

Just when he'd solved one form of frustration, he'd created another, the dratted man. Not a single breast, chest, calf, or hand appealed, unless it was Robert's rough callused palms smoothing or pinching or his broad chest lowering to tantalize her with his mouth.

Like it or not, she needed to hear what he wanted from her. She was too invested in him to let it play out over time.

From what he'd shared of his childhood, she understood his desire to avoid the scrutiny of the Ton. That and their time apart had allowed her to see that she'd overreacted. She could accept his preference for multiple models if there was no touching involved, especially as she'd received a reply from Helen

Montague indicating interest. She also wished to discuss expanding the use of the catalogue.

Robert put his work aside when she let herself in. "Hullo, love." He bussed her cheek. "Come, sit with me. Sherry?"

"No, thank you." She perched next to him on the settee, which had been cleared of leather designs. Apparently, he had planned for their conversation. Was that a good sign or bad?

He sat angled toward her and took her hand in both his.

Uh oh. Feels like a bad sign.

"First, I want to be with you, to spend more time with you. For instance, I should like your continued help in blacksmith shopping. But privacy is important to me. So can we keep things somewhat quiet for now, and I will consider a path forward?"

Ugh. She'd just resolved that she did not want this to drag out, as she'd subject herself to more hurt the longer it did. On the other hand, she'd seen how private he was and understood him needing more time. Mayhap a trip to the school could give them more time together, as Peterborough had.

She gave a reluctant nod.

"Thank you." He raised her hand to his mouth and brushed a kiss on it. "Second, I apologize. I was somewhat abrupt that night about the catalogue."

She arched a brow. What part did he regret?

"You did not give me a chance to explain."

Possibly true. But she stayed silent. She'd wait for the explanation before coming to any conclusions.

"I wanted to create the catalogue to please you. It was an excuse to spend more time with you."

She beamed, then frowned as she replayed his words. He still wasn't excited by the idea.

"But the more I contemplated it, the more concerned I became regarding exposure. I should not have laid out mandates, however. I am happy to discuss ways to ensure anonymity." He stared at her expectantly.

"You do not need an excuse to spend time with me. In fact, I planned to discuss that with you this evening. But let us address the catalogue first." She took a breath. "I feel sure we can find a way to keep your identity a secret."

"I appreciate your help with the designs so much." He squeezed her hand. "And I know you are enthusiastic about modeling and care little if the Ton recognizes you. Can you understand my worry over the association?"

"Yes. My first reaction was defensive, I admit. But, Robert, consider this. Whilst you find me unique, and I love that you do, I am not. No one looking at a sketch figure would recognize me. Even among the Ton, I am not the only short, round—"

"Voluptuous, please."

"—voluptuous woman." She rolled her eyes but sent him a grateful smile. "Certainly, the audience admiring the catalogue will not be thinking of a lady modeling anyway, which leaves it wide open to any serving maid, spanking wench, or cook around."

He tilted his head, nodding slowly.

"However, I understand the preference not to have faces, as it may facilitate sales. May I at least get to choose the specific creations and number of them that I model? Please?"

He took a deep breath in and whooshed it out, narrowing his eyes. She knew that look from Althea.

She'd never been above bargaining to get her way. That look said he was wondering how much further she'd push if he gave in on this negotiation. She attempted innocence, smiling demurely and holding his gaze with a serene countenance.

"I really would prefer different female forms illustrated, so everyone can picture their partner in place of the sketch."

"I understand. I find I dislike the idea of you fitting other women, though. Would you consider allowing me to do that at your direction?"

"Certainly. Especially if I can watch?" He gave her a mock leer, and she grinned.

Their conversation about Lady Peterborough—Charlotte to him, for godsakes—and his reticence regarding his clients gave her an idea. "Mayhap even a male model if we can find one?"

"Oh." He nodded slowly. "Yes, that might be good, although *I* shall fit him for pieces."

Excellent. Whilst he is in an agreeable mood, I shall raise my other idea. Helen's letter had indicated she'd be interested in hearing more about the leatherwork for both the School of Enlightenment and to offer to select sponsors.

"I shan't ask to model more than…half of the designs?" she asked as much as stated.

"Thank you, Beth."

"If you're making a catalogue, I wonder if there are other uses for it than only Sarah's," she mused, trying to ease into the subject.

He frowned. "What did you have in mind?"

"For one, mayhap a wider set of private parties. 'Twould be easy to have people pass it along with no one knowing the original source."

"That is too risky for my tastes." He shook his head, his brow still furrowed. "There is a reason Sarah vets her clients so thoroughly and why I remain anonymous, particularly for sales outside of her club. The Ton is a quagmire of rumor. A single person's poor judgment could put the book in the wrong hands with sketches appearing in the gossip rags."

"Oh." She thought for a moment. "Still, even if it was through my network or Evan's, you could expand the private parties beyond what you do now." She took a breath. It was now or never. "Or there is another channel I considered."

He gulped. "Right." A pause. "What is it?"

"'Tis extremely confidential. I needed special permission to share this with you. I told you I was wild. When I came to live with Althea, I was still reeling from the death of my parents, and I acted out. Within weeks, she was exhausted and knew she needed to find another solution. That is how I attended the School of Enlightenment." Knowing he wouldn't have heard of it, she rushed on, "'Tis a private, secret school for girls. They can learn anything from maths to Latin to politics to sexual pleasure."

He stiffened, his hands dropping from hers as he sat upright.

"There are courses for marriage," she rushed on, "for servants, even for courtesans, and advanced courses for those who want to learn more." She took a second to grin at him. "And you know I am all about the learning."

His smile was fleeting.

She explained the school in more detail before summing it up. "My volunteer work at the charity school allows me to identify students who might be best suited for the School of Enlightenment and vice versa. My network in part comes from there. 'Tis of the utmost importance that you do not share this with anyone, please."

"I understand. You know I can keep a confidence."

"I do. I trust you, or I would not have told you. The reason I did is because I had a fantastic idea. Again." She smirked at him.

He laughed under his breath before sobering to say, "Right, then, let's have it."

"We could sell through the school the same way we sell through Sarah's. With a catalogue. Think of the expansion."

His hands dropped away from her, his muscles turning to stone under her fingers and thighs.

She peered up to find his expression steely.

Oh no. I pushed. Why do I always do that?

He had only just agreed to the catalogue for Sarah's, a known quantity for him. This was too much, too soon. She'd risked the confidentiality of the school and her future with him when they'd barely reunited.

****

Robert had contemplated how to explain his concerns and preferences to Beth for days. He thought he had found the balance with her willingness to compromise on the catalogue.

Then she took it further.

There is a secret school for girls? Heaven help the men of England.

He swallowed thickly, battling sorrow as he realized their differences were too great to safely continue the relationship. Beth would always push for more.

215

Networking and connecting people was her passion. She would never understand that he did not wish to be connected.

"I confess, I am at a loss. I cannot believe such an education exists."

"Why shouldn't it?" Her back snapped straight as she built up a head of steam to defend the concept.

"No, you misunderstand. I have no issue with its existence. Indeed, I am pleased to hear of it. Clearly, its creation has been a well-kept secret. However, they do not know me, and if 'tis run by women, they are more likely to trust women." He recalled her words introducing the school. "Wait, Beth, did you give them information about me?" His heart thundered in his chest at the thought.

"No, Robert. I would not," she hastened to reassure him. "I gave them a general idea of the products and noted that my associate preferred anonymity."

"Ah. Right, then." He breathed a sigh of relief, but that did not allay his remaining concerns.

"Just as they do not know me, nor do I know them. Having a catalogue there means a significant number of people would be aware of my designs. 'Tis similar to my concern about private parties. All it takes is one untrustworthy person getting my name."

"But Robert, 'twould also mean quite a bit of growth in your sales."

He grimaced. He preferred not to talk about his wealth. It led to people looking at him differently when his prosperity was Bags's doing. Just like in school when Bags's friendship led to more social invitations. If people did not like him for him, he did not want to befriend them or even work with them.

That's not fair. She has already proven that she likes you for you. She just finished saying that you needn't find excuses to continue the relationship.

He sighed. She deserved an explanation after all she'd done to help him. Here goes nothing. "This school sounds wonderful. And I would be happy to support it any way I can. However, it has too many unknowns for me to venture there for business. I hope you will understand."

She nodded again. "Right, then. Mayhap I will think of something else."

"I do not want to expand my business to that extent."

"I thought with a new blacksmith..." she asked.

"Thank you, but you needn't worry about me. I can afford to decline the school. I can more than afford to. I do not need to work at this. 'Tis more of a hobby or, really, a passion."

Beth's eyebrows rose. "I wasn't aware. I don't know that I've ever met a nobleman, even a second son, who worked a trade if he did not need the funds."

"Allow me to clarify. I told you Bags managed my money. Well, he made me a very rich man. You know his nickname was earned whilst we were still at Oxford for that very reason?"

"I did not. Interesting. I wonder if Althea and Penelope know..." She tilted her head in thought.

"What I mean to say is, I can be particular about my privacy."

Her head still cocked, she frowned at him. "But if you have scads of money, then why do you care what the Ton says or thinks?"

His jaw nearly dropped. Had she not listened to his description of his childhood? Could she not see past her own paradigm?

Her upbringing was too different, and she's spent too long shunning society's rules. She will keep prodding you further and further until your preferences are out of sight over the horizon. You'll be living in her world by her rules, prancing around like a puppet on a stage.

No. This stops here. I don't need anyone's approval, but nor do I care to listen to their condemnation.

"Beth, listen to me, please." He took her hand again. "I tried to explain that the other night. It should be my choice, and I choose anonymity. I choose the shadows. They are comfortable. I know what to expect, and I am happy."

"Are you, though?"

"Are you?" he retorted. Really, he couldn't imagine having to field gossip directed at one's actions constantly and pretending to ignore it or that it didn't hurt.

She tugged her hand away and stood to pace. "I do not seek out public attention."

"Mayhap not. But nor does it bother you when it lands on you. It bothers me." He sighed again. She was going to make him give voice to their differences. "Your questions indicate that you struggle to accept me how I am. I have tried to meet you partway, right from discussing the undergarment at Evan's dining table to our play at the theatre. Did you think 'twas comfortable for me? It does not seem to be enough for you. I am not at all sure where we go from here. Even your recitation of the school's existence makes me worry about your ability to keep my identity secret."

He knew as soon as he said it, he shouldn't have. But it was too late to take it back.

"That is not fair," she cried, her hands fisting on her

hips. "I had permission, and I did it because I trusted you. Godsakes, I thought you might know, given your friendship with Cheltie."

"What?" What did Evan have to do with anything?

"Half his servants are from there, and I am quite sure he's funded the school, although to what extent I have no idea."

"What?" His voice was incredulous. His best friend had kept such an enormous secret from him? Well, that proved his point. "That supports what I said. Evan has never breathed a word about the school in all these years, yet here you are."

Lud, what am I doing? I am running her off. Am I sure this is what I want?

Beth stamped her foot. "You dratted man! I was trying to help you. How was I to know you did not need it or want it?" Her eyes held tears, but her voice was firm. "You've made it quite clear now, I assure you. You don't want me or my help." She strode to the door. "Good night, sir."

Letting her go, both literally and figuratively, was the right thing. They were not compatible. Beth's behavior was always going to edge on the outrageous, and despite her good intentions, she'd struggle with his need for normalcy.

But then why did his chest hurt so much, as though something in it had broken?

****

Robert tossed and turned all night.

His thoughts circled around everything he'd learned from Beth.

He felt naked, in the worst possible way. He'd peeled back his layers of protection, baring himself to her a little more each night, trusting her to protect and accept his weakness.

She had not been able to see that vulnerability. He'd shared his creative visions, his unprepossessing body, even his dreams of buying a manor home, although he never told her he was waiting to have a wife to pick it out with for fear of her laughing at the idea of someone marrying him.

For all that he'd revealed, perhaps he had not shared his history in enough detail. 'Twas not a lack of trust, despite what he'd said in anger. He simply hated to speak of the past, the bullying and taunting, the disdain for a second son, another layer of rudeness.

Mayhap she would not have pushed so hard to expand his business if he had shared more of his fears or his finances earlier. At least then she'd have known he did not need to worry about growing his business. He'd told her he worked because he loved it, not because he needed to, but he hadn't shared the extent of it. He'd seen too many women pursue Evan for the weight of his purse.

She'd said the school had a variety of programs and had been open several years. That equated to too many people who might judge him on his profession or laugh at the idea of such an ungainly creature creating beautiful sexual pieces. When she'd compared it to Sarah's, suddenly Sarah's no longer felt safe.

He flopped to his other side and worried anew. He'd given in on the catalogue for Sarah's to please Beth. He'd thought he'd do just about anything to make her happy. Only then she'd wanted more. Now, he was unsure if he'd pursue a book for Sarah's, especially without his favorite model.

Come now, you are a member at Sarah's. 'Tis the safest of places; no one there will judge.

His focus turned to the school. Were there other outlandish women like Beth walking around because of this secret education? Well, mayhap not like Beth. There was no one like her in beauty, kindness, caring…

Then why did you push her away, nitwit?

We are simply too different.

Yet she seemed to want to continue seeing you.

He missed her already. Her succulent form, all soft and begging for his touch. Her creative ideas, put to naughty use just as his were, improving his designs. Even her outrageousness, at least when it was in company he felt was safe.

Which brought him to Bags. The school had been open for a few years, but they'd been friends for fifteen years. Yet his closest friend had never seen fit to tell him about the school. Evan's secrecy hurt. Intellectually, he understood that silence had been a mandate. He even approved of it. If he'd been judged, he could only imagine how girls attempting to improve themselves might have been, should the information land in the wrong hands. But it still felt like a betrayal.

One step at a time. He needed to talk to Bags. He'd consider the catalogue further. If he pursued that, the effort would take time. And who would model for him? In the meantime, there was a demi-monde party in less than a month, hosted at Sarah's, and he'd already committed to provide implements for a demonstration room.

Chapter Nineteen

Robert wound his way through the seating areas at White's to his group's favorite niche. Michael and Evan were already there, facing away from him at right angles to each other. They leaned close, and their conversation was murmurs.

As he approached, he caught random words. "Pen…Enlightenment…scholarship you are sponsoring."

He slowed. He'd never heard the word enlightenment used in conversation with his friends—or anyone, for that matter—before Beth described the school she'd attended.

Wait. Did Michael know about it, too? And Penelope? Who else?

"…girls like Pen to have a path out of poverty."

Damnation. They did both know about it. And were discussing it in White's of all places. She wanted him to parade his wares and thus himself at this not-so-secret school? *Hell, no.*

He sped up, circling around them to plop into his usual armchair.

They both looked up and sat back, reaching for their drinks.

"Gentlemen." He nodded, his lips pressed flat. "Pray, do continue." He waved a hand in a circle.

Evan arched a knowing brow. "What's the matter,

old chap?"

He was too angry to mince words. But if somehow this was still a secret, he wasn't going to be the leak. Rumors had harmed him too many times.

He angled forward and hissed low, "Does everyone in White's know about the school? Or just you two and, apparently, your ladies…and their friends, and God knows who else?"

Evan's brows had shot up at his first question, and he leaned in again, as did Michael. "I suppose Beth told you about it?"

Robert growled.

"I'll take that as a yes." Evan remained calm. "It is a very closely held secret, I assure you. No one who isn't directly connected hears about it, or you know I would have said something. As for talking about it here, consider the background noise. No one can hear us. 'Tis the perfect foil."

"So how did he learn about it?" Robert flung a hand toward Michael.

"A group connected to the school hosted the auction that Penelope participated in, and the girls came from there." Michael's tone was matter-of-fact. "If you had bid on someone, you would have been brought into the fold."

Evan held up his hand when Robert started to reply. "Really, Ford. I am sorry. Even students who know one another are warned to be careful when they discuss it. And those they meet after attending are not aware of their shared past."

"If you'll remember," Michael added, "Sophia and Penelope reunited well after I won her. They only discovered their mutual education because one of the auction leaders specifically approved it."

"The new Lady Peterborough?" Robert was momentarily distracted from his ire at Evan—and Michael—for keeping secrets. *A countess?* Beth spoke of a marriage course, but for the Ton, the biggest gossipmongers of all? His anger at her inability to grasp his concerns reignited.

"You'll remember Peterborough dropped his membership to Sarah's around the time of his marriage." Evan arched a brow. "Either way, why is it shocking for a countess to attend the school and not for an earl to visit a spanking club?"

"Good point. Well said," Michael added, nodding.

Robert threw up his hands, still glaring at them.

"Now that you know, what questions do you have for me—us?" Evan asked, glancing at Michael.

Michael nodded, elbows on his wideset knees. His hands hung between cradling his drink.

"Anything, man. I'm an open book."

"Hmph," Robert grumbled. But he recognized that most of his anger was at Beth for thinking he'd sell there when it was a far wider audience than he'd imagined. From what Evan said, the number of people who knew wasn't as large as the men's conversation had first made it sound. He considered his questions. "Who else knows of this school?"

"Sophia's husband, Peterborough." Michael ticked them off on his fingers as he cited names. "And her cousin and his wife, Suffolk and Lady Roslynn. Sarah Potter. My theatre manager and the other ladies who ran the auction."

"Oh, and a good number of the servants at Greenborough are graduates." Evan grinned at Robert, who knew of his policy regarding the staff there and had joined him in partaking in more than one naked and sweaty evening.

Robert nodded slowly. It all made sense. If one spouse knew, the other would. Beth, with her incredible skill at connecting people, would have made friends and friends of friends. After all, she'd connected the charity school she worked at with the School of Enlightenment. His rage ebbed, morphing to resignation. He'd made the right choice in parting ways with the little peach. His chest hurt again, and he rubbed it distractedly.

"Wait. Sophia was gentry, even before Peterborough married her. Penelope was…not." He slid a careful glance to Michael, who nodded. "And…servants?"

"Yes," Evan replied. "Three separate courses, but with overlap. The ladies of the Ton or destined for Ton marriages are of course in separate classrooms and dormitories but have leeway in choosing the subjects. And every student has a sponsor to help direct them. I am presently working on adding a fourth program."

Robert glanced at Michael, who frowned and shrugged.

Then Michael's forehead smoothed, and he chuckled. "An enterprise path, mayhap?"

Evan grinned and responded, but Robert's thoughts turned inward. Beth had had a sponsor. A past lover? Her parents had died before she'd reached the appropriate age for the school, from what he understood of it.

"So who was Beth's sponsor?" He interrupted the other two discussing Evan's latest idea.

"Althea."

"And Althea's?"

Evan shook his head. "She did not attend. But she fully supported Beth attending."

"So there are people directly connected to the school who have never attended, floating about the country as well?" Alarm bells began ringing again in Robert's head, as the theoretical pool of people with knowledge of the school rippled outward.

Evan arched a brow at his strange phrasing. "Yes. You're looking at two of them. Why?"

"Never mind that for now. How did you first hear about it?"

Evan grinned. "How d'you think?"

Robert rolled his eyes. "Of course, you probably contribute funding."

Evan wiggled his brows. "I helped found it." He raised his glass. "And you're welcome. Cheers."

The other two gave reluctant chuckles as they raised theirs to toast him. Robert's smile hid his grim thoughts. As much as he'd wanted to find common ground with Beth, this discovery had scared him away from venturing forward with a catalogue at all. He suppressed the urge to cancel the demo at Sarah's and wondered whether he should scale back and produce less. That would minimize his need for a new blacksmith, although he'd already gotten a response from the smith Hunter had referred him to. He'd hoped to take Beth with him to meet the tradesman, but that was unlikely now.

One thing was certain. He needed to keep a suitable distance between him and that not-so-secret school…and its lovely but conspicuous alumna.

****

Beth considered the last line of Helen Montague's letter.

In her last note to the headmistress, Beth had asked for the direction of an alumna of the charity school who was an excellent artist and had attended the School of Enlightenment. Beth had hoped to see if she'd draw the sketches for the catalogue, with Robert's permission.

A week had passed since Robert had rejected her, calling her a gossip who could not be trusted, and she was still furious every time she remembered it. In fact, she'd avoided thinking of it for that very reason. Determined to put him out of her mind and get on with her life, she'd thrown herself back into the charity school. If she sketched cuff configurations when she had a few moments between helping students, then no one need know.

However, Helen had sent the name and likely address of the student, and the information niggled at her. In the past, she'd helped people whether or not she liked them, agreed with their outlook on society or did not. The fact that she had not connected Robert with the sketch artist as she'd have done for anyone else weighed on her mind.

It also brought the feelings she'd been ignoring to the forefront. After a student had caught her in a compromising position testing a new design, her first inclination had been to regale Robert with the tale. Of course, in all likelihood he'd be appalled rather than amused. The threat of exposure seemed to tint his outlook of all activities. She did not want to live that way.

However, she was not at all sure this was living. The dull ache in her chest that never went away detracted from her usual sunny outlook. It also killed any desire for intimacy with anyone else. No one would make her the center of their world for hours on end, only allowing her to pleasure them if she begged, and only after they'd brought her to the pinnacle several times.

Every time she recalled her nights with Robert, her core wept even as her eyes did. How could she be aroused and miserable at the same time?

Each new design she dreamed up built eagerness to see it brought to life in leather at Robert's hands and tested on her.

She was miserable. There was no way around it. This was not living, 'twas torture. She needed advice. As different as they were, Althea understood her and accepted her. More, Althea's attitude regarding privacy and circumspection about her reputation was closer to Robert's, making her the perfect person to ask.

Finding her cousin in her office, Beth knocked and wandered in, all in one motion.

Althea glanced up. "I haven't seen you in days. How are you?" She put her paperwork aside. "Most importantly, did you ring for tea on your way here?"

"Of course." Beth's could barely muster a smile. "Can I steal you away from your work for a few minutes, please? I could use your counsel."

"You never need to ask, you know that. Come, let us move closer to the fire." She led Beth to the wine-toned settee and chairs by the fireplace as a servant brought in a tea tray and set it on the low table in the center.

"Cuz, I told Robert about the school," she blurted out as she accepted a cup of tea.

"Oh? What prompted that?" Althea's tone was mild.

"You're not upset? No chastisement?"

"Well, I can if you'd like…" Her cousin grinned.

"But I prefer to understand your reasons. They are generally sound."

Beth burst into tears. Althea had faith in her judgment. Why could Robert not feel the same? Instead, he'd called her reckless and untrustworthy.

"Oh no." Althea switched from a chair to the settee beside Beth, putting an arm around her. She took Beth's cup and saucer from her and placed them on the table. "Let's not dilute the tea."

Beth managed a watery smile at her cousin's attempt at humor.

"Come now. Tell me what happened. I will support you however I can."

She leaned her head against Althea's shoulder and explained her idea for the catalogue, his acceptance, his backtracking. Then his apology, their negotiation, and her suggestion regarding the school.

"He completely rejected the idea, cuz. No discussion. Simply a no thank you."

"Hmm."

Twisting her head to frown up at her cousin for the noncommittal answer, she could only see an open gaze and listening expression. Deciding to ignore the hum for the time being, she continued. "Then he told me he's wealthy, thanks to Cheltie's investing on his behalf. But then why is he so obsessed with anonymity?" She straightened from her cousin's shoulder, throwing up her hands.

"Did you ask him?" Althea's question paused her forward motion to reclaim her teacup.

Her head swiveled. "No. He said I hadn't accepted him as he prefers to live. I was trying to change him. And that he struggled to do the same with me. I only wanted to leave."

"He said that? I can understand you wanting to leave then." Althea nodded. "You deserve to be with someone who wants you as you are. You are magnificent and deserve the amount of care and respect you give others."

"Aww. Mayhap 'tis a shame you don't like girls, cuz." Beth managed a smile and a wink. "In fact, are you sure you don't like girls?"

"I am serious, Beth. However, I also wonder if he is right about your struggle. At least he is aware of his."

Beth frowned but stayed silent to hear the rest.

"Consider this. There are many reasons to dislike the Ton's attention. No matter how much money one has or how much easier it is for men"—she ignored Beth's snort—"being exiled from the Ton can be lonely and limiting."

"He hates social activities anyway," Beth grumbled.

"Ah, but at least he has the choice. Evan and Michael would also be affected by his identity being associated with the designs. Whilst Evan likely would not care and his reputation could sustain it, there would still be an effect, possibly even a financial one. And you know Michael's family tries to avoid being the topic of gossip. So Ford might care on behalf of his friends. Furthermore, he might not have 'more money than he needs.' What if he dreams of doing something with his savings? Marriage, babies, a country estate, whatever he might be planning."

Marriage? Babies? Beth pictured Robert holding a son in his arms, a leather cap on the baby's head hand-stitched by his father. Robert would sit the boy down when he reached the right age and give him scraps of leather to practice stitches on. Or a girl. To be sure, Beth would not be the right person to teach their children stitching.

With a start, she realized she was picturing Robert married to her. Shaking her head to clear the thought, she replied to Althea, "Mayhap, but to call me untrustworthy when I have been the pillar of help and respect for his work is unfair."

"Hmm."

"Stop that! Do you agree with him?"

"'Tis not a matter of agreeing or disagreeing. I see both sides. For instance, consider his point about secrecy. I have heard you mention his creations to Penelope. Did he give you permission to do that?" Althea asked.

"She is married to Michael, one of his best friends," Beth protested.

"You did also share information about the school when even Evan had not divulged that in all their years of friendship."

Beth gritted her teeth. Althea echoed Robert's exact thoughts. Godsakes, she'd had permission.

"Also, what if Robert inserted himself into your quest to place a charity school graduate? Say he'd met her twice and then assumed he could do a better job of it, against your wishes."

She seriously hated it when her cousin was right, and it happened far too often for her tastes.

"The question is, what do you want?" Althea asked.

"I want…him to see life the way I do."

"Why?" Althea raised her brows expectantly.

"Because…" Ready to spout her parents' philosophy, Beth shook her head. At the core of it all, she simply wanted to be wanted.

The taller woman reached for her hand. "Because you can be sure you're accepted then."

"Yes." She nodded and looked down at their joined hands. "And loved."

"Ah. Let us flip this situation, cuz." Althea borrowed her affectionate nickname to show her love. "What are you doing to adapt to his preferences, to show your love?"

"I snuck around in coarse wool, for godsakes. I have remained faithful, even when he was away, without him asking."

"Faithfulness is a baseline, my dear." Shaking her head with a rueful grin, Althea squeezed Beth's hand. "What about positive gestures of caring, rather than abstinence from negative actions?"

Beth's lips pressed in annoyance before she answered. "I've helped him grow his business and supported him in that. I've even found a potential blacksmith for him. Althea, I appreciate what you're trying to do, but I have bent over backwards to please him and to not draw attention to myself or to us, to no avail. He said he doesn't trust me. Until he changes his mind, there is nothing more I can—" She caught Althea's glance and corrected herself. "—am willing to do."

Changing the subject, she told Althea about the letter from Helen Montague and her thoughts on the artist for the catalogue. "What do I do now?"

"Before you do anything, consider your reaction if Evan did not choose any of the nursing candidates you arranged for him to interview."

"I would have tried to understand why and endeavored to find a better fit."

"You would have respected his decision?" Althea

prodded.

"Yes, of course." Beth's answer was immediate.

"Be sure you're willing to do that for Robert. I think you have two choices. I can understand if you want nothing to do with him, after he's stepped back from your personal relationship. On the other hand, connecting people is your passion. So if you direct him to the people you think are right to help him but he declines their participation, be prepared to step back as you would for any other person you helped."

He is not simply another person I am helping find a connection for. I want his approval. I want his respect and admiration.

Always before, she'd shaken off rejection as the person being another judgmental aristo. She'd buried her hurt and disappointment at not being chosen and moved on to the next conquest. This time, however, hope continued to bombard her heart, hurling it against her ribs in a tantrum of wishes. This time, 'twasn't disappointment she'd end up with, but heartache.

Chapter Twenty

Beth was not surprised to receive another invitation to a demi-monde party. It was the off-Season, and the weather was less predictable, keeping many aristocrats at their county seat from Michaelmas through Christmas. Those who remained in London liked to take advantage of the absence of Society rules and play dress-up. And possibly dress-down, depending on the exact nature of the fête.

She'd convinced Althea to attend, despite the risk of Robert being there. She hoped the gathering would spark her interest in a new bedmate. All the better if he was there to witness it. She still had not decided what to do about the artist and was dying of curiosity about his search for a blacksmith, but there had been no communication between them.

As the day of the party approached, she rethought her decision. Still upset by Robert's reaction, she was in turn furious at herself for pining for a man who did not share her beliefs. On top of that, she had belatedly realized she might see Robert's creations, and possibly even some of hers, on another woman if there were models for the demonstration.

Althea's comments had not been helpful. "You're jealous. Of some stranger having sex with another stranger. Why did you design these pieces if not for people to enjoy them?" And "Can you imagine if I was upset every time I thought of someone washing their hair with my shampoo?"

For that one, Beth gave her a withering look. "You know 'tis not the same, especially now you've been with Evan."

Althea smiled. "Ah, I am glad to see Robert has changed your mind. I swear you treated sex like washing your hair until now." She ducked when Beth threw a slipper at her.

By the day of the party, she was in a lather. She'd made eyes at her favorite stable hand, only to decline his generous offer clutched in a fist between his legs. Later, she'd lingered in her bath and allowed her maid to wash her but found herself uninterested in stepping out into the girl's arms. Unexpected irritation surged at Althea for taking her suggestion to hire more open-minded servants from the School.

She finally came out of her own thoughts to see Althea's nerves that afternoon. "What is the matter, cuz?"

"If Robert is present, Evan is likely to be."

"Yes…is that a problem?"

"I am still concerned about people connecting us, to the detriment of both my business and my reputation."

For the first time, Beth realized how similar Robert's and Althea's concerns over privacy were. Her cousin's advice and ability to see Robert's side of things stemmed from that. Of course, she did not have to like that fact, but it lent credence to Robert's reactions.

On the other hand, at least she could help her cousin. "Given Robert's concerns are similar, the one positive aspect to my annoyance with him is that I can reassure you 'tis a safe crowd. He would not offer pieces to show there unless he was confident of the clientele."

"Right. Thank you. And you are sure you want to attend?"

"I darned well do. I am tired of pining for him, and self-pleasure is not at all the same."

Althea blushed at her bold words but carried on, "Then I suppose you should help me decide what to wear."

After helping Althea dress in her most daring gown in a rich wine color, Beth perused her own choices, her mood vicious. That dratted man would not hold her heart hostage any longer. She'd find someone to play with at the party and enjoy herself, for godsakes. She'd revel if Robert saw them. Mayhap he'd realize what he was missing.

Deflating, she acknowledged that if she was doing it to show him what he was missing, she was still not over him.

Beth had taken one of Robert's corsets home with her weeks ago, as he'd wanted to test its wearability for longer periods. She had hidden it in the bottom drawer of her writing desk and sporadically pulled the drawer out to stare at it. She really should return it.

Shutting the drawer on the lovely corset once again, she nonetheless chose her gown to show off her greatest assets, to him and to anyone else who cared to look. The butter yellow gown was hardly demure even with the proper undergarments. With no corset, even one of satin, and her nipples rouged, it was provocative.

Even her own touch as she smoothed the makeup into her nipples made her moan. She dropped her head back and tugged at them.

"Miss. There isn't time." Her maid drew her hands

away, holding the chemise out for her, then the dress. Ah, the bounce without a corset. If the unabated arousal didn't kill her first, it was sure to convince Robert—er, someone—to play. Her body was humming like a tuning fork, and while it preferred Robert's pitch pipe to truly resonate, she was determined to quiet it one way or another.

She smoothed her curls in the mirror then stepped back for a last check.

'Tis perfect to encourage play and pleasure. Of course, it will draw attention, but what do I care. She'd never worried about that before. *Dratted man.*

After donning their masks in the coach, they entered the unmarked door, gave their cloaks to the servant in the entryway, and made their way to the small ballroom.

Both women's heads swiveled to see who they recognized, both looking for their men, first and foremost.

Knowing Althea would spy them more easily than she, given the women's height differential, Beth catalogued other men there who might be her maestro of pleasure later if Robert's instrument was out of tune. She was determined to overcome her recent missishness regarding changing partners without communication. Just because she hadn't done so with a stable hand did not mean she couldn't or wouldn't at the party, if only she could muster the slightest interest in another man or woman.

Grabbing two champagnes from a passing server's tray, she passed one to Althea and motioned. "Shall we promenade?"

A gentleman engaged Althea in conversation, so Beth turned to search the shadowed corners, refusing to admit she was checking for Robert. She spied Penelope and Michael lounging in a dark niche and smirked. Michael had been taught to avoid scandal since childhood, only to succumb to Penelope's beauty one night. Even married, the pair seemed unable to give up the allure of the demi-monde balls but attempted to keep a low profile.

Penelope squealed as Beth approached. "Beth. How are you?"

They exchanged cheek kisses, and Michael bowed over her hand.

"Such earlish manners, so trainable." Beth loved to tease him. She'd made up "earlish" early in their friendship.

He shook his head with an indulgent smile.

Penelope volunteered the information Beth was looking for. "I haven't seen Robert or Evan, but I have no doubt they shall make an appearance."

Beth turned to watch the entrance.

Within moments, Robert entered with Cheltie and stepped aside to speak with Sarah. He gestured behind him toward the door and the hostess nodded, no doubt arranging for whatever items he'd brought to be taken up the back stairs to a room for display.

She wandered upstairs, unsure if she wanted to talk to Robert or what she'd say. Her body's hum of arousal intensified from the mere knowledge that he was in the building. Brushing her hands over her dress intensified the ache, her skin sensitive to even her own touch.

Most of the doors above-stairs stood open. Assignations were more likely later, from what she remembered, although they would not preclude the doors remaining open. Toward the end of the hallway, a couple wandered out of an open doorway, whispering with their heads together.

As she walked by each room, she envisioned people in them, enjoying all sorts of acts. If only Robert were more like her, they might be one of the couples. He'd strip her dress off, leaving her breasts in only a chemise above the cut-out cups of the leather corset that she'd have worn for him. He'd untie her petticoats, letting them drop and then mayhap simply tug her short chemise out of the corset, allowing the warm supple leather to mold to her skin. Producing a set of straps, he'd open her to his desired position and buckle her into immobility. Then he'd strum her and pluck her and build to a crescendo, made even more titillating given the audience.

Her excitement dulled at that last thought. Always before, a crowd had enhanced her enjoyment. Their appreciation of her appearance and performance increased her arousal.

Now, only the lure of Robert's care and skill with her, not just her body, had her nervous, excited, and wet.

A servant approached from the back stairs with a pile of leather, disappearing into a room.

Her mood morose as she realized her bluster about other partners was just that, Beth lingered in the doorway to watch the footman lay out Robert's wares.

When he placed a set of cuffs attached to a collar by a long strap upside down, she stepped in to correct him.

****

Robert turned through the doorway to the usual "sales" room and stopped short.

Beth stood at a table against the wall, running her hands over an arrangement of leather straps with a collar.

His cock surged in his breeches.

They'd never played with collars. Robert had used them, but only occasionally, and almost always with cuffs closer to the collar to keep the person's hands out of his way. The ones she touched had cuffs down a long strap, allowing the hands to sit near the waist.

Peaches—Beth—had advanced to rarely needing cuffs to remain still for him after the trip to Peterborough. When he did want her tied, he preferred her spread, so he could feast on every gorgeous inch of her.

His cock pulsed, jerking upright, poking against his clothes.

Beth turned and gasped.

He hardly heard her over the roaring in his ears when he caught the shadow of her areolas through the pale gown. His mouth watered, and his teeth ached to close over those tips.

Good lord, he had missed her. Her voluptuous curves made his palms itch to smooth over them, but her mind... He wanted to lay sketches at her feet and beg for her thoughts. He had questions about the blacksmith as well. *Ugh.*

Reason reasserted itself.

She's here with rouged nipples, deliberately drawing attention to herself.

Even in the improbable likelihood she was trying to garner his attention, it was a perfect example of her not worrying about others'.

"Beth." It came out as a rumble, and he cleared his throat. "Did you wish to purchase that?"

"No, thank you. 'Tis not one of my preferred styles." She flipped it over and set it down again. "It had been laid incorrectly."

"Ah. You have my gratitude then."

She lingered, walking the length of the display, trailing her hands over the pieces. Here and there, she'd finger the leather, testing thickness or suppleness.

His gaze and his cock followed her progress hungrily. Mayhap a quick tup in a back room with the door locked? No, their interludes had never been rushed, and he wasn't about to change that now when it might be their last time together. To leave her with less than his best effort would exacerbate their issues, not lessen them.

"Aren't you concerned about someone finding you in here?" Her tone was contemptuous, and one lip curled in a sneer.

"Few people come up this early. I wished to check on the same thing you found—that items were properly displayed."

"Why do you care?" She stepped closer so the servant could not overhear. "If you're so rich, why even sell these? Just give them away to your friends." She flung out a hand and stamped a foot.

His eyes nearly crossed as her bosom jiggled with her stomp and her scent wafted toward him. He was so distracted by her proximity, he could not form a reply. Thankfully, she hadn't seemed to notice his cockstand.

Then her gaze, as hungry as he was sure his was, traveled down his body.

She took one more half-step so her skirts brushed his bulging breeches, her breasts brushed his waistcoat.

"See something you like? There are plenty of rooms here available." Her finger ran across her decolletage, then skimmed the buttons of his waistcoat until she fisted his erection through his breeches.

"Hunh."

"If you are so worried about gossip, why do you attend these parties?" She squeezed, a hardness in her gaze that he'd never seen before.

His eyes drifted shut. Even if he'd been coherent enough to say that Evan dragged him most times, it was clear she was not in a mindset to listen. Whatever small amount of blood that was left in his brain told him her question was rhetorical.

"Unless you've changed your mind, mayhap?"

His eyes flew open, gazing at her in alarm.

She squeezed him harder, as she knew he liked.

He bit his tongue to avoid moaning.

"What say you, Robert? We could borrow a room for you to taste my peaches."

She was baiting him. He knew she was, but he could not help his response. No matter her reason, she was also reinforcing the issue between them. Their location and a possible audience did not bother her. Worse, she did not seem to care that he did mind.

She leaned in, her mouth mere inches below his.

He sucked in her scent, and his knees went weak with desire.

"Robert. No one here judges. I've done everything I can to support you. Why can't you at least try this and see if you like it?"

His cockstand wilted like an unstarched handkerchief. *And that is precisely why.*

He wrenched out of her hold, gritting his teeth. "Beth, I appreciate your support. In turn, I have tried to support your penchant for risking more than I am comfortable. I cannot do this."

"Will not, you mean." She stomped her foot again.

"Temper, temper." He chided, but his tone was mild.

"Do not condescend to me!"

What? He was bewildered.

"I am allowed to be mad. You are judging me for my unwillingness to succumb to the Ton's stupid rules. My desire to live my life the way I choose, out in the open."

"No, I—"

"Yes, you are. Or you wouldn't care what people think. You'd try this."

He'd never seen her this mad. He wasn't sure she would listen to any defense he offered. Reaching to cup her arm, he lowered his voice. "Beth, please. Let's discuss this later. Or tomorrow. I—"

"No. Either be with me here, tonight, to watch or be watched, or I shall find someone else to play with tonight. I am tired of sneaking around in the dark. Of thinking 'what would Robert say?'"

His eyebrows shot up at that. He hadn't known she'd ever thought that. He caught a flash of fear in her eyes before she continued. Distracted for a moment, he wondered if she worried she'd have to act on her ultimatum.

"Of picturing you fitting someone else with designs I helped create." She folded her arms. "Choose."

Huh. No wonder she didn't like my options. Neither of those are palatable choices. Can I get a third? He looked at her arms crossed under her breasts and was momentarily distracted by the sight before taking in her tight jaw and furrowed brow. *Likely not.*

His throat tight, all he could manage was, "Please don't do this."

Her frozen wide-eyed expression told him she did not mean her words, but it didn't matter. He had nothing to offer her in counter. He dropped his hand from her arm.

Her eyes welled with tears.

Unable to hold her gaze, he bent his head. Staring at his feet, he clenched his fists as he heard a receding swish of skirts fade from the room and the doorway was empty. As empty as his heart.

Chapter Twenty-One

Given Beth's challenge, Robert chose not to linger at the party. The risk of having to watch her become intimate with another man made him nauseous. Even remaining in the ballroom held the possibility of seeing her ascend the stairs on a man's arm or flirt outrageously on the dance floor.

He stared through the dark at the bed canopy most of the night, wondering if Beth had found someone to replace him, speculating if that person would take as good care of her as he had.

Finally, morning dawned, and he forced his mind to the meeting he'd planned. Deciding not to take samples with him, he hailed a hack to visit Hunter's friend. If the apprentice was there, even better. But how would he overcome his shyness without Beth there?

Might as well ask yourself the same question about everything you do. He grunted. He'd done just fine before he knew her, and he could relearn to move forward and be happy without her again. Eventually.

Arriving at the forge, Robert asked the tradesman for Noah Cooper.

A man approximately David's age came out of the back, wiping his hands on a greasy rag. He'd likely been oiling pieces to ensure they did not rust. "Can I help you?"

"David Hunter suggested I talk to you. I need a

blacksmith to supply small specialized items regularly." He cast a glance at the younger man working on a thin strip of iron over the anvil. "Is there somewhere we can talk privately?"

"Come on back." Despite the high cost of space in London, the smithy had a small nook off the back room with a narrow hob that backed on the smithy forge, a tiny table and two chairs, and mugs for tea.

"Drink?" He gestured to where a tea tin shared shelf space with a decanter of amber spirits.

"Thank you, but no."

"Right, then. What sort of pieces and what volume are you looking for?"

Robert started the way he and Beth had with David, accenting the need for privacy and keeping the description of his goods vague. He added, "Hunter actually thought your apprentice might be a good fit."

"Oh?" The man's eyebrows shot toward his hairline. "Why?"

"'Twasn't an issue of quality or anything like that," Robert hastened to assure him. He did not wish to offend this man who might have a solution for his needs. "'Twas more…" *Gah, Beth would know how to word this delicately.*

Cooper grinned. "Ah. Mayhap the, shall we say, nature of the goods?"

Robert's breath whooshed out. "Yes." His face heated, and he hoped Cooper attributed it to the forge flames.

"Right, then. Acknowledging your need for discretion, I still think we need Folly for this discussion. Trust me, if anyone values his privacy, it's my apprentice. The few of us who know about the items he creates in his spare time tease him mercilessly."

Robert nodded. "Fine. I will follow your lead on that and on how directly you wish to be involved. I am not trying to steal him away from you."

"I appreciate that. But the idea of an apprenticeship is to teach them to fly, and that little birdy is ready to leave the nest. I've already begun looking for my next apprentice, someone who will be more accepting of the lesser jobs I hand off."

"Excellent. So…Folly, you say?"

"Ha. Nathaniel Follett. We call him Folly because of his hobby, as we termed it Follett's folly."

Robert frowned. He did not want someone who did not take it as serious work requiring skill.

"Do not worry, man. He is excellent. Like I said, he's ready to leave the nest, and I have high standards, as Hunter likely told you."

"We shall see." That was why he usually brought samples. He preferred to judge for himself.

Hunter stepped to the doorway and called, "Folly, finish that up and come back here. And bring a few of your toys."

There was an off-tone clang as though the hammer had landed wrong and slipped off the piece the young man was creating.

Within seconds, the lean six-foot frame of Nathaniel Follett ducked through the door, wiping his brow with the bottom of his shirt as he went to a corner of the storage area and dug out a bundle wrapped in an oiled rag. As he straightened, he added an iron rod almost three feet long.

"Sir?"

"Sit down, Folly." Cooper remained standing.

"Meet Robert Orford. He is a friend of a friend and would like to speak to you."

The young man's brows rose in surprise. "Why me?"

Cooper nodded to Robert, and he turned to the teen. "I make leather goods for—" He searched for an appropriate term. "—personal, private use. In order to put them together, I need specialized metal fasteners that are small scale and intricate. Think furniture level detail, but to be joined to leather rather than wood."

Grateful Beth had helped him narrow that description to be so succinct, his heart twinged at her absence.

Nathaniel nodded. "I understand. Do you have any pieces here?"

"No. My business is extremely confidential. Most of my clientele are Ton." The boy's eyes widened. "And yes, before you ask, the profits are excellent." He turned to include Cooper with his smile. "The volume is such that I could keep a smith busy about thirty percent of the day right now. But—" He gulped. "—I am considering expanding my sales, so that will likely increase."

Another twinge. He had almost reconciled himself to creating a catalogue, although the thought of Beth not modeling sent arrows of pain through his heart.

"Are you looking to keep your current blacksmith then?" Cooper asked.

"Only during a transition period," Robert said, shaking his head. "He wishes to retire and spend more time with a new grandchild."

"Hmm." The blacksmith's tone was contemplative. That was a lot of new business, Robert knew. The man might be sorry he said he was prepared to let his apprentice go.

"I will leave it to you two decide how to handle the workload. 'Tis a good bit of detailed work for one man's eyes and hands, as I can attest." He held up his calloused, scarred hands, and the other two chuckled in commiseration.

Beth loved the texture of my hands, as rough as they were against her satiny skin.

"What I need to know is whether your work is to the standard I require and whether the nature of it will offend your sensibilities."

Cooper laughed out loud at that and gestured to Nathaniel. "Folly, show him some of your pieces."

The young man's cheeks went ruddy, but his back remained straight and proud as he unwrapped the bundle.

He placed two small items on the table. Made up of narrow ribbons of metal, they were hollow squares with the ribbons curled into decorative metal scrolls at the corners. Tiny screws arrowed toward the center through each of the four sides.

"May I?" Robert gestured.

Nathaniel nodded.

He picked one up, turning it. Impressed with the workmanship, he admired the scrolls in such fine strips of metal. But he had no idea of the item's purpose.

"Care to guess?" Cooper asked.

Nathaniel's face held a mix of pride, defiance, and nerves.

"The detail is excellent. You did this?" Internally, Robert wondered if Beth would be able to identify the piece. If she were with him, she'd have her own questions, then they'd return to his house and discuss all the configurations. Well, they'd discuss after a long romp in the sheets. This would be so much more exciting if she were here, but even without her, he was focused on her as a model as well as a partner.

The teen's shoulders dropped an inch as he nodded.

Robert turned it again. He tried to fit a finger into the center opening, even unscrewing the tiny screws to make the aperture larger, but he could not.

"Wrong body part," murmured Nathaniel, his cheeks even redder.

Robert tilted his head. If a finger was too thick… *Oh.*

"Nipple screws?" he asked, his voice hopeful. Hellfire, to see these on Peaches, her nipples pinched and turning a deep rose. He stifled a groan. This was not the place for an erection.

'Tis not the time for an erection, either. She lost her patience with your fear of publicity. You need to stop fixating on her.

Follett nodded, watching him warily.

David was right. 'Tis a better fit than I could have imagined.

Again, his first inclination was to share this triumph with Beth. Her imagination combined with this young man's would know no bounds. But no, 'twas not to be.

He forced himself to refocus, saying, "My compliments on your vision, as well as the execution. I wish I had brought my own pieces now, to get your take on a few things."

"Really?" came in unison from both men, one incredulous and the other excited.

"Yes, really," Robert answered in a mild tone as he fished out the fasteners he had brought to leave as tests of their work.

"I'll explain these in a second, but first, may I see more of your pieces, please? And what is the rod for?"

"Of course." Nathaniel grabbed the solid length of iron and set it across the table. There were small loops on each end. "I was debating iron for the shackles," he said, pointing to the ends. "But leather would be so much kinder to the person's ankles wearing them."

Robert sighed in awe. No more needing bedposts or wrapping around table legs. A person could be spread-eagled in comfort with leather next to their skin, but this rod holding their legs apart. "'Tis ingenious. I will send a runner over with a set of cuffs for you today." He stroked the bar with envy.

If only he had a reason to order one. He'd never get to try this on his Peaches.

Desperate to head home to curl up and wallow in his misery, he muscled through the rest of the conversation. As he departed, he was mentally choosing samples to send, although he was quite sure none would be a challenge for Follett to recreate. The three of them had hashed out a tentative plan toward partnership, with a meeting set for a fortnight hence to consider any new questions and share design sketches.

Follett's ingenuity regarding sex accessories complemented his own. Despite that, Robert could not conjure even a modicum of excitement at the new alliance. He missed his old partner too much.

****

Beth wallowed, dragging herself to and from the charity school and spending inordinate amounts of time in bed—alone.

Evan had broken things off with Althea again at the same ill-fated party, so she'd gathered her energy and attempted to be upbeat for the older woman's sake. She wished she had advice for her cousin, but she was too heartsick to see a path forward for either of them. Too, her counsel was not reliable given her reckless ultimatum to Robert, when she'd known she would not follow through. The hurt and sorrow in his eyes haunted her still.

After a fortnight, she found herself unable to continue the charade. Skipping supper, she huddled in bed and lamented her sorry state. Tears dribbled down the sides of her face as she stared at the bed canopy. Lying in the dim light of a few candles, she imagined all the positions Robert had twisted her in on a bed. She'd never gone this long without an orgasm, but she had lost all interest in sex or even self-pleasure. She missed Robert.

Inevitably, Althea came to check on her. She perched on the edge of the bed. "What is amiss?"

"You are having enough troubles with Evan. I do not want to burden you."

"I keep telling you, you are not a burden. You are my family and my closest friend. Now what happened?"

"I told Robert he had to choose. Have sex with me at the party or not at all."

"What?" Althea gasped, her mouth dropping open. "Why would you do such a thing?"

"Because he needs to love me as I am," Beth wailed.

"Oh, Beth." Her cousin leaned in to hug her before straightening to give her a hard stare. "He does, though, don't you see?"

"No, he doesn't. He judges me for flaunting society's rules."

"Don't be ridiculous," Althea replied with a snort.

Beth glared, although she suspected it was less effective from her prone position.

"He loves you to pieces. He gives you all sorts of leeway, just as I do. We may not always know what to do with you, but we love you. And that man is in love with you."

Beth pressed her lips together in a suspicious moue.

"Do you think I judge you, simply because I do not make the same choices?"

"No."

"So?"

"You've found your own vice, with watching."

"And he has his, with the leather pieces—" Althea paused for emphasis. "—which he shares with you."

Beth looked away from her cousin, unable to meet her eyes and acknowledge that parallel.

"So you gave him an ultimatum. He declined. 'Tis been weeks since then. Usually, you'd at least have had a dalliance with a stable boy by now. Why haven't you, I wonder?"

"Haven't wanted to," Beth mumbled.

"Why is that, though? Are you hoping he will come around? Or is it that you've found someone who is more important than the freedom to do as you please? Mayhap 'tis now more important to do as *he* pleases on this one thing. 'Tis called compromise, and it is a necessary part of any relationship."

Beth gave her a wry look.

"Yes, well, I tried to compromise with Evan. Our differences were too great. That is not the case between you and Robert, though."

"We are quite the pair, aren't we?" Beth asked with a sigh. "We may yet end up as two spinsters, pinching the footmen's bottoms and vetting new maids for their figures."

Althea grunted and shook her head. "Speak for yourself. What are you going to do now?"

"I don't know. I need a plan."

"You'll think better with supper in you. Come on, now." Her cousin dragged her up, waited while she dressed, and accompanied her down to their waiting supper.

Beth's mind churned. Did she flaunt society's requirements out of self-defense, rejecting them before they spurned her? If so, then Robert was far more important. Mayhap her reactions were reflexive or, worse, just plain stubbornness. But could she break that pattern of reactive behavior? Even if she could, she needed to formulate a plan to win him back.

Chapter Twenty-Two

Unable to find any interest in Sarah's club, even to test the small pile of new designs he'd completed, Robert went to White's. He could not stand to be in his house any longer, staring at pieces Beth had helped him create and furniture he'd used to worship her beauty and ingenuity.

Neither Bags nor Michael were there, but the earl who'd attended Evan's house party was.

As Robert wound his way toward his usual corner, the man approached. Robert's stomach knotted when he stopped to talk.

"Orford." The man nodded, looking uneasy.

"Smythe. 'Scuse me, it's—" he searched for the man's title.

"Never mind that. I saw your designs at Greenborough. They're ingenious." He gave Robert an awkward slap on the shoulder that could have been friendly or mocking. "I never knew you had it in you, old chap."

"No, you wouldn't have, would you?" Robert held himself rigid, his words bitter through a clenched jaw. He wasn't the forgive and forget type, and declined to give Smythe a free pass simply because time had passed.

Ready for the man to cut him down for his attitude, he braced.

But the earl surprised him. "You're right. Not well

done of me at all. That is why I came over now. You have my apologies. I have a son of my own now, and it has given me new perspective."

Robert's jaw nearly hit the floor in shock.

Ignoring his speechless gape, the earl said. "Think on it. Perhaps you could call on me and meet my son. I'd also like to place an order with you, if you're amenable."

Robert took the proffered card with the man's address in numb fingers, and managed a nod as the schoolroom tyrant strolled away.

Still in shock, he settled in his usual seat facing his two friends' empty chairs and ordered a drink. Nursing it, he contemplated the peculiar turn of events. One of his bullies had not only complimented him, but had requested one of his designs. He wasn't sure he trusted the earl, but Evan did, else earl or no, he would not have received an invitation to Greenborough Park.

Mayhap the School of Enlightenment needed classes for men. Could he find his way past his childhood fears? And Beth was right—with his wealth and wares in high enough demand, he could afford not to care about rumors or disparaging remarks. But decades of first his father lavishing his older brother with love, then peers who denigrated him for the lack of a title, his shape, or anything else they thought up, could not be undone at one little peachy woman's behest.

Lost in thought, he jumped, spilling a few drops of whisky onto his hand when a deep voice asked, "May I join you?"

He looked up to find the Earl of Peterborough smiling at him.

"My lord." Robert stood quickly to make a shallow bow. "Of course."

"Thank you. Are you waiting on your cohorts, then?" Edward was still smiling. Of course, he could smile and joke at Evan's and Michael's expense. They were all Peers, not just peers.

"We had not scheduled anything." Robert shrugged. "I came on a whim."

"May I ask what had you so deep in thought?"

"'Tis something of a long story, I'm afraid."

"Ah, the universal polite way of saying mind your own business. Right, then. How have you found the weather?" The earl sat back and crossed one leg over the other, making himself comfortable.

Robert rolled his eyes but attempted courtesy. "No, it truly is a long story. About a woman." Why had he said that last part?

"I should have known. Right, then. May I ask who the lucky lady is?"

"Lucky because she's no longer with me," he muttered. "Beth Jenkins."

"Beth?" Edward stared at him in shock. "And…you?"

"Thanks ever so much. 'Tis been lovely talking with you, but I think I shall take my leave now."

"Sorry, sorry. Wait, please. I didn't mean that to be unflattering. Rather that she's a handful." The earl rocked his head. "Actually, an armful."

"I beg your pardon, my lord—"

"Edward, please."

Robert ignored him. "I'll ask you not to disparage her figure in my presence."

"What? Oh, armful. Geez, I'm making a muddle of it this evening, aren't I?" Edward chuckled. "'Twasn't a reference to her shape or size. She's a lovely little thing, a friend of my wife's. I alluded to her attitude, energy, personality…" He waved a hand in a helpless circle.

"Right, then." Robert was still indignant, no matter how friendly the earl—Edward—wished to be. "And you think I can't handle her?"

"Not at all. I was simply surprised. I would not have put you two together. But opposites attract. Look at Sophia and me. I wouldn't have put us together either."

Robert's shoulders loosened.

"So what seems to be amiss?"

"She sees my desire for privacy as a statement on her disregard for society's opinion of her actions."

"And discretion is that important to you?"

"Well, that is what I was sitting here contemplating," Robert admitted.

"You may recall that certain secrets can exist even in the Ton?" Edward asked, glancing around.

"The school?" Robert nodded. "Yes. Although that seems less and less secret the more people I speak to." His lips twisted. "I assume you're now aware of my trade, then, too?"

"No, actually. Nor do I need to know if you prefer otherwise."

"'Tis not important to this conversation, I think."

"Right, then." Edward was silent for a long minute, sipping his drink. Then he leaned forward. "I shall tell you something private, that only Sophia and Suffolk know." He referenced his best friend and Sophia's cousin, the Earl of Suffolk. "Because they both have needed to help me with the issue."

Robert's brows rose in curiosity.

"I cannot read." The earl watched him.

Robert's jaw dropped before he quickly recovered.

If Bags's and Michael's complaints about their responsibilities were any indication, the man must read piles of Parliamentary bills and correspondence just for his membership in the House of Lords. "How can that be, sir?"

"Please, 'tis Edward. I can struggle through a brief note when I need to, but the letters and words sort of stir themselves into a knot and by the time I've undone a longer missive, I've lost the thread." He sat back, crossing his leg again. "Suffolk helped me get through Cambridge, and Sophia helps me every day now. I was so ashamed I swore never to marry because students at school had made fun of me. And when I was a free second son before Charles's passing, I did not need to marry. Even after we adjourned to Peterborough as man and wife, I hid my weakness from Sophia."

This earl had been bullied too? Aloud, he replied, "I had no idea. I shan't say anything, of course. But why tell me this?"

"Because I fear sharing this information with others less now that Sophia discovered it and still loves me."

Robert sat back as Edward's words settled over him. Beth knew about his dislike of attention. She cared for him anyway. She'd pushed him to overcome the fear because those people were not important to his happiness. He would still prefer that she had not pushed, but he also understood that her actions had stemmed from her own fears.

Mayhap there was a compromise for them.

"I am not certain she loves me," Robert voiced his greatest worry. "Or can accept my aversion to public interest."

"What I am saying is that her support may give you

courage to overcome that to a small extent. Meeting her in the middle, so to speak. As for the rest, there is only one way to know, is there not?"

****

Robert knocked on the front door of Evan's townhome. He greeted the butler and strode the length of the main hall to Evan's office unaccompanied.

Rapping lightly on the door, he poked his head in.

"Ford. How are you?" Evan tucked an unopened letter into a drawer, looking distracted.

"I've been better. Do you have a few minutes?"

"Always for you. Drink?"

"Tea?" Robert requested.

Evan rang for tea. "Right, then. How can I assist?"

"I am not even sure what to ask. You know more of my reluctance to be in the public eye, and my reasons, than anyone."

Evan nodded.

"Beth wanted me to sell through a catalogue—"

Evan raised a brow, looking interested.

"No. Do not start on about that, you investment-minded sod. Focus, please. We can discuss the catalogue later."

"Promise?"

"Yes. Now, as I was saying…to Sarah Potter's girls and clientele, beyond at parties. She also thought the school and—I don't know, people related to the school? Sponsors? Alumnae?—might be another opportunity for expansion."

"That girl. So much intelligence in such a petite package." Evan shook his head in amazement.

"I balked, for understandable reasons, particularly when I realized how many school-adjacent people there were. I suppose I'm asking if you understand and respect my concerns."

"Of course I do." Evan tilted his head at Robert. "I also have no doubt that Miss Jenkins does as well."

"I am not so sure."

"Look, you'd never heard of the school. Yet you have no idea how many balls you've attended with servants trained there. For that matter, how many Ton ladies have you spoken with who attended? Hellfire, I am involved in the school oversight, and even I don't know."

"Really?"

"Yes. More to the point, you likely know things about Ton members that I do not. Whilst I host those crazy parties every summer, I do not see the details of their orders. And I certainly do not know who buys from you here in London. I'm sure some of their choices would shock me."

Robert considered Lady Charlotte's order when she was married to Edward's older brother, Charles. Evan was aware of that as he'd directed the lady to Robert, but there were many similar intimate preferences that only Robert and the couple—and mayhap their servants— knew. Then there was the recovering bully at Whites, and Edward. And Evan's mother's illness, which was also a well-kept secret.

"Look," Evan said rather forcefully. "Secrets can be kept. That is my only point. But you have every right to choose how private you want your life. Beth has a particular kind of bravery. Why do you think that is?"

Robert frowned and said, "Because she does not care what others think."

"I think 'tis more bravado than bravery," his friend

shook his head. "She is so damned smart and so loving. But she is easily hurt, too. So she puts on a show with outlandish behavior and pushes people away before they can reject her. Sometimes I wonder why she continues to help so many titled nabobs who have been mean to her. The size of her heart is amazing."

"I agree—"

"But," Evan cut in over him. "You, too, are brave. 'Tis simply a different sort of courage. You create masterpieces of a nature that would bring horrific backlash should the wrong people discover your work. You needn't even work, much less expand, but here you are considering it. Yes, 'tis a passion project. Why? And why have you contemplated how to make pieces more affordable? Because you believe every couple deserves happiness."

Robert took a breath to reply, but Evan held up a finger.

"You and Beth are not so different, after all. You both believe in sexual freedom, you both are zealous in helping people find joy, and you both want someone to accept and love you as you are. There are worse starts to relationships."

Robert stared, silent. Sometimes he forgot how insightful Evan was because of his friend's lighthearted nature. Until he said something like this.

Could it truly be that simple? Did she push me away for fear of rejection?

Dunce, she as much as said that's what she was doing. You simply couldn't see it over your own anxiety.

Evan did not stop there, however. "My next question is one we both know the surface answer to. I want you to think about it with fresh eyes, so to speak. Why are you so focused on your privacy?"

Robert grimaced and sent him a glare.

"I know, I know." Evan raised his hands placatingly. "Why now, though? Why still? No one can hurt you. You do not need alliances for the House of Lords." He ticked each thought off on his fingers as he itemized them. "You've more blunt than half the Ton. You've not gone out of your way to garner a larger circle of friends, so I imagine you have the friends you want. When and if you marry, you'll do so for love and want a quiet life, much as you have now. So why do you still care what others think of you? Or is it more a habit than anything?"

Robert's thoughts whirled like a cyclone. He almost felt dizzy with them. Evan's intelligence was hard to keep up with at the best of times, but when he was putting forth insights about Robert's psyche, it was overwhelming. His thoughts also kept returning to Rose's marriage and mental health cut short. If there was ever a reason to take happiness where one found it, her example was better than most.

He mumbled his thanks and goodbyes to his friend, then wandered home in a daze.

Would his life really change if Ton biddies found fault with the way he looked, dressed, or designed leather? It would still hurt, and he did not wish to partake in Beth's outlandishness behavior, but with his friends and her by his side, mayhap he could ignore the gossips for the most part, just as he did now.

Damnation. Peaches was right—or at least more right than he'd been.

****

Robert was still contemplating how to approach Beth as he strolled to his next meeting with Cooper and

Follett. Sending her one of his pieces or even one of Follett's would not demonstrate any readiness to handle the public. Nor did he have a coherent plan for either showing comfort or becoming comfortable. He supposed it took practice, like most things. He only knew that being with her was more important than what others thought or said.

With Beth on his mind, he sidetracked past Penelope's bakery to indulge his sweet tooth. As though he'd conjured her, Beth stood outside the bakery door.

Focused on his thoughts, he took a minute to notice that two Ton matriarchs blocked the door. He narrowed his eyes at them, trying to recall their titles. They were not part of the set that flirted with propriety and attended demi-monde parties in the off-season. These ladies were all about respectability.

He slowed. These were the female equivalent of the bullies he'd experienced at school and were exactly the type of people he preferred to avoid.

Then he heard one sniff and exclaim, "Don't you feel that dress is a little low-cut for daytime, dear?" Her voice was as sweet as any of Penelope's confections, but her expression belied that tone. Mouth pinched, she'd lifted her chin as though Beth's bountiful bosom offended her.

Beth laughed.

How can she laugh? But the laugh sounded forced to his ears, so attuned to all things Peaches.

"Are you out alone, dear?" The other woman chimed in, peering around for Beth's maid.

The "dears" grated on Robert's nerves. He caught sight of Beth's balled fists buried in her skirts and worried there might be a brawl.

Without further thought, he stepped up beside her.

Huh. He still could not recall either of the women's names, but one of them had purchased a rather sturdy collar, that he suspected was for her husband or a male lover.

"Ladies." His bow was brief and likely not low enough for their station. He cared not at all. His only concern was Peaches.

"Pea—Miss Jenkins," he sketched a more lingering bow. "How was your visit with Lady Mansfield?" He raised the volume of his question on Penelope's title.

"Oh! Mr. Orford. What a lovely surprise." Beth beamed at him like he was a pastry. "It was lovely, but so warm in there with the ovens on all day. I had just stepped out when these lovely ladies were kind enough to say hello."

"Really? It didn't sound like hello to me." He leveled a hard stare at the ladies, then turned back to Peaches. "Miss Jenkins, I was admiring your gown from a block away. You look luscious."

Her grin gained a few degrees. The two ladies ceased to exist for that moment.

Then he swung his gaze back to the one with a collared something or someone and asked, "How is your pet doing these days?"

The woman blanched. Her friend turned to her with a confused frown. "Letty? I did not know you owned a pet. All those visits to your house and I've never seen it."

Robert stifled a smirk. He bet she had, and simply not known it.

Letty stuttered and swallowed, appearing ill.

He let the question hang for a moment, then smoothed it over. "My pardon. I may have misremembered."

She glared at him. "Indeed. I do not own any animals, other than my husband's horses, that is."

She didn't deny having a pet, though. He stifled his grin with an effort. His only care then was Peaches, however. He wanted her away from these hypocrites. He might not always have the power to put someone in their place, but he found he was less concerned with that possibility than he'd expected.

Indeed, Evan and Peaches were both right.

It felt empowering to stand up to a bully. He would never have dared for himself. In fact, he was sweating and tense. But for Peaches, he'd fight whatever battles were necessary, and damn the consequences.

Beth was watching him, looking almost as lost as Letty's friend.

"Shall we return to your visit with Penelope?" He gestured to her, as though the ladies were not standing in their way.

"Yes, please." She bent her head demurely.

Ha! She wanted to see how he'd navigate around the women. He cocked his arm, accepted her hand, and stepped forward.

The women scrambled sideways, crablike.

Beth snickered under her breath, and he squeezed her hand on his arm in warning.

He thought he might hyperventilate. The exchange had been confrontational and stressful. Meanwhile, his Peaches was laughing.

This is how it could be if I can win her back. She balances my reaction. I really hope it gets easier with repetition, though.

He gave a tiny shrug to release the tension in his

shoulders. He'd passed his own test. It turned out that he'd needed the right incentive to overcome his concerns regarding exposure or criticism.

"Good day, ladies." He didn't even bother bowing.

****

Beth had spent days after her conversation with Althea conjuring plan after plan.

Finally, after her millionth unsuccessful attempt to guess Robert's reaction to any number of scenarios, she decided she was not good at planning. Her strength was spontaneity. Mayhap when she found her courage she'd return to his house and…what? Apologize? Try to compromise? That is where she lost the thread of the plan.

To stop the spinning thoughts, she'd set out for Penelope's bakery. Where two Ton biddies had snared her. Usually, she'd laugh them off, but she was raw enough from Robert's rejection that she felt their barbs more than usual.

Then he was there, saving her. Standing up for her when she'd have expected him to shrink back in the shadows. Especially after he'd told her of his aversion to Ton attention.

She fell in love all over again on that sidewalk. Barely able to follow the thread of the conversation, she let him lead her inside the bakery.

He turned toward a table, murmuring about getting her fortification.

Coming to life, feeling as though her heart might leap out of her chest just to be closer to him, she tugged him toward a door at the rear of the customer area.

Stepping into the kitchen, she pushed him against the wall next to the door.

"Robert." His name came out on a sigh. "My savior."

He snorted.

Shocked, she stared at him.

"My word. If only I'd known how to render you speechless." He grinned and winked.

She smacked him, smiled, and reached up to yank his head down to hers, kissing him thoroughly to whoops of encouragement from the bakery staff.

He looked up and blushed as he realized they were the center of attention.

"Really? *Now* you blush?" She shook her head. "I need you to explain all that, please."

"I am on my way to a meeting. In fact, you should accompany me. We can discuss it all more later, but the short of it is that—" He gulped. "—I am in love with you."

Beth gasped. *He is in love with me? He is in love with me!*

She struggled to believe that everything she'd dreamed of was within reach. Wanting to jump for joy, she realized he was still speaking.

"I find 'tis more important to be with you than it is to avoid censure." He cocked a brow, oblivious to her internal circus flips. "Ideally, we can do both most of the time, but I shan't expect miracles."

She tried to laugh but instead burst into tears, shocking Robert and herself. No one had ever been in love with her before, and only Althea had ever defended her like that. She'd almost stopped hoping she'd find love. To have the person she'd fallen for months ago return the feeling was beyond her wildest imaginings. And her imagination was no shy miss.

"Peaches? Peaches! Talk to me. You have my apologies. I did not mean to overstep."

"Oh, shut up. Say it again."

He chuckled. "Er, which would you prefer?"

She glared at him.

"Right, then. I love you more than—than my privacy."

She gasped, tears still streaming down her face. Then she threw herself at him, pressing her whole body against him to hug him hard.

"I love you, too. I'll try to be good. I can't promise I always will be, but I'll try."

"Peaches, I love *you*. Not some well-behaved society miss or a version of you I wish you to be. It simply took me an unfortunate amount of time to realize it."

"I have so many questions and things I want to tell you."

"Let us see what sweets Penelope has to offer and hail a hack. You'll like this meeting."

Her thoughts were so muddled, her emotions in such turmoil, Beth did not question the meeting's purpose until they were in the hack.

As she started to ask, Robert spoke. "What did you want to tell me?"

"First, I must apologize for my behavior at the party." This was more important than the meeting. "I was goading you, thrusting my wishes, or what I thought were my wishes, on you rather than respecting yours. Just as you said."

His brows twitched, his frown deepening momentarily, but he remained silent, listening as she'd requested.

"Althea pointed out to me that she has quite a different notion of what should remain private than I do, yet we are as close as sisters."

He nodded.

"And—" She took a breath for courage, gratified as always when his gaze dropped to her bosom for a second. "—I have realized that you are far more important to me than some perception of independence. Indeed, I feel quite dependent on you and quite like it. The rules for women were too confining, and I acted out. Yet you don't suffocate me. That was my fear of being hurt or rejected when you'd never given me any reason to think you'd do that. I mean, I'm not asking for forever—"

He smiled, and she broke off in confusion.

"I might be," he started, taking her hand to hold it on the seat between them. "Asking for forever, that is."

She gasped, her eyes shining.

"Let us get through this conversation first, though. I need you to find some balance with my desire for privacy. Whilst I find it is no longer a need, per se, 'tis still my preference."

"It doesn't matter—"

"Ah, let me finish, Peaches. I appreciate your sentiment. It may matter later. I cannot promise I can overcome it, but I shall try in small amounts. It helps to hear that you're less focused on being outrageous..." He arched a brow.

She sniffed, indignant, then reluctantly grinned.

"Regardless, I find myself willing to try just about anything to keep you in my life. I miss sharing design thoughts. I want you to meet my potential new blacksmith and help me locate a sketch artist. In short, I quite depend on you as well. Not for any of that, I don't *need* any of that, but I want to share it with you. I wish to find a country manor to raise children if and when you're willing. I simply need you, because I am completely, irrevocably in love with you."

Tears welled hot, swimming in her eyes again. She tried to blink them back.

He groaned at the sight. "Please, you must stop crying. You're killing me." His arms went round her to cuddle her to his side.

"They're happy tears," she mumbled.

"You know, I've never understood those."

She sniffed and wiped her nose on his jacket sleeve before raising her head. "Robert, I love you so much. Thank you for loving me."

"Shh, never thank me for that. You are warm and caring and beautiful, and you deserve all the love in the world."

"Nevertheless. Thank you for your love, as it is the most important love in the realm. You are in control, Robert. Of my heart and of our privacy."

"And of your orgasms." He grinned at her hopeful look. "Speaking of which, let me tell you about this meeting."

Epilogue

Robert leaned back in his chair. His gaze roamed the hall of Greenborough Park as he stood waiting for Beth. This was where it all began.

Beth and Folly, as she loved to call him, had become fast friends. Robert did not know whether to be impressed or frightened by some designs they dreamed up together. Some were more metal, such as the bar to keep legs or arms apart, while others were more leather, like the corset with attachments she'd sketched just the other day.

He fingered the nipple screws in his pocket. He and Beth had tested them several times and discovered they should not be worn for longer than an hour or two. Which meant that if he put them on her on the ride home, she'd be begging by the time they returned for dinner. He wasn't sure if he'd allow her fulfillment before dinner to tide her over or if he'd make her wait.

He hadn't shared the purpose of this outing. As they climbed into the barouche, he pulled a folded piece of paper from his pocket.

"Robert"—her voice bordered on a whine, but she was careful as she knew whining resulted in punishments and delayed pleasure—"please. You must tell me now. Where are we going?"

"I want to show you something first." He unfolded the real estate flyer and handed it to her. "I have had an estate agent watching for properties in this area. It is familiar to me from spending so much time here with Evan, and 'tis close enough to London to allow me to come and go for leather and accessories as needed."

She perused the sketch and details of the property.

It was a medium-sized house, with a nursery and servants' quarters on the top floor. A small ballroom could be used for country dances, and a lovely garden with both flowers and vegetables was just beyond the kitchen. The surrounding land included open fields and others that were leased to tenant farmers. It was a fraction of the size of Greenborough Park but less than two hours' ride and had as much land and servants as Robert wanted to manage. However, he needed to know her feelings on the house, country life, and more.

"'Tis lovely, Robert."

"I hope so. I felt we needed to see it in person to be sure."

They had lunch in the nearby town, then met the agent at the property and toured it. Robert's excitement and nerves climbed. He loved the house and the land. The size and location were perfect to him, and he could almost picture cinnamon-curled children running about, full of Peaches's energy. However, if she did not love it as much as him, they'd keep looking.

Back in the small carriage, he took her hand. "So? You seemed to like the house and the fact that it didn't need work to make it comfortable."

"I really did, and the little town was pretty, too. You said you'd been thinking of a country manor, but I didn't know you were set on being near Cheltie. This was unexpected and quite fun. Thank you for including me."

His eyes widened. His reasons for including her had

not occurred. She was so smart, he'd thought she might guess. "I prefer this area, as I said, but the choice must be yours as well."

"What? I cannot choose for you. 'Tis your house and your money." She tilted her head, half-smiling in confusion.

"Not if I can help it." He tugged her hand closer, holding it in both of his as he leaned in. *'Tis now or never.* "Please, Peaches. Marry me and make it our house and our money. Help me choose, not only this house but this life, children, friends, everything."

Now she was crying again, dammit.

Gads, I hope those are happy tears. His hands shook with nerves waiting for her answer.

After an eternity, she sniffed and nodded.

His exhale was audible, but he'd prefer audible confirmation, just as when he handcuffed someone. "Er, is that a yes?"

She smiled. "Yes. Oh, yes, Robert, please let's. I never thought I'd have such a wonderful life. I love you so much."

He held out the nipple screws with a smirk. "Enough to wear these for me, so I can enjoy the view through dinner?"

"You know I hate being tortured that long without your touch, but right now, I will do anything for you, even this." She plucked them out of his hand. "Anything, Robert. Are you sure this is what you want?"

He smirked and nodded. They both knew she'd do anything for him any time, just as he would for her. Marriage and their own house created a whole new host of places and ways to torment his Peaches.

"Well then, I think I shall wear them with my lowest

cut corset and my palest gown. Do you think Cheltie or Althea will notice?" she teased him.

"As I gave him a set just this morning, I think Althea will be concerned with other things. But Cheltie and I can compare how well-behaved you both are."

"That is mean. You know I struggle not to squirm when wearing these."

"Exactly." Once he'd gotten over his fears, he loved this balance of public and private play. She could be counted on to control her outrageous behavior, though he knew it would be an effort, and he'd reward her…eventually.

****

Want to read some unpublished scenes from Beth's time at the School?
Sign up for Maggie's newsletter here:
https://dl.bookfunnel.com/5re3shswfg

~*~

And if you haven't read the other books in this series…

SOPHIA'S SCHOOLING

An innocent country girl...a jaded earl...an education in pleasure.

Orphaned at eighteen, Sophia has learned love means loss. Now she must leave her country home to navigate the opulence of the London Season, although she has no desire for romance or a husband.

Edward, the newest Earl of Peterborough, is struggling with the business of his family estate. He has shunned marriage due to a shameful secret, but with his title comes the need for heirs.

Despite their misgivings, Sophia and Edward cannot resist their attraction. When she accidentally discovers his penchant for spankings, her curiosity is her undoing. A clandestine meeting risks a scandal. Only marriage to a reluctant bridegroom can save her reputation. But perhaps the School of Enlightenment can give her an education in love.

PENELOPE'S PASSION

Schooled in the art of pleasure, her real passion is baking. Required to marry, the earl's heir finds his new courtesan more to his taste.

After her mother's death, Penelope Wood's hope of opening a bakery falls victim to the real need to support herself. When four retired courtesans present her with a temporary yet lucrative path back to her dream, she wants to hear more. Attending the School of Enlightenment, participating in a Virgin Auction, and becoming a courtesan all sound feasible. The most important rule--do not fall in love.

Lord Michael Slade, heir to the Earl of Mansfield, loves his family above all else, cooks for relaxation, and revels in his membership to a discreet spanking club. But his father is ill, and his mother is pushing him to marry. Even so, when he meets a dark-haired beauty who doesn't mind a good spanking and discovers she's up for auction, he can't let her go to another man. He has to have her...at least until he finds a wife.

With an inevitable marriage looming and a vow to remain faithful to his hypothetical bride once he's engaged, both Penelope and Michael must protect their hearts, even as they find a connection they cannot deny.

<u>ALTHEA'S AWAKENING</u>

A widow with no knowledge of carnal desire, a rake bored with even the most hedonistic pleasures, and a game of truth or dare...

Lady Althea Egerton's late husband secured her independence when he left her his apothecary. After two years of growth, she is ready to expand the business...if she only had capital. Finding a wealthy husband would solve that problem, but Althea refuses to subjugate herself to another man. She prefers an investor.

Unfortunately, the only one she knows is the golden god of hedonism, and his help comes with a price.

Evan Gardner, Earl of Cheltenham, is bored. At twenty-eight, he has no equal in business, politics, or seduction. None of them hold his interest. Even his annual week-long orgy disguised as a house party leaves him cold. Yet the prudish widow, who wants only his money, intrigues him. As neither of them wants the trappings of marriage, a dalliance with the elegant widow might be just the challenge he's been searching for.

Though Althea cannot resist the lure of ecstasy he offers as condition for his assistance, a continued liaison could risk her reputation and her store's profits. To win this negotiation, Evan will have to ensure she can have both independence and pleasure.

<u>ANN'S ANGEL</u>: A Regency Christmas short story

December 1812—London
Two courtesans looking to get out of the game…

Ann Dockree wants this Christmas to be her last as a courtesan, but learning that her latest investment did not return the expected funds crushes her. Especially since her dearest friend Mary Hale has enough saved to quit the life and leave London.

But when, only days before Christmas, Mary is hurt at the hands of her so-called benefactor, Ann must care for her. Touching Mary is its own sweet agony, torturing Ann with fantasies of what might be. If only Ann can summon the courage to confess she wants more than friendship with Mary before it is too late.

A warm bath, a compassionate touch, and an unexpected yet longed for taste of pleasure might inspire the Christmas gift that offers happiness to both.

Acknowledgments

This is my first self-published book, and I needed extra help with many aspects of this.

Special thanks to my editor, Diana Carlile, and my cover artist, Lisa Dawn MacDonald, for sticking with me. To Marie Tuhart (read her books, they are great!) for spending hours with me helping me master some of the technical steps to put this book in readers' hands.

For the story, I am grateful to Jena Doyle (who also writes excellent books!) and Michelle Tucker Crum, one of my advance readers, who both fielded half-crazed messages from me when I had a crisis of confidence about Beth's journey, and who made this book better.

Always, my real-life romance hero, my husband, gets the biggest thanks of all.

About the Author

Maggie Sims began her love affair with romance before her teen years, drawn to the Regency by her mum's British influence. In her twenties, she did her best to live the Carrie Bradshaw life in New York City, albeit with less expensive shoes and more books.

Despite reading hundreds of romance novels in her life, she was still blown away when she met the love of her life, an ex-Marine cinnamon roll with creative woodworking and culinary skills.

Having retired from corporate life, they live in Central Texas and are parents to a varying number of dogs and cats. When not writing, Maggie is a wine enthusiast, a travel junkie, and a romance reading fiend. She also sporadically crochets for KnotsofLove.org and does just enough exercise for that second glass of wine at night.

To find out more about Maggie's latest reads, favorite wines, and travel destinations, sign up for her newsletter.

~*~

Contact Maggie at
www.MaggieSims.com